After Love

After Love

THE LIFE OF ANNA GENNUSA
A NOVEL

Mary B. Patterson

Scribes Unlimited, LLC Cleveland, Ohio

Edited by Scribes Unlimited
Cover Art by Mary B Patterson

Scribes Unlimited, LLC
2652 Ashurst Rd
Cleveland OH 44118
www.scribesunlimited.com
info@scribesunlimited.com

February 14, 2021
First Printing, 2021

To the most awesome and strong sons, a mother could have.
I dedicate my novel to you,
Daniel, Joseph, and Matthew Patterson

CONTENTS

Prologue

I felt the winter wind nearly blowing me over. It was so cold, and the snow was massively heavy, weighing us down. The winds were without mercy, and we were all shivering badly. I could barely see a foot in front of me. What a first night in our new country.

Since early in the morning, we had not eaten, and all six of my daughters were hungry and upset. My baby, my Maria, was crying. I picked her up and held her as tightly as I could to try and warm her up. Even though I could barely see her, I heard her voice crying out, "Momma, where is my Papa? I want my Papa."

I held her in one arm as I rubbed Innocenza's back, trying to reassure her that she was safe and protected. I was lying, of course, because I had no idea what to do. I had to be strong, in any case. I had six young girls who depended on me. Teresa, Pina, and Vincenza were all huddled around Francesca, who was also crying. I wanted to hold her too. I tried to keep all of them safe and in my arms.

I wanted out of this situation. I wanted to be home – in Sicily in my house or my farm kitchen. Not here, now when my stomach was growling from fear, and I felt a pit of despair growing in me. I've always feared the unknown. My body was shaking. My head and back throbbed. What was I going to do? How was I going to get them out of the cold and heavy snows? Where could we go?

I watched my older daughters comforting their sister, and I felt such pride in them. They were my strength and did not complain because of the nasty conditions

I took my hand from Innocenza's head and put it in my pocket. And there it was. My old friend. I took it out and raised it. My spool of pure white thread, reminding me that I had an inner strength. I was part of this country and could be so again.

I held a spool of white thread and said aloud so my daughters could hear me, "We will be fine!" Louder, I repeated it with more definite conviction. "We will be fine!"

From ages three-and-a-half to eighteen, my daughters and I were still huddled together in front of the Port Authority building, shivering. Without any money, I had to figure out what to do next.

That three-week voyage on the Marine Perch was hellish. A decommissioned war tanker converted to a passenger transport was not an ideal way to arrive.

Here it was, December 15, 1947, we were now completely exhausted and hungry. I had been seasick, and my children were unable to eat that awful food. Luckily, one of our bunk-mates shared oranges, figs, and nuts, with us. But that night, in front of the Port Authority Building, we had nothing but our simple baggage and nowhere to go.

I never thought I'd be stranded on the streets of New York again. It was so many years had passed since I lived here. Now this land was now foreign to me. Even though I studied English when I was here before, I hoped I had enough to get by. I wondered how much of American society I knew anymore.

"Stay close. Shuuuuu, Maria, stop crying. I will take care of you."

"Francesca," I said to my third youngest child, "Thank you for not crying." And saw her wipe her tears quickly.

As my daughters huddled together, I made up my mind. I unbuttoned my coat and the first three buttons of my dress.

Teresa asked, "Momma, what are you doing?"

I ignored her and walked to the street. Since the snow was so heavy, visibility was tricky. Then I saw the headlights and held up my hand.

The taxi driver spotted me and pumped the brakes to slow the vehicle down. The taxi skidded and stopped inches from my legs. The driver rolled his window down and started to yell. As I went around to the driver's side, he shouted, "Hey lady, what the fuck are you doing?"

"I need you to take me to 1851 Greene Avenue in Brooklyn." I saw him staring at my breasts and knew I had him. I could feel his lust.

"Okay, lady, but I could have killed you."

I smiled shyly and complimented him, "That would never happen. I know how skilled you New York taxi drivers are."

He looked me up and down, and I could see he wanted me. "Let me help you with your baggage while opening his door.

The snow blew viciously at the cab driver when he got out of the cab, making it hard for him to close the cab door. He was a heavy-set man with a smelly cigar hanging from his mouth. He barely kept his hat on as he walked around the cab to the passengers' side. I walked in front of the cab, slipping several times before reaching the passenger side. I opened the back and signaled my daughters to move fast with a quick hand gesture.

I pushed them into the car before the cab driver could stop me. I grabbed all our bags, and bundles piling them on top of the five girls crowded in the back. I grabbed Maria and got in front before he could protest.

"Hey, lady! Sorry, but I can't take all these people in my cab. The law..." He got into the driver's seat.

"It's so cold, and the wind is so brutal." I ran my free hand through my hair, shaking out the snow, acting helpless. "Please, can you help me?"

The cab driver glanced at the children and hesitated. Then he started up the car and turned the heater on high. It warmed us.

The driver turned the heater up higher, and the burst of hot air instantly filled the cab. It warmly blew on our cold bare legs.

I felt the heat touch my bare legs, so soothing and relaxing. Even Maria calmed down and rested. When the driver told me to tell the children that if a cop came by to duck, I relayed this to them in our Sicilian dialect. They did not reply, for they were simply happy to be warm and out of the wind and snow.

"Where to again?"

"181 Greene Avenue, Brooklyn!"

I checked my daughters in the backseat to see if they were comfortable. Teresa and Pina cuddled the two younger ones on their laps, keeping them warm. My Vincenza, my Cenza, was behind the driver, looking out of the window, amazed at the falling snow. On occasion, there had been snow in Sicily, but not like this. As always, Cenza began asking questions, but I put my finger to my lips and told her to be quiet and not disturb the cab driver. For once, Cenza was obedient and did what I asked, even though I knew this was hard for her because she was the inquisitive one.

As we drove, the cab driver began flirting. I smiled so that he would keep talking. He rattled on and on. I was comfortable for the first time all day and looked out of the window at the snow. I started to daydream. My mind wandered back to when we were in Sicily, my real home. I imagined the sweet scent of the untouched mountain terrain. I remembered the laughter of my daughters at the farmhouse. How they played happily, running after the chickens and splashing cold water from the well onto each other on a hot summer day.

Then I replayed how we got from our beloved warm island to here, in the frigid New York City winter.

Her husband demanded that they all move to America. "Anna, why do you think I married you?" he asked. "I married you because you are an American citizen. I had a lot of offers that begged my parents for my hand in marriage. I owned my village home! I leased a farm that I worked on!"

That same night, after dinner, Anna followed her husband to ask him about his announcement that they were moving to the United States. She knew that she had no right to question him. Women in her station never asked their husbands. They did as they were told. However, she knew that working in America was more difficult. She did not think she could handle the responsibility that would be conferred upon her because she was no longer young. She also knew that life in the new world would be vastly different. She realized that everything from the modern stores with their beautiful things would be out of reach for them financially. She knew they would not be able to attend the theater and eat at the many ethnic restaurants that the city had to offer. Anna felt that she had to question him for her daughter's sake.

They were settled in their simple, uncomplicated lives, and the older daughters were in school. In America, her older girls would have to go to work in a factory. There would be no education for them.

Franco, Anna's husband, was sitting against the water wall in their backyard when she approached him. He was drinking wine as usual and smoking. She asked him why he insisted on going to America when the scars left after World War II started to heal.

Slurring his words because he was inebriated, he said, "I could have married a woman who owned land and who could have given me many sons to help me work my farm. Did you think that having so many daughters would not cost us? I could have married a woman who I did not have to show how to please me when she touched me." The pain was still sharp in her heart, remembering his words. She had thought their love for each other was bottomless and dependable.

She had trusted him with her whole being.

Franco said, "We will go to America!"

Anna, shocked at her husband's demand, protested angrily, "No, Franco, I will not go. My daughters and I belong here!"

Franco lifted his fist and struck Anna hard in her face, and she fell to the ground, semi-conscious.

Franco asked, "Who is Innocenza's father, Anna? Who is my fifth daughter's father?" Angrily, Franco repeated for the third time, "Who?"

That question continually rolls around in my head. I remembered the pain from his hand. I touched my face, where Franco had hit me and rubbed the spot.

How could he think that one of our daughters could not be his? Yes, that daughter was different from the others. Yes, she had darker olive skin and hazel eyes. Our other girls were all light-skinned like Franco. Most of the girls had light hair, and a few had dark hair. Some girls had his blue eyes, and her second had her hazel eyes like hers, but Innocenza was dark. Yes, Innocenza was more content and quieter than the others.

Franco knew that I was innocent when we married. I never had another man because her parents, religion, and society would at no time permit it. Why would he think that of me? Because one before we met, I had liked a boy from a nearby village? But that was nothing. I adored Franco, and I cannot believe he thought I could ever be with another man. My poor Innocenza, always to bear her father's suspicion.

"Momma, I need to go to the bathroom."

"What did you say?" I was startled.

"I have to go to the bathroom," Maria repeated.

I looked at the cab driver. He was still babbling on.

"How long before we arrive?"

"Not too long. It's just the weather is making it slow going."

Suddenly, the cab slid across some ice and started to veer off the road. The cabbie tried to control the car. However, it slid across the street, hitting the curb. The passengers swayed from side to side, squealing. The cab driver braked; we all fell forward. I held onto Maria tightly, almost hitting my own head on the dashboard. The cab driver stopped the cab. We flew backward onto our seats. After a few seconds, the cab driver caught his breath. He asked if everyone were okay as he feared that one of the children would be hurt. I turned to the daughters in the back seat and asked if they were all right. I assured the driver they were unharmed.

Maria began crying. I rubbed my little daughter's back to console her. At first, I thought it was because she was scared, but I felt warm water running down my dress and between my legs from the near-accident.

I whispered, "It's okay, that happens sometimes, and we can't help ourselves."

I was angry that I forgot clean underwear and guilty for not taking care of my daughters' needs before we left. Being under such stress was still no excuse for not packing the proper clothes.

As we turned onto the road towards the address, I tried to remember the building I was seeking. They all looked alike, and the snow made the search more difficult. I randomly pointed to one I felt was right and directed the cab driver to it. He stopped. We got out of the cab, and I sent them loaded with all their bundles into the building. It was tough going since the snowdrifts were huge.

I watched the girls as they opened the door and entered the building. Then the cab driver told me in a flirting way what the fare for the cab ride was.

I waited until the girls were safely in the building. Then I asked him to wait for us since I'd be right back. Before he said another word, I shut the door and hurried quickly inside.

The dark entrance way made it hard to see.

Teresa asked, "Momma, what are we doing here?"

I put up her finger to her mouth to indicate to be quiet. Maria started crying, and she picked her up. Innocenza clung to her coat, and I took her hand. "Follow me."

Frustrated, Pina asked, "Please, Momma, can we just sit here and wait for you? I am so tired."

"No, Pina. It is too dangerous. I want all of you to stay with me and do as I say. We need to climb up one flight of stairs, and I do not want any complaints. Now, pick our belongings."

Teresa whined. "Momma, "Please, I can..."

I let go of Enza's hand and turned to my oldest daughter. I grabbed Teresa by the coat and pushed her up to the stairs. "I am tired too. Pick up your bag. Do you hear me complain? Now move!"

I led Enza up the stairs, and the others followed. I walked over to Apartment 2B and knocked lightly on the door. Then I knocked again a little harder. A deep hoarse voice behind the door said, "I don't know who you are, and I don't fucking care! Back away from my door. I have a shot-gun, and I have no qualms in putting a bullet through the fucking door and killing you."

I froze. We all backed up, and I led everyone back to the foyer. I was shaking when we reached the entrance to the building. I was grateful my daughters did not understand what the man behind the door had said. I scanned the foyer. Between fleeing the cab and the snow, I picked the wrong building.

"We are leaving this building because it is the wrong one."

Cenza asked, "It is obvious that you are looking for someone who is it... Momma?"

I ignored Cenza and ordered my children to pick up their belongings. They protested as I began shoving them out of the door. She told them not to go near the cab and that she was going to talk to the driver. "Teresa, you and Pina take care of Maria and Innocenza. Now go and hurry; it is getting colder outside. Get into the building next door."

It was ten minutes since we left the cab, and I knew the driver would be edgy. I trekked back through the snow and heard him yell, "Hey, lady, What is up with you? I need my money!"

I bent down to the window, flashed my cleavage, and apologized to the cab driver. It was the wrong building. I will be right back." Before he had a chance to argue, I shut the cab door and rushed as quickly as possible to the next building.

We stood in a similar foyer as the last building. Everyone's shoes and socks were soaked from the snow.

As soon as I looked around, I realized that while this building seemed right, it wasn't the building I wanted. I sat on the step and put my head between my legs. I knew I was scaring my daughters.

For the first time that day, they felt insecure because their mother was frustrated and beside herself.

Cenza said, "Momma."

"Cenza... please... be quiet, I need to think!"

"Momma, I think we are on the wrong side of the street." Cenza raised her voice so I would acknowledge her.

"Cenza, stop yelling. Why are you questioning me? You are always questioning." I barked. "I told you to..." Then I asked, "What did you say?"

"I have been watching the streets and the numbers to the houses, Momma, and when we approached the entrance of this street, the cab driver couldn't get down the street because there were piles of snow that blocked the way. He went around the buildings and entered the other way."

I lifted my head as Cenza was talking. I realized that while I daydreamed, I had lost all concept of our direction. I suddenly realized that I missed the cab driver going around the block.

"Cenza...my dear daughter... I think you are right." Once again, I ordered my children out of the building. They all moaned and complained, but they did what I said.

Meanwhile, the cab driver had driven to the new building where we had gone and waited. I went to the open window across from the driver's side and explained again I had the wrong building.

"Look, lady, I need my money. I need to bring the cab back to the station. The snow is getting worse, and all the cabs are being recalled to home base." Angrily, he demanded, "So, give me my money!"

"Sir, if you could give my family and me a little more time, I will get you your money."

"Fuck!" He screamed, "You mean to tell me you have no money to pay me?"

He stepped on the gas pedal and sped off, swaying from one side of the road to the other, spraying icy snow all of us.

Maria started crying again. When I picked her up, I realized the child was freezing from her wet clothes. I had to get them into a warm building because they were in danger of frostbite.

I panicked and peered in all directions. I stared into the heavily snowed road. The wind was now becoming bitterer, and it blew on us and our bare legs, biting our skin. All our extremities were ice cold.

I finally spotted the building. Cenza was right. We were standing on the wrong side of the street. I held Maria and Innocenza's hand and slowly stumbled across the road. As we approached this other building, it appeared familiar. I kept checking that my girls were keeping up with me. Each one of my daughters had to pick up their ice-cold wet feet and had to take huge steps in the snow, balancing themselves and their packages. The wind blowing made the process more challenging for them to move. But they followed me. They still believed that I was going to protect them and take them to safety.

We stood in front of this last building. As we entered, I recognized the building's well-known, homey walls and knew I was in the right place. The foyer had a familiar smell I remembered from times past. Although the hallway was cold, at least I had my family out of the bitter blowing wind.

"We are home."

Cenza started to question me again, "Cenza, please. Wait for your questions. They will all get answered."

I knew my inquisitive one was frustrated, but she quieted down as we all walked upstairs. My headache grew worse, and my back was aching. The cold, stuffy hallway made it hard for me to breathe. I pushed myself, so my daughters wouldn't know how fatigued I was. I was sweating despite the cold because I knew that this was our last stop, and then there was no place else to take my family. I prayed hard, asking God for help.

We went up one flight, and in the dim hallway, I stopped in front of a door that said 2B.

My knocks echoed down the hall.

1947-1948

On December 5, 1947, Tennessee William's premiered "A Street Named Desire." This playwright, also known for his screenplays and poetry.

Frank Capra was known to the Gennusa family. Not for his directing "It's a Wonderful Life" and other films, but because he was born in Bisacquino, Sicily, their home village.

Jackie Robinson, hired by Branch Rickey, broke the color line in Major League Baseball.

Al Capone dies of syphilis.

One

∾

The door slightly opened, and Anna saw a part of a man's face looking at her. The person asked, "What is it that you want?"

"Excuse me... Sir... I apologize." Anna stopped, exhausted, took a deep breath, and then continued, "But I am looking for a person. Her name is Angelia Costa?" Anna said.

"Who did you say?"

"Please, Angelia Costa? She used to live here."

"Who?"

Anna started to repeat herself, "Her name is. An..."

"Yes, yes, I heard you."

He shut the door, leaving Anna and her daughters wondering why he hadn't even taken the time to tell her that he did not know Angelia Costa. Anna stared at the door and became scared. After all these years, why would the same person still be living here?

Anna wondered whether they could spend the rest of the night on the stairs leading to the third floor. She questioned if they would be safe and if they could survive the cold, long night. She knew there were dirty socks for them to change into, to keep them dry and somewhat warm.

As Anna tried to figure out how they would survive the night, the door opened wide. A small, middle-aged woman with dark graying hair stood with the man, staring at them. Both wore their night-clothes, and the woman had a shawl wrapped around her.

"Why do you want Angelia Costa?"

As Anna answered, the woman squinted her eyes, stared at her, and exclaimed, "Anna!"

"Angie?"

"Oh," Angie put her hand at her heart, took a deep breath, "My God, what are you doing here? And who are these children?"

Angie saw that the girls and Anna were utterly drenched. From their icy soaking hair to their thin, dripping clothes and sodden shoes, they were shivering and wet from top to bottom.

"Angie," Anna said, "I need your help. These are my daughters, and we have nowhere to go."

"These are your children?"

"I have no money and nowhere to go," Anna said, shaking for fear of rejection.

The man moved Angie gently aside, "Angie, for heaven's sake, we have guests, let them in! Hurry... Hurry, children, get out of the cold hallway." He smiled sweetly and exclaimed, "Angie, these children look hungry!"

The man attempted to take Maria out of Anna's arm, but the little girl resisted. He glanced at Innocenza, bent down, and opened his arms. Innocenza seeing his sweet, cheerful, pink face, ran to him. Happily, he picked her up and bounced her in his arms as they entered the apartment. "Come, come," said the man as he reached out his one free arm to the rest of the family. "I am Angelo. Please come in out of the cold hallway."

Then Angelo asked the little girl, in Sicilian, "What is your name?"

"My name is Innocenza."

"Did you know that your name means innocence?"

Innocenza gazed at Angelo, surprised. She smiled because he knew what her name meant. She giggled and snuggled into his arms.

Angie hugged Anna, who held onto Angie tightly. "Come into our home, Anna."

The Gennusa family walked into a modest apartment after many hours of uncertainty and finally felt safe and warm. The kitchen was wonderfully cozy and inviting.

Angelo said, "Look at these children. They must be hungry. This sweet child in my arms is cold. I will get the soup from the refrigerator and heat it." He looked to his wife, "You get the children out of their wet clothes. I bet the bread is still warm."

The young girls removed their wet coats, scattering them onto chairs and hangers to dry. They changed into their dry but dirty clothes.

"Angie, my daughters need to use the bathroom."

"Of course," Angie said. She grabbed the bathroom key, led the girls out of the apartment and down the hallway. She unlocked the bathroom door with her key.

Angie said, "Be quiet not to wake up the supervisor downstairs. When you finish, lock the door, and quietly come back to the apartment. Be sure to stay together. Don't take long for the bathroom can get very chilly."

While Anna waited for her daughters to return from the bathroom, she studied the familiar three-room railroad apartment. The door opened into the kitchen, which led into a living room, and then into a third room that was the only bedroom.

When the daughters returned, Angelo hurried them to sit at the kitchen table to eat. The soup had fresh vegetables and plenty of meat. The bread was homemade, served warm with melted butter. It had been the best meal the family had had since they left Sicily. The food was familiar, and they all ate heartily. Exhausted from their day, the family was ready to sleep anywhere.

Maria fell asleep in Anna's arms. Anna placed her on one of Angelo's jackets beside Innocenza on the living room floor. That little one had her feet tucked in one of Angelo's wool hats for warmth.

Angelo giggled as he tickled Innocenza's feet while putting her feet into his warm cap.

The four older girls wore Angie's wool socks willingly. Francesca slept on the couch, and the other three girls slept in Angelo and Angie's bed. Warm and exhausted, they fell asleep quickly.

Angelo knew he was no longer needed by his wife. Before he settled down in a living room chair, he checked each of the children to ensure they were warm. He pulled a coat over him and slept soundly in a most uncomfortable chair, occasionally making a soft snoring sound.

Angie and Anna sat at the kitchen table, drinking hot demitasse coffee. The only light in the apartment was a candle between them.

"Tell me, my friend, how did you get yourself into this situation? Your daughters do not speak any English, so I am assuming that you have just arrived in the city? The last I knew you were in Sicily."

Anna sighed and told Angie how she traveled to the U.S. despite protesting her husband's demands. She had no choice and took her children aboard the ship. Franco caught pneumonia and died last night.

"Whenever I asked him how we would survive, he told me it was none of my business."

"Anna, did your husband have money with him?"

"I did not think so, but after he died, I took a satchel that he guarded, and in it, there was money. I did not know this until we reached the dock. I showed the official my papers, and I was told to go to a particular building, room 410. They told me people were waiting to sponsor Franco into the country.

"I had no idea what they were talking about, but I did what I was told. I went into the building, and these people I never saw before called me by name and came to us like they were family. The man whispered to me that he and his wife were paid to sponsor Franco to get into the country and got part of a retainer. I explained that Franco died. He whispered that he wanted the rest of his money, regardless if Franco was alive or not.

"I looked into the satchel, found a bundle of cash. The stranger signed some papers and kept a copy. He handed me a copy and led us out of the room with his wife following. When we were out of the room and in the main Port Authority building, he grabbed my satchel, took the money, and ran. When I realized what he'd done, I ran after them. After catching up with them, I grabbed the satchel back. During the fight, the woman grabbed the money. Then she and her husband ran through the crowd. I had no idea what to do. I knew that my children could be taken away from me if I asked the officials for help."

"Where is Franco's body now?"

"The ship's doctor who took care of Franco told me that New York State would bury him in Potters Field. He told the city Franco was traveling alone and would take him and bury him. The doctor assured me that there would be no inquires made. After we got through the inspection and those sponsors stole all our money, we were alone with no money and no place to go. We stayed at the Port Authority Building as long as we could. Then as it was closing, they told us to leave the building. I found myself outside in this blistering weather with my daughters, destitute. I never felt so alone."

"What made you come here?"

Anna drank some of the intense hot coffee. She held the cup to her nose and smelled its rich aroma, and its warmth felt good on her cold, trembling hands. She sipped some more, enjoying its luxurious taste. "MMMMMM. This coffee is so good."

She leaned back, "I was standing outside the Port Authority when I put my hand into my pocket. I pulled out my white spool of thread, and you came into my mind... I thought of you and remembered the days that we worked together."

"You mean to tell me you still carry that silly spool of white thread?" Angie asked, "God in heavens! You could have frozen to death! It is so cold outside."

"Somehow, my instincts came back to me how to survive in this city. That is when I hailed a cab."

"You did what?"

"I hailed a cab,"

"You mean to tell me you got a cab driver to drive you here in this weather with no money? Do you know how dangerous that is?"

"Well, I did have to use some feminine persuasion." Anna laughed, blushing, "I was fortunate that he was a nice man. He and the cab smelled bad, but it felt so good to get out of the cold wind, we did not care how it smelled."

Anna hesitated. "Angie. I have no money, and I have nowhere to go. I know I should not impose on you and your husband, but I have no one to ask for help. Can you help my children and me? I will work and pay you back as soon as I can." Anna closed her eyes and asked, humbly, "Please."

"You don't have to ask, of course. I can help you." Angie went over to Anna and hugged her.

Anna returned the hug, swallowed hard, "Thank you."

"I don't think my husband is going to let Innocenza go."

"I hope you don't regret this. Enza is quiet, but Maria, when she gets her sleep and is fed well, will be running around this apartment. I will try to keep her calm."

"Wonderful. That is wonderful. Angelo is a child himself. He can be running around with her."

Anna and Angie stayed up talking the whole night and watched the sunrise and the blizzard still raging outside.

"When I married Angelo, we moved into this apartment because my parents were old and needed care. As you can see," Angie said, "Not much has changed here, not even the furniture. I am still in the same apartment that you left me in. My sweet Angelo adapts, God love him, to any situation. "

Anna told her about her marriage to Franco and how they weathered through World War II together. The strain that her husband felt during and after the war was massive. They had some bad weather, and the olives that they harvested last season were small. That was why her husband decided to come to this country. "He thought it would be best for us to come here and put the older daughters to work. After working for a few years and saving some money, we would return to Sicily. He was concerned that if we stayed in Sicily, we could never save enough for our daughter's dowries, and they would be forced to marry beneath their stations. It was of great concern to Franco." Anna took a deep breath, "His intentions were good."

"Anna, did you explain how hard it is to live in this country and save money?"

"Yes... I did, but Franco would not listen. He heard from my father that the streets of America were paved with gold.".

Anna told Angie how hard it had been to leave her family and their home. She and her daughters were happy in their simple lives.

As the sun rose, the storm had subsided but left mounds of snow in the streets and buildings. The women still at the kitchen table watched as the sun showed its bright face and shined through the windows, making the snow glisten. The news reported over the radio said that New York's city was completely shut down due to the weather.

Angelo awoke and joined the women for coffee. He was delighted to hear that their company was staying with them. "I will start looking for a job as soon as the weather makes it easy for me to look."

"That is not a problem. I will get you a job with me. With all your sewing talent, they will pay you more than me."

"That would be wonderful."

"Angelo, what do we do about the Superintendent of the building?"

Angelo saw Anna's concern. "Don't worry, my friend, we will find a way to get around him. Wonderful! Wonderful!" It is about time we had some life in this apartment."

Angelo heard a sound and turned to see the little ones waking up. He strolled over, tickled Enza's toes then opened his arms to her as she ran to him. They laughed when he threw her up into the air and then hugged her. Anna was shocked to see how Enza lovingly reacted to this stranger. Angelo held one arm open for Maria, but she was sleepily rubbing her eyes and slowly walked toward her mother.

At around noon, Angie came into the apartment with her arms loaded with winter gloves, boots, and wool hats. She walked across the family room calling the children and told them to try them on.

"Where did you get all the clothes?"

"This morning early, I went upstairs to my neighbor, Mrs. Carney, and told her I needed clothes for my company staying with me. I told her about your situation, and she spread the news - not only in our building but throughout the neighborhood. We should have enough winter coats and more boots by tonight, which our neighbors donated to you and your family. They will not be new clothes, but they will be warm and comfortable. Your children will have proper clothes for this cold winter. I know that there will be plenty of clothes for you too."

"I don't understand. How does something like this happen?"

"We are not a rich neighborhood, but we have all been in your place with no place to go. We are not a neighborhood but a family. When one is in need, we all help. When the snow melts, and it is clear for us to, we will have a party so you can meet the neighbors."

Angie put her arm around Anna, "We just ask that when you can help with donations, please donate."

Anna put her hand on her heart, "Really... you people truthfully take care of each other?"

"Yes, by tonight, we'll also have enough food to feed all of us for weeks. All donated by our neighbors."

Angelo said in a joyful voice, "Angie... tonight, the children will be fed well! Enza, where are you?" he turned and spotted her, "Ah, there you are, my sweet friend, you said you know how to cook French toast? You said the cook taught you how to cook it when you were on the ship, and that was your favorite American food. Well, tonight, my child, you will show me how to cook French toast!" He raised his arms, "We will have a French toast dinner for all!"

Angelo turned to Angie and took a hat from her hands. He turned to Enza, "Here, my little one try this on." Enza smiled and went to him, followed by Maria. Angelo saw Maria following her sister, and he laughed with delight. "Okay, a hat for the littlest one!"

The older girls rummaged through the clothes, trying them on and handing big or small items to their sisters.

Cenza walked over to the window, thinking, *"How could this be? How could people be so kind and generous?"*

Anna saw Cenza looking out the window and knew not to disturb her. Her daughter was mulling over things on her mind, and it was always loving and enterprising. She turned to her other daughters, smiling. It had been the first-time Anna had seen her children smile since they left Sicily.

"Angelo, do you think we will have enough room in this apartment with all the donations that will be given to us today? Will there be enough room for us to sleep?"

With joy in his heart, "Well, we can use the bread given to us as pillows, and we can use the coats as blankets!" Angie gazed at her husband with a smile on her face, shook her head.

Anna turned to Angie with her hand to her heart, "How can I ever repay you for all you are doing for us?"

Angie poured her a fresh cup of coffee. "You already have."

"How is that?".

"By coming here to me with your family. You can see how happy you have made my husband with your children. Not having any of our own, you have helped me give him what he has always wanted." Angie hesitated, "Not having any children of our own is another story...I owe him happiness, Anna."

Angie smiled, "Look at him. I have not seen this happy since I can remember."

It was late evening as the daughters were getting ready for bed and needed to use the bathroom. "Remember," Angie said, "Only flush the toilet once. We don't want to make the Superintendent aware of you being here." Angie handed Teresa the key, and the daughters tiptoed to the bathroom.

Anna was amazed at the clothes and food donated to their cause. She promised herself if she were ever able to help this neighborhood, she would. She was indeed indebted to these wonderfully warm people she just met.

The daughters came back from the bathroom, giggling. Anna told them to go to bed. Angelo helped them get under their covers. He promised that tomorrow they would go outside after breakfast, and if it were a sunny day, build a snowman.

Quite somber, Enza asked, "What is a snowman?"

Angelo picked her up and hugged her. Then laughing, he tickled her. He explained to all the daughters what a snowman was. "And when we're are done with the snowman, I'll show you how to make a snow angel."

"Angelo, what is a snow angel?"

Angelo gave Enza another hug. "You'll see!"

As Angie and Anna listened to Angelo's description of what a snowman was, they realized that he had the children laughing and had them already tucked into their blankets on the floor. He was telling them tall tales as they drifted off to sleep

Angie took Anna's arm leading her to the final set of blankets. "Get a good night's sleep. You'll be no good for your daughters or yourself if you don't get some rest!"

Anna down on the soft blankets and quickly fell into a deep sleep.

The smell of strong wine and stale cigarettes filled the air. It was sexually stimulating, and she could not get enough of that smell. She felt the wet and pleasing kiss for which she yearned. She engulfed herself in the scent and then could no longer breathe. She started to choke from the surrounding smell. She tried to wipe the scent from her nose, trying to remember the kiss, but her hand would not move. She wanted to run, but her feet would not move. Franco's mood was bitter. His temper was bold. He kept reminding her that he did not love her. She stretched out her arms to him but could not reach him.

He turned away from her. The pain! The pain she was feeling was profound. She tried hard not to experience it, but the pain was severe. She twisted and turned in her bed, trying to escape the loss of his love, when finally...

Anna woke up, startled from her nightmare. She was hot, and sweat ran down under her arms. At first, she did not remember where she was. Sitting upright, she finally recognized the room. Throwing off the covers, she stretched her back and then lay down slowly on her pillow. Resting her head and letting her body become cool, she thought about her dream. She remembered the last time she was with her husband on the ship as they gazed deeply into each other's eyes, still in love. She wanted so much to reach out to him and tell him how much she loved him. She had stared into his captivating blue eyes, and she saw his deep love for her.

Then a split second later, he turned from her.

Anna stared at the ceiling, wondering what went wrong. He had ripped out her heart. What did she do to lose his love for her? Why did she not confront him instead of staying in her place as a compliant wife? She tried several times, gently without overstepping her bounds, to get him to open to her.

However, at her every move, he resisted her. What was tormenting him? What had happened that he could not have come to her? She would have forgiven him. She thought about how amazing their sex life was together in the early years after their marriage. She longed for him to touch her. After the hard delivery, when her youngest was born and was yet another girl, no more passion ever came from him.

She watched the sunrise. She reached for her blanket and covered herself. She again wondered why she was not in Sicily, her homeland, waiting for the birth of spring to arrive.

Two

~~

December 17, 1947

Dear Momma and Papa,

It is difficult to tell you that Franco caught pneumonia and died on our last night of our trip. After my daughters and I reached this country, I contacted a friend. She and her husband have taken us in. The city is truly cold, and the snow is remarkably high. Unprepared for this harsh weather clothes-wise, Angie and Angelo, my friends, told their neighbors. Within several hours, we were dressed for the coldest environment. The people here have been amazing. Please do not worry, for we are doing fine. I am getting a job and will write soon to tell you about it. I miss you very much. Tell my sisters that I miss them too, especially Gi.

I will write soon.

Anna

After writing the letter to her family, Anna was heartbroken. She missed them all, especially her sister Gi, whom she loved dearly. When they were young, Anna and Gi shared all their secrets. She had proudly named her second daughter after her and their mother.

Early one morning, five days after their arrival, Anna and Teresa got off the subway. Anna was thinking of her home island. She knew that the fertile soil would bloom with its fruits of olives, dates, oranges, and many other foods in a few short months. She longed for her island as she knew her daughters did too. Her village, still cold from winter, was milder than what she was experiencing today.

When she was in New York before working with her father and sister, they used the subway as their primary transportation. The noise and scurrying of the travelers on their way toward their destinations were still the same. Even the smell had not changed. Maybe the city's scent was a little thicker from all the cars and buses. For some reason, she did not feel like a total stranger anymore, which made her feel a bit more secure.

Anna and her oldest daughter followed Angie as they walked on W36th Street and 7th Avenue towards a large old brick building in the garment district. Along with a crowd of workers, the women emerged from the subway into the biting winter weather—harsh icy winds whipping around them. Everyone veered in different directions, fighting to keep their coats and scarves wrapped snugly around their shivering bodies as they struggled to reach their jobs.

Angie had gotten Anna and Teresa jobs at the company where she worked. As they approached the building, Anna saw the enormous three-floor establishment rising above her. She touched the chiseled words on the brick front, "Simon and Simon." Anna knew the garment district because this is where she and her sister Gi had work years before.

Angie, Anna, and Teresa entered the building, shivering from the frigid outdoors. They climbed a flight of stairs to the second floor. It was chilly, cold, and damp and smelled of mold Anna and Teresa remained by a large door that led into a vast sewing room. A booming vibration of sewing machines tapping away came into the hallway. Angie opened the door, and the sound was deafening. It hurt their eardrums. Anna and Teresa cringed, but not Angie. The noise was al-most nonexistent to her, as she had worked for this clothes company for many years.

They looked at many rows of sewing machines being worked dili-gently by women. All heads were down intensely working in a dimly lit cold room. Each woman wore a coat or a heavy sweater -with a shawl over their shoulders for more warmth. Anna was again ex-tremely grateful for the warm clothes that Angie's neighbors had given her family. She scanned the room, noting each sewing machine had a light on it, directed onto the fabric. There were bundles of neatly stitched clothes placed in boxes by every device. Behind the sewing machines were piles of fabric waiting to be put together into a garment.

A woman in her early fifties, who seemed much older, stopped working and approached them. Like Angie, she had been with the company for many years. They saw that she was slightly bent over. Obviously, in great pain from her back condition, she did not com-plain, fearing to lose her job. She greeted Angie warmly.

Angie introduced Mrs. Barkowitz to Anna and Teresa. Then Mrs. Barkowitz led Anna over to an empty machine across the room. Meanwhile, Angie led Teresa to a flight of stairs to the third floor.

Where Angie led Teresa was identical to the vast room downstairs. A large woman with gray hair rose from her machine. She joined them and escorted Teresa to her sewing machine.

Angie returned to the second floor and went directly to her sewing machine across the room from Anna. She quickly got to work because she had lost time helping Anna and Teresa settled in their new jobs. She worked extra fast that morning to make her quota or lose her job.

Anna saw Angie start working. She peered around the room and watched the other women. Memories of her and her sister Gi working long and hard hours flooded through her. She thought this building looked much, such as the one where they worked many years ago. She wondered at the many years between now and her first job in New York doing the same trade. She sighed, turned to her machine, and started to work fast, remembering her responsibility to Angie and Angelo.

The lunch bell rang, and Anna, with the other women, stretched their tired backs. They rose from their machines, grabbed their lunch pails, and walked into a small room. Angie accompanied Anna to where they would eat lunch. Angie also told Anna that one of her friend's daughters, who worked on Teresa's floor, would care for her. They entered a crowded room with a few tables and chairs. Most of the women ate lunch standing up because they had been sitting all morning. The older women sat at the tables. The room was filled with women chatting.

Angie squeezed by a group standing by the door, and Anna followed her. They reached two other women leaning against it, talking away.

"Sadie, this is my friend Anna!"

Sadie, a small, pretty woman, Anna's age, shook her hand. "Hi Anna, welcome to our hell-hole."

"What did you say?"

"Anna," Angie turned Anna to the other woman, "This is my other friend, June. She lives in our neighborhood at the end of the street."

June, a tall, a once-beautiful faced, blonde-haired beauty, was in her late twenties. Her bright green eyes were sad and empty. Her face's dry skin showed she didn't care to keep up her looks. She waved slightly and elevating her voice over the sound of the background noise, "Angie has told me so much about you, Anna. It is nice to finally meet you."

Anna thought how much lovelier June could be if she combed her hair and wore softer and more feminine clothes. This sad face in front of her looked like life did not go well for her.

Anna wondered why a pretty person like this was so unhappy. In Anna's creative mind, she had June dressed in a softer look. This sad, sweet spoken girl evidently did not care about herself.

Anna started to put her lunch pail on the floor when Angie stopped her and told her to hold it. She explained that anything, including lunch put on the floor during lunch, was a free-for-all.

"I don't understand."

Sadie said, "It will get stolen and stolen fast. You will never see who did it. Some of the women here don't bring lunch because they don't have the money to buy food. Some can't even afford breakfast. They are lucky if they eat one meal a day."

Anna's body shook listening, and it was at that moment that Anna decided never to complain about the pain she had in her lower back. She was grateful to be working and for a good friend to help feed her and her daughters.

A loud bell rang, and some of the women walked out of the lunchroom. Angie explained the signal was for anyone needing the bathroom to do so now. "If you have to go into the bathroom during working hours, you have to ask our floor manager, and that can be embarrassing."

"Who is our floor manager?"

"The short, fat ugly man over there," Sadie pointed to him, "The one with the big pants hanging off his stomach." Anna peeked in the direction that Sadie pointed.

Sadie continued, "That one with the round face and hanging jowls like a bulldog. He has scars all over it. Don't get too close to him. He is dirty." Sadie made a face. "He smells so bad like he has not taken a bath in weeks, and when he does take a bath, he still smells." Sadie made another face, "He looks right through your clothes to your naked body when he looks at you. Every time I think of him, he makes me want to throw-up."

"I saw him this morning going by me and watching me on my machine," Anna said.

June said in a low bitter voice, "Bastard... You stay away from him, Anna. Don't even look into his eyes or let him see you watching him. He can make your life miserable here. He will strip you of all your dignity."

"Stop it, June," Angie said. "She may be beautiful but is too old for him. His taste is for the younger ones."

"You're right; he likes them young," Sadie said.

"I am sorry, but I don't understand?"

June, with hate in her eyes, said, "He's a filthy pig."

Angie told Anna, "Hurry, if you need to go to the bathroom, we don't have much time. When the second bell rings, we have to go back to our machines."

The women moving from the lunchroom turned right and hurried to join a long line for the bathroom. Anna glanced around at the large room again. Several feet beyond the toilet, there was a door that said, "Manager." The walls had worn paint on them and were very dirty. Along the wall were double windows that were large and dirty. On the opposite end of the room, a set of stairs led to enclosed loft rooms with big windows. Anna asked, "Angie, who is up there?"

"That is where the owner of the factory has his office and office help." She pointed at the door on the stair said, "That door goes out of the back of the building. The owner and his office help use that door to come into the building."

Anna wondered what they did in the main office. Before she could ask, she heard a woman standing in the middle of the line shout to them to hurry up so that everyone could get in the restroom before the bell rang. When Anna's turn to go into the bathroom came, she found Angie and her new-found friends mingling in the crowded room. Her stomach turned from her lunch because the air smelled awful. The toilets and sinks were filthy. Trash scattered on the floor was stepped on so many times that it was ground into the tiles. The walls were painted a dark gray, and they too were filthy. Several dirty windows across the room were tightly shut. Anna was appalled at the conditions of the room. The women had to bring in their own toilet paper.

Angie forgot to tell Anna to bring paper for her use, so Angie gave her half. The bell rang, and all the women returned to work. Anna was grateful to get out of the bathroom into the large open room even if it was chilly because the bathroom smelled horrible. The machine pounding resumed, and Anna realized less than twenty minutes had passed between eating lunch and bathroom break

At the end of the day, Anna, Teresa, and Angie reached home and were completely exhausted. Anna endured a severe backache, refusing to admit it weakened her. When they entered the apartment building, Anna noticed that Maria, Enza, and Francesca were hiding under the foyer's stairway.

"What are you doing? You are supposed to stay at the apartment."

The children giggled when Angelo stuck out his head from around the corner of the second-floor landing.

Anna said, "Stop being so silly and go inside the apartment."

Maria ran up the stairs, and Enza slowly followed.

"Maria... Stop running so fast you are going to fall and hurt yourself." Anna shook her head, knowing that Maria was not listening.

Francesca exclaimed, "Momma. We are torturing the Super!"

Anna put her hand on her hip, surprised at the word torture coming out of her daughters' mouth, "Do you know what the word torture means?"

Before Francesca had a chance to answer, Angelo waved to her, "Come, Francesca...come on, child, before I get you into more trouble. Your mother doesn't want us to have fun!"

Angelo waved Francesca to him.

Angie laughed, "Anna, don't yell at your daughters for being mean to the Super,"

Angie led the way up the first flight of stairs keeping her head turned to Anna. She continued speaking, hitting the second-floor landing step when she says, "He deserves it. He is drunk all the time and always accuses us of not paying our rent when we pay on time the first of every month." They reached the apartment door. "He sometimes locks the bathroom doors on each floor to save money on water and electricity. When we come home at night, there are no lights on any of the floors because he tries to save money to get more money in his paycheck for his drinks. Besides, I know that Angelo put the girls up to it."

Angie opened the door up to the apartment, "Angelo, did you go to work today?"

Angelo faked a cough, saying he was not feeling well. Angie laughed, "But you are well enough to play among the children in the cold, damp hallway?"

"We just left the apartment for a few minutes to get a little needed fresh air," Angelo replied lightly, coughing again.

Francesca said, "Angelo, that is not true. We have been playing."

"Quiet Francesca, I am in enough trouble,"

Francesca was giggling in the apartment's warm kitchen that smelled so good. Pina and Cenza made the evening meal - a chicken with roasted potatoes.

"What? No mashed potatoes with butter for us for dinner?"

"No, Momma," Pina said, "Mrs. Carney, the lady from upstairs...Oh...Momma, she is so nice. She showed Cenza how to season a chicken and the potatoes. She gave us a recipe on how to cook the gravy for our meal. The Irish call it pan-gray. We spent most of the afternoon with her, and she showed us how to make an American apple pie."

Angie walked over to the kitchen counter, put her nose to a pie, and sniffed it, "You made an apple-pie today with Mrs. Carney?"

"No," Cenza said, "Francesca made it."

"Mrs. Carney makes the best apple pie," said Angelo.

"You made the apple pie?"

Francesca smiled. Anna gave her a big hug, and Francesca said excitedly, "Tomorrow, Mrs. Carney will teach me how to bake chocolate-chip cookies."

Dinner was over, and all was quiet in the apartment. All the residents were in their sleeping area, enjoying a belly full of oven-roasted chicken and the best apple pie. Anna was the last to settle down, lying on her blankets. She was grateful to be resting her aching back. The thought of her having a second helping of Francesca's apple pie made her feel guilty. She had better watch herself, for she could become a fat lady and easily enjoy it. She lay for a few minutes with a smile on her face. She remembered Angelo's face when he got caught skipping work and playing hiding games with her little ones. She needed to talk to him and make sure he did not miss work again. She did not need Angie to get cross with her children. Angie had to make sure that Angelo went to work the next day as his job was desperately needed to help feed this enormous family.

Anna became very sleepy. Her last thoughts were about her day, and she recalled something that she needed to ask Angie about. She wondered why June became hostile when the factory manager was mentioned. Why did her face grow red with anger, even looking at the manager? It bothered Anna, for she could not imagine why this girl reacted this way.

Several days later, Anna noticed a stunning young woman in her late teens, leaving the manager's office in tears. It was before lunch when she happened to lift her head. Picking a piece of fabric to sew, she saw this young woman walking to her sewing machine, not too far away from hers. The girl's long dark hair was pulled up into a scarf.

She clutched her stomach as though she was trying not to vomit. Sobbing, she sat down at her machine and started working.

When Anna met up with Angie, Sadie, and June at lunchtime, she had to ask. "Angie, there is a pretty girl who sits near me by my machine, and after she left the manager's office, she was crying hysterically. Do you know why she was crying?"

"That bastard!" June started crying. She put her head down, staring at the floor. Then she rose and left the room. Anna was shocked at June's reaction.

"Angie," Anna said, "What did I say to get June so upset?"

Sadie answered, "You should tell her. She has the right to know about what goes on here."

Angie whispered, "Tonight, when we are alone, I will tell you about June."

Anna heard the first bell, and she took the last bite from her sandwich. She followed the crowd to the line to stand in front of the bathroom.

When the house was quiet, Anna confronted Angie about the girl who came out of the manager's office crying. Angie poured them a cup of hot coffee and made sure that no one was listening.

Angie took a deep breath, "The manager, DogFace, as we call him, has a thirst for beautiful innocent women. He likes them young and naïve to control them. He frightens them into having sex with them by threatening to fire them. Most of the women who work in the factory need the money badly. He chooses the prettiest girls and takes advantage of them. He strips them of their innocence. He gets great pleasure seeing them leave his office frightened and ashamed. They never complain because this job is their only livelihood, and they need the money badly. Many are teenagers who have been abandoned or live with parents unable to take care of them. Some have younger sisters and brothers who need to be fed and housed. They're the only ones who bring money home for their families."

Anna was appalled. "Is that right for someone to do this?"

"What can they do? Complain to the owners? These girls need these jobs badly. One victim's father even accused his daughter of provoking the situation. There is nowhere for them to turn."

"June... did this happen to her?"

"Yes," Angie said.

"Tell me about what happened to her."

Angie squirmed in her seat. She told her when June came to the factory, a young exquisite blond child, that DogFace could not take his eyes off her. He slobbered in front of her whenever he walked by her workstation. "We all knew that she would be next. The last girl he forced to have sex with him killed herself. We found out after she died that her father had sexually abused her at home too. So, when she was gone, Dog Face was looking for his next victim."

"That was when June came to the factory needing a job badly because her father had just died, and she was alone and needed to support herself. She was at the factory for one month before he summoned her. You could tell that June was frightened because she did not know what she had done. We all stopped our machines and watched her walk into his office. He stood at his door and glared at us. We knew what that look meant. We knew that if we said a word or talked about what went on in his office, we would lose our jobs. After the door closed, Mrs. Barkowitz told us to go back to our machines. We had no choice, so we all continued to work."

"What happened when she came out of the office?"

"When she came out of the office, out of respect, no one looked at her."

With tears in her eyes, Angie continued, "When she left his office, she was crying. She ran to her machine, so ashamed. She put her head down and vomited. One woman helped her, cleaned her dress with rags lying around on the floor, and held her tight. She told her to be strong. June raised her head, turned to her machine, and started to work.

Months later, after many visits to DogFace's office, June lost some of her looks. She was never the same again. The spark in her eyes and her sweet smile was gone. She stopped taking care of herself. She broke off her engagement to a young man because of her shame. Sadie and I never asked her about him because she becomes cold and hostile when men are mentioned around her. Sadie and I stay close to June in hopes that some of the life we saw in her years ago would come back."

"Maybe you should have told the owner?"

"Anna, we couldn't tell anyone because we all need to work. It has been hard since the war ended. All of us at the factory had decent-paying jobs during the war. We worked industriously for the war effort with little pay but happy and proud to have our jobs and help the cause. We wanted to win the war and did our part. After the war, jobs were plentiful. Factories, construction, and all the food industries flourished. There was work for everyone in this country except for us, the uneducated and unskilled laborers. There was steep competition, and we can always be replaced with much stronger and younger, more aggressive personnel. There was a woman who got a job at the company by showing her skills. She put a little flair into our clothes without adding cost to the garment. Of course, they hired her. We all worked faster to make the company profitable so as not to lose our jobs. We did what we had to do to survive and still do. Even June had no choice but to put up with this for many years...until he broke her, and when she got older looking, he moved on to his next younger victim."

"Angie, you should have told me about this before I agree to have my Teresa work for the factory.

"Don't worry about Teresa. She will be fine. Because she works upstairs, he will not touch her. He is smart. He only picks the ones from his floor because he doesn't want owners to know what he is doing.

He does very well production-wise. He brings in more than the other floors in the company. That is why he can do whatever he wants. The owners never question him on how he runs his floor."

"Don't the owners see?"

"The owners only look at their books. They, too, have fallen on hard times because of the war and are trying to recover. Besides, Dog-Face is smart enough to do his dirty deeds when the owners are away – at a meeting, at lunch, at the end of the day, or by the weekend, when they are gone."

The women finished their coffee, hugged each other, and went to bed. Anna lay on her blanket, feeling sick for June. Now she understood why she hated DogFace so much. Anna tossed and turned in her bed and took a long time to fall asleep because she could not get June out of her mind.

Having daughters in this country was a burden on Anna. She always worried about their safety. She worried about them during the war, but she had their father help and somehow knew that he would protect them. Here she was alone. Even though Angie said that Teresa was safe, Anna feared for her.

Anna was so pleased to get her first paycheck. She went to the corner store and made her first American purchase since she had been in the country - donuts for the whole family. It was only one donut for each person within the family but still - a donut. She would not eat hers but cut it into small pieces for the little ones as an extra treat. She knew it was extravagant but made the purchase anyway. That became a family tradition that the children and Angelo loved.

Three

⤫

The New Year of 1948 dawned upon the great city of New York with its people ready to celebrate. The town rejoiced by bidding good riddance to the old and becoming hopeful of more jobs and larger wages for the New Year. The New Year also distanced its people from World War II, and the scars were finally starting to melt into the past.

Regardless of the brutal winter weather, the city still celebrated with the crowd-gathering around Times Square to witness the globe dropping at midnight. Estimated at around seven hundred fifty thousand people, it was small in comparison to past years. However, the city's revelers still cheered and snake-danced together through the streets. The crowd danced, waiting for the massive glowing globe on top of the Times Tower to slide down the pole to welcome in the New Year at midnight.

The bars and nightclubs charged eighty-cents to a dollar for a drink. Champagne cocktails cost up to two dollars. Drinks were outrageously priced but worth it to the people gathered for one massive celebration to get rid of the doldrums from the past year.

In the following months, Anna and Teresa brought in enough money to help pay with rent and food. Anna felt so good. The little ones still hid from the Super of the building, and he never knew that Anna and her family moved in.

The youngest children loved to play disappearing tricks on him. They would knock at his door and afterward run away. He would come out of his apartment, look down the hall, and then go back inside. The little ones did this for a long time, which confused the Super. He would come out of the apartment and start to mumble curse words out of frustration.

The little ones hid under the stairway and giggled. Of course, Angelo was the one to show them where to hide before the Super came out of his apartment. Angelo, on occasion, joined them to help torture him.

"Angelo," the Super said one day when Angelo came home from work and was heading up the first flight of stairs to his apartment,

"Yes, Mr. Hechman,"

"I know you are hiding people in your apartment."

"What did you say, Mr. Hechman?" Angelo said innocently. He looked at the Super, "Why would you say that? Do you think that Angie or I would do anything to spoil our relationship with you? Do you think we would want to jeopardize our home that we have had for many years?"

Angelo put his arm around the Super, "Why would Angie and I have people living with us when we can barely support ourselves? Of course, if you want to help us and lower our rent, that would be wonderful. We accept your offer. How generous it would be of you."

Angelo tried not to get silly.

The Super looked at Angelo and was confused, which he always was whenever Angelo started to double talk him. "Here is a present for you, Mr. Hechman," Angelo pulled out of his coat pocket and handed Mr. Hechman a small bottle of whiskey. Mr. Hechman took the bottle willingly. Angelo skipped up two stairs at a time to his apartment, hurrying away from the Super.

"Angie, children, where is everyone?" Angelo said as he entered his apartment, covering his eyes. The little ones ran to him, jumped into his arms, and he kissed and hugged them. He put them down and walked over to Angie. He opened his coat without the little ones seeing to show Angie that the bottle he carried in his pocket was gone. She pointed to the top cupboard to indicate that there were more hidden there.

The younger daughters were attending a neighborhood school and adjusting well except for Francesca. She hated school and cried every day. She did not want to go to school, and Pina had to push her. At the end of the school day, they walked home together. When they arrived in the afternoon, the older neighbors in the building waited for them. They would be in the building entrance-way, making sure that the Super did not see them. It became fun for all the people inside the building. The Super was a cranky old man who never worked on the apartments when they needed him. Because the Super was too drunk to do his job, hiding the daughters was sweet revenge for the tenants. Even though the older ones did not need babysitting, the residents took care of them too. They knew that these inexperienced girls needed guidance and taught them how to be safe in the neighborhood. The girls had won all the hearts of the residents who lived in the building.

The renters loved the entire family. Anna repaired the tenants' clothes for nothing in return for watching her daughters and feeding them snacks after school. These children never caused any trouble and brought much joy and less loneliness to the older tenants. After school, the tenants would have milk and cookies waiting for them. Sometimes the older tenants would get together and wait for them to come home from school in Mrs. Green's apartment. She lived in the apartment across from the Super. If one of the tenants could not be home when the daughters arrived, she would give Mrs. Green cookies for the sisters.

Whenever Cenza had free time, she sat in the family room cuddled up on the couch, reading one of her many books. She was teaching herself English. Cenza, with her excellent math skills, budgeted all the money that came into the house, even Angie and Angelo's. Cenza's ways to save money made her perfect for doing all the food shopping. She brought home some of the best foods for practically nothing. She looked at the foods' condition, such as apples, and often got them cheaper because they were too ripe to sell or food in a damaged bag or can that customers would not buy.

One day, Cenza came home from the grocery store when she met up with Anna in front of the building. "Momma," Cenza said excitedly, "Mr. White at the grocery store offered me a job after school. I have been watching his customers in his store when I am there shopping, and I have made a few suggestions to help him sell his goods. He liked my suggestions and asked if I would like a job."

"What about your schoolwork?"

"Momma, I would really like to do this. I know how important my studies are. I will handle both."

"Of course, you can take the job, but schoolwork comes first."

As they walked together into the apartment building, Cenza was quiet. Anna knew that her daughter was already thinking about the changes needed at the store. Anna was pleased with Cenza's enthusiasm.

As spring arrived in the city, the people's spirits rose enormously, breathing in the sweet air of spring that made everything better. The neighborhood residents walked and talked with each other even as their children played in the park, enjoying the long sunny days.

Often the neighborhood gathered in the park. Mothers oversaw their children as fathers gathered around to exchange their opinion about the first African American baseball player breaking into the Major League.

Anna, Angie, and Angelo slipped the daughters out of the building and headed for the park. Anna and Angie sat on the park bench while Angelo held Innocenza's small hands walking to the swings, and Maria ran.

"Maria, stop running, you are going to fall! I swear, Angie, that youngest child of mine does not know how to walk."

Angelo and the little ones got to the swings and sat on them. Angie yelled, "Angelo, don't swing Maria too high."

Angelo waved.

"That husband of mine, he is just a young kid himself."

"You say that so often about Angelo, and it troubles me because sometimes you say it with just joy as you do now, and other times you say it with such sadness. Why is that my friend? Why when I can see that you love him so, and yet you are quite sad at times?"

"Yes," Angie said, "I do love him, but not in the way you mean. I love him like a mother who loves a child, and I sometimes have regrets because I don't want to be a mother to him or a mother to anyone."

"I am sorry I don't understand. You are wonderful and a second mother to my children."

"Oh, I know what love truly is. I loved deeply once. I loved with all my heart and thought it would be forever."

"Angie, I am sorry, I never meant to pry."

"You haven't. It feels good to talk to a good friend."

Anna knew what it was like to have a good friend to talk to, a good friend who did not question but listened. Anna thought about her sister Gi, whom she missed and left behind in Sicily. Angie was indeed her good friend.

Angie just kept on talking, and Anna, out of respect, listened to her. "When I was in my early twenties, my brother married and moved to the other side of the city with his new wife. He became involved with his wife and her family. He worked in his wife's family business and was too busy to visit. I missed his company. I was living at home with my parents. It was just the three of us. I was lonely. My parents hated each other and never spoke to each other unless they had to. Our home was quiet, as you know, and was sad all the time."

Angelo waved.

Angie waved back. "I stayed out as much as I could because I was so lonely. I went out every night with my girlfriends. One summer night, we stopped outside the corner store." Angie pointed to the corner store across the street. "When we came out of the store, there was a group of boys. And I saw him. His name was Tony. His black curly hair was slicked back, and he was the most impressive person I had ever seen. He was smoking a cigarette when he turned and looked my way. He was tall, dark-skinned, with big dark eyes, and very handsome. I was hooked when I looked at his face. I fell in love. I didn't know his name, where he lived, or who he was.

"That didn't matter. I was in love. I forced my girlfriends to go every night to the corner store and made them drink sodas until they were ready to burst. I couldn't take my eyes off him. I wanted him. Of course, I didn't know what I wanted because I was inexperienced, but I thought I liked him. The beginning of summer was warm, so one early night my girlfriends and I were coming out of the store. We had drunk so many sodas that I started to burp. He walked over and stood in front of me. I was shocked and so surprised that he even noticed me. The night air was sweet and cast a tranquilizing spell that lowered my inhibitions. I was floating when he stood in front of me.

"Hi," he said, "I'm Tony. What is your name?" I looked into his dark eyes and said my name after I burped again, feeling dumb. I put my hand to my mouth, embarrassed, "Gina, I mean Angie...Angie Costa

"Hi, Angie Costa," he said and smiled. His smile was wide and warm. I almost fainted. I thought, why would a handsome boy like him ever notice a short skinny person like me? I smiled back, and he asked if he could see me the next night. I was shocked, but I said yes.

I knew my parents would disapprove because he was Puerto Rican. I knew they would never allow me to see or get involved with anyone unless he was Italian.

"So, the next night I sneaked out when they were asleep and met him. The date was wonderful. He bought me ice cream, and we walked through the park and the neighborhood streets, just talking. When we stopped right here, before our date was over, he kissed me. I never thought that love could feel so alive. I saw him every night that summer. I felt so at ease with him. The first night we made love was in his friend's car, and it felt right."

"Angie, you don't have to tell me this."

"Yes, I do have to tell you. I need to tell someone. It is time to un-bury my feelings. I will never be free of the past if it is still deep in my heart. I haven't had a good friend for a long time, and now I have you. I need to talk about my past and hopefully put it to rest."

Anna felt sad. She already figured out where this story was going.

"It was that following winter that I became pregnant. I wasn't worried when I realized why I was sick every morning because I knew he loved me. I didn't care what my parents would say or what people would think because I loved him. I did not doubt that we would be married. Only things were changing. Tony started making excuses about seeing me. He said he was working at night at a new job. I believed him because I trusted him. When I told him I was pregnant, he was surprised and asked me if I took precautions. I said I didn't know what he was talking about. He said didn't you know that you can prevent pregnancy. I looked at him, shocked, and said no, but it doesn't matter because I said we could get married.

"He looked at me, "What do you mean get married? How do I know if this baby is mine?"

"I was stunned. I did not know what to say. I ran home. I was sick for several days when I convinced myself that Tony didn't mean what he said. I found out he was working in a meat packaging factory, making good money. I knew we would need the money for the baby.

"So, I stood outside the building one night. When his shift ended, I saw him come out of the building. I was about to call out to him when I realized he never saw me. Instead, he looked at a pretty girl standing by an expensive sports car. When he reached her, they kissed, and he got into her car. I was so hurt. I ran. A week later, I learned that Tony's new girlfriend's father owned the meat-packing business where he worked and that her family was rich. His new girlfriend had gotten him the job and was "putting out" for him. I asked my friends what putting-out meant. They told me that she was having sex with him. How naïve was I?

"Sadly, I was putting out for him too."

Angie said nothing more, staring straight ahead.

That night Anna was grateful for this time to be alone with her thoughts. She thought about Angie and the story Angie had told her. She felt Angie's pain and wondered what happened to the child.

Anna had written several letters to Gi, who never wrote back. She told Gi about Franco's death and asked her to assure their mother that she and her daughters were all right. It hurt her very deeply when Gi did not answer. Anna knew that her beloved sister was angry at her for allowing Franco to force her and her family to come to America.

Franco had promised Gi on their wedding day that he would never take Anna away from her. Now, all she could do was write and hope Gi answered her. At least, Anna's parents were grateful for the letters.

Anna then thought about Lucia, her other good friend. Her husband and sons worked on their farm. One bitterly cold winter day during World War II, this family appeared at their farmhouse looking for work, cold and hungry. She and Franco took the family in, and they lived at the farmhouse. Franco was grateful that the husband and his two sons helped with the farm work. Along with Anna's daughters, they all worked the farm leased to Franco by the nuns at Muccune Di Povire Tarucco (Mouth of the Poverty Farm).

Anna and Lucia also shared the day's work of cooking and cleaning with the older girls. During that time, Lucia gave birth to a daughter whom Anna adored. Anna smiled at the thought of Lucia's delightful daughter's tiny smile.

The two families cultivated olives and sold the oil to supplement their livelihoods. They planted vegetable gardens and sold their goods. They shared fresh eggs and milk. At first, Lucia and her family were employees, but soon both families depended on each other. Together they worked hard to provide for each other's family, making for a more comfortable survival through the war.

Anna imagined the damp olive groves' sweet scent during harvesting as she lay alone on the floor. She recalled how her daughters hated working the olive groves because it was cold and damp. All her older daughters wanted were to be back at school. The little ones cried because they were cold, but it was not safe for them alone at the house because of the dangerous times.

Anna remembered the nuns from the monastery who leased them their land. She thought of Sister Maria, who cared for the poor, and the sick. There was a special bond between them, and whenever she thought of the nun, she felt a sense of peace and love come over her.

Anna dreamed of the warm summer months with her family growing vegetables for the winter months. She visualized Cenza and Francesca and knew how happy they were there. Cenza's happiest times were selling and bargaining with customers.

Francesca enjoyed digging in the dirt and collecting vegetables for the market to sell. Anna missed the monastery land beneath her feet. She missed its smell, its feel, and its abundance.

She was tired from her day and finally fell into a troubled sleep.

June 1, 1948

My dearest daughter,

It is wonderful to hear from you again. Knowing that you have good friends in America to help you and your daughters are a great comfort to your father and me.

The island is beautiful now, and its people are happy from the warm days. The village streets are busy with vendors selling their wares just like it was before the war. It is wonderful to see our homeland getting rid of the disfigurement that the war left behind. The island is almost normal. The unwanted blemishes are fading away from the many years of not caring for them. I miss you and your daughters very much. Papa sends his love and wants you to tell Francesca how much he misses her tears. Please stay safe. Please write soon, for your letters are gold to us.

Momma

Anna finished reading the letter aloud one night after dinner in the family room, surrounded by her daughters with Angie and Angelo.

"Oh," Angelo said as he turned to Francesca, "I see that you are famous for your tears in Sicily too."

Francesca looked at Angelo and started crying.

"No, no little one, I say that to you with love not to tease you. Come here and let me hug you."

Francesca ran to Angelo. She put her head on his shoulder and sobbed. "What is it, my sweet, dimpled child? Why do you cry so hard?"

"I miss my Grandmother and all my Aunties... I should be with them... they need me."

Anna watched her daughter cry for her home in Sicily and shared the pain in her heart. The other daughters were quiet and sadly feeling their emptiness for Sicily. They, too, missed their home.

Pina said, "Don't cry, Francesca, we will all work hard, save our money and go back to Sicily."

"Well, enough of all these tears and sadness. It is time for ice cream. Who wants chocolate?" Angelo said with cheer.

Francesca said, while wiping her tears, "I love ice cream."

The sisters got up from where they were sitting, and Maria said, "Me too, I want chocolate!"

"Angelo," Cenza asked, "Do we have any vanilla? I don't like chocolate."

"Of course, would I forget you, my Cenza?"

> *June 15, 1948*
> *Dear Momma and Papa,*
>
> *Your letters are becoming dear to me too. Please do not stop writing. I know you want my daughters and me to return to Sicily. I feel a great loss not to be with you and my sisters. It is difficult knowing that my daughters are growing, and we are not there for you to watch them mature into young women. Francesca cries for both of you and her Aunts.*
>
> *At this point, it is impossible to return home because of the money. My daughters and I are working hard to maintain life here. If it is at all possible, we will save and come back.*
>
> *I long for the island smell and the feeling of the warm sun upon my shoulders. I hear the people talk of the warm weather and speak of the few flowers around the city as a miracle after going through such a harsh winter. I laugh because they have never lived upon an island to know what spring has in store for its people.*
>
> *My daughters are doing well. Give my love to all my sisters, especially Gi.*
> *Anna*

Four

∾

A nna!" June hurried up to Anna outside the lunchroom.
" What is it, June?"

"It's Teresa. I just saw her follow DogFace into his office."

Anna dropped her lunch box and ran to the door of DogFace's office.

Angie, coming towards the lunchroom, saw Anna racing to the manager's office. When she reached June and Sadie, they told her about Teresa.

"Oh my God... I didn't know that Teresa transferred to this floor."

Anna knew that DogFace never locked his office. He did not need to since no one dared enter uninvited. Anna flung open the door so fast and hard that it hit the wall, making a loud noise.

The women watched Anna throw open the door. Those near DogFace's office jumped as the sound echoed back to them. DogFace was startled when he saw Anna rush into the room.

Anna's skin crawled when she saw her daughter pinned against the filthy wall. He pulled his hand out of Teresa's skirt and stepped back. DogFace's pants were down to the floor, and his penis was erect.

Teresa, in tears and shaking, cried out. "Momma!"

Anna said, in Sicilian, "Leave us. I will take care of this."

Teresa ran from the office, and Anna shut the door behind her.

DogFace was furious. He began cursing and threatening her job when Anna walked up to him and put her hand on his penis. She pulled hard. He stopped cursing after she touched him, and his ragged, ugly face had softened. Anna then worked him over gently, slowly, and precisely. It took all her energy not to throw up on him because he smelled disgusting. Not bathing for many days and wearing soiled underwear was very revolting and made her sick to her stomach. However, she looked into DogFace's face and his dark, creepy eyes. She knew that he liked a strong woman who was not afraid of him and took over. She intrigued him by her power over him because the girls he molested couldn't look at him.

DogFace felt Anna's hands working, and he moaned like the whores that he used to pay for sexual enjoyment in his younger years. Continuing to tug at DogFace's cock, she started to be more aggressive, pulling and tugging harder. He was fully aroused and never felt this kind of deep pleasure when having a sexual encounter. Anna came close to him as she worked him and put her breast to his chest.

Anna's soft breasts lay across his chest, and he could smell her clean skin. He breathed in her smell, and it captivated him. She was in full control over her actions and of the predator she had captured. As she pulled and stretched his penis, he moaned and grunted. She got closer to him and put her mouth to his ear, said, "You will never get the satisfaction from my daughter that you will get from me."

Anna stood outside DogFace's office. Feeling and aware that everyone was staring at her. Only Mrs. Barkowitz was at her machine, bent over.

She watched Teresa sobbing. June had her arms around her.

Angie covered her face, trying hard to control her emotions. Sadie stood beside her with hate and anger in her eyes.

Teresa, crying, asked, "June... what has my Momma done?"

"Your Mother did what she had to do."

As Anna walked to the bathroom, Teresa started to follow.

June stopped her, "No, leave your mother alone. Wipe your eyes and get back to your machine."

Mrs. Barkowitz came close to June and Teresa, "Okay, ladies...we all have a quota to make. Get back to work."

As all the women returned to their machines, June led Teresa to hers. Mrs. Barkowitz, slower and humped over, even more, sat down at her sewing machine and started to work.

Anna stared at the old worn mirror in the bathroom and did not recognize who she was. A stranger glared back at her. She bent down to the sink and threw up. She splashed cold water on her face and took a hand full of water, sipped it, and rinsed her mouth out. She spat out the water and stood up. She looked at herself in the mirror once more and felt nauseated.

Again, she bent down and threw up. She took off her smock full of semen and threw it under the sink with the garbage and debris. She took a deep breath, opened the bathroom door, not looking, and walked over to her machine. She sat down and started to work fast, for she had her quota to meet.

Except for the appalling act of copulating with DogFace, she loved the morning and its promise of the coming day, whether it was cold, rainy, or a fresh spring sunny day. But now, as she rested nightly on her make-shift bed, she didn't want to see the next day. She found solace staring at the dark ceiling.

How did my life get so complicated? What will become of my girls in this cold, cruel place? No matter what, I'll protect Teresa's innocence, even with that disgusting man.

All she saw when she closed her eyes was DogFace's face. She would defend her Teresa, no matter the price. Mornings no longer held any promise.

Angie was also unable to sleep. She wept, feeling responsible for what happened that day. She never thought that Teresa was in danger since she was working on the third floor. She did not know that Teresa had transferred until June, and Sadie told her. Angie felt guilty for not telling Anna about DogFace before she and Teresa ever entered the factory.

Months passed, and DogFace stayed away from Teresa. Why would he look after this inexperienced child for sexual favors when he had Anna fulfilling all his sexual desires? Anna satisfied him more than he expected. He never felt as good as he did with her. He took advantage of her every minute that he felt the desire. His desire was great, and many encounters occurred between them. He even smiled sometimes and was pleasant on several occasions to his workers. There was less stress among the women, but their lethal hatred for him rose daily.

By summer that Anna pleasuring DogFace was gossiped about among the women at the factory. They mentioned it at lunch or during bathroom breaks. Work at the factory went on as usual. Still, Anna had won respect from the women by sacrificing herself to protect her daughter. All the women admired her and, in their small ways, showed it.

They never discussed Anna's situation when Teresa was with them. Even though the second-floor women tried to protect Teresa through this horrible ordeal, her sadness was evident. The grief was there whether Anna was in DogFace's office or not. The women stood by her, touching her hand as she cried. These gestures gave Teresa the strength to endure what her mother had to do.

During the summer months, many people sat out on the stairs of their apartment buildings early at night and socialized. If they were not outside, they would be in their apartment with the windows open. Their radios were on, and that gave more life to the neighborhood. The super of the building was drunk all the time.

Anna and the children stopped sneaking in and out of the building. In his confused state, the super acknowledged Anna and the girls thinking they were paying tenants. He assumed that they were living in the apartment on the second floor. The little ones missed torturing him with the silly games.

Along with Pina, the tenants took care of the younger daughters during the summer months while Anna, Teresa, and the Pertuccis were at work. Mrs. Carney and Mrs. Green would sit on the building steps happily, overseeing their playing. On hot days, the girls and other neighborhood children played in the fire hydrant's cold water. The ladies listened to the laughter of the children playing and enjoyed their sounds. The daughters were safe, cool, and watched closely.

The residents shared a loving bond. Often, they would get together on the weekend to do the repairs to the building. They even paid for the repairs with their own money when they could afford it, just to keep the Super in his job.

During that summer, Cenza worked all day at the corner grocery store. The grocer stocked up on merchandise because she sold everything to everyone who came into the store. No customer ever left empty-handed. By the end of the summer, the grocer gave her a small bonus, which Anna insisted that she keep.

Cenza opened a bank account, and she was thrilled to have her own money. She carried her bank book with pride. Although she gave Anna all her paychecks, that small bonus was hers. She had no wish for material things; however, she liked tracking the numbers in her account. She loved watching the numbers grow with the interest that the bank gave her

Cenza's interests were in math and history, but not herself. She had no interest in fancy clothes and high-heel shoes. When not in school or working, she was in a corner somewhere reading as many different books as possible. She stored piles of books given to her by her neighbors and read them all.

As she got older, she began collecting books on art and music. Her skills were many, but her most precious time was when her nose was close to a book. She felt rewarded and was a completely fulfilled person. Of all the girls, she adjusted the best in this new country. She not only adapted to this new land with its vast knowledge and opportunities, but she also experienced all that was available to her.

The older Gennusa daughters were slowly accepting their fate except for Pina. She remained sad and stayed in the apartment. She refused to adapt to the city and its customs.

Pina blossomed from a lovely young, long-legged girl into a stunning tall, thin, dazzling woman during those first few months in America. Her hair was long, wavy, and golden blond. Her skin was creamy, smooth, and naturally pink, and her high cheekbones gave her perfect facial features. She, like Cenza, never saw her beauty. Her love did not lie in books, high fashion, or the adventures available to her. Her passion was for her home island, walking through her village or out on the islands' farmlands.

Pina's large hazel eyes failed to appreciate spring's color as it flowed into summer that first year. Her bright gaze did not rest on the few green trees the city had to offer. Her long hair flowed whenever the warm summer breeze blew through it. However, as she pushed it away from her face, she often closed her eyes and floated back to her island and its smells.

Pina had enjoyed the crisp winter weather. She loved the snow, remembering her island during World War ll. Snow rarely fell in Sicily. She recalled the rare occasion when it did fall, and the children from the island with their parent's protection played in the few snowflakes that fell from the sky. But now, in the summer, she only longed for her Sicily home.

She loved her family and Angie and Angelo. How could she not love them? But she could not find her place in this country.

Pina worked hard at school and took care of her sisters, and asked for nothing in return. Despite this, she still felt empty with all around her, and in a crowded room, many times felt alone.

Anna had noticed how quiet Pina had become since they arrived in the U.S. She was placed in a classroom with children much younger than her to learn the language. Anna knew being with younger children embarrassed her. In Sicily, Pina was at the top of her class. It was not easy for her to adjust to this new situation, but Anna knew that this daughter did her best.

When winter arrived, sometime after Thanksgiving, Angelo dragged a tree upstairs to the apartment. He stood in front of his apartment door, placed the tree in front of him, covering his entire body, and knocked. The door opened to a full-size green spruce tree, with the little ones wondering what a tree was doing standing in the hallway.

Angelo jumped to the side of the tree and shouted. Maria and Enza jumped when they saw a figure, and then after realizing it, Angelo started to squeal. The little ones showed so much excitement as Angelo dragged the tree through the kitchen into the living room and placed it on the floor. The tree dragged in dirt and left needles behind in the room.

Pina saw the mess and went to get a broom.

"Hurry girls, before Angie and your Momma come from the store. We must put up the tree and decorate it."

As she was sweeping the floor, Pina said, "Angelo, how will we get the tree to stand up?"

Angelo looked at Pina and was puzzled by the thought. "Well, how about we get a bucket and put the tree in it?"

Pina brought a large bucket from the kitchen. She and Francesca helped Angelo stand the tree up. "We need something in the bucket to keep it straight."

Angelo thought, "How about we put heavy blankets in the bucket around the trunk of the tree. I think that would steady it."

Angelo held the tree in the bucket while Pina gathered blankets. When Pina returned, Angelo held the tree while Francesca helped

Pina put the blankets in the bucket. The tree was holding steady as they all stood in front of it. The little daughter's eyes were big as they looked at this huge tree that took up a large part of the living room.

Enza asked, "Angelo, how will we decorate it?"

"Ah. That will be the most fun...we will be creative. We all must think of things about this house to put on the tree. Something must be small, and a few things can be larger." Angelo went into a dresser drawer in his bedroom and pulled out a splendidly embroidered linen tablecloth. He came out of the bedroom, went under the tree, and put it around the bucket to cover it.

"Ok!" said Angelo, "It is up to you to do the rest..."

Laughing, he added, "Remember, we need to get done before Angie and your mother come home."

They all scurried around the apartment, picking up whatever they could find to put on the tree. Several hours later, Angie opened the door and entered with Teresa and Anna. The little ones gathered in the kitchen. Anna looked at her children and wondered why they were looking sheepish and trying not to giggle. Maria, unable to stay, still jumped up and down in one spot.

"Okay," Anna said, "What is going on here?"

Enza had her hands over her mouth, ready to burst. Anna had never seen her so excited. Finally, she could not contain herself, "Momma, it is beautiful!"

Angie had now passed by the daughters and had no place to put her packages on the kitchen table. She could not help seeing the mess. She put her parcels on the floor, turned, "What is?"

"That is!" Enza said as she turned to the living room and pointed her finger to the decorated tree in the living room. Angie and Anna turned to the living room and looked at a huge tree. They walked across the room to inspect the Christmas tree with Angie looking at her husband. He had a big smile on his face. His face shone like a little boy just getting caught playing a prank.

"Momma!" Teresa, catching her breath, said. "It is beautiful...Look at it!"

Angelo announced forcefully, "It's Christmas, and we will have a Christmas tree in this house!"

The three women were amazed at the decorations. The daughters put small kitchen utensils like small forks and spoons with ribbons tied to the handles. They shared the tiny dolls Anna had sewn together. The older girls made bows from the leftover fabric of all different colors and textures. Some material was cut slim and long and hung from the tree-like tinsel. There were crocheted socks of all sizes and the small little mittens lying against the tree base. The girls cut up snowflakes out of newspapers that Angelo had shown them how to make.

The kitchen door opened, and a cold draft of air wafted into the apartment. Cenza was home and starving, for she had the healthiest appetite of the girls.

"Hi!" She yelled as she entered the kitchen. "What is for dinner?"

Maria ran through the kitchen, grabbed Cenza's hand, and pulled her into the living room.

Cenza saw the Christmas tree, touched its fresh, crisp needles, and started to sob. She walked over to Angelo and hugged him, "It is gorgeous."

Pina said, "Cenza, we waited for you to come home to put the top on the tree. Your job is to come up with an idea for its crown."

Cenza walked back into the kitchen without a word and pulled from her bag a large red satin bow her boss had given her. She stood on a kitchen chair and tied the bow around the top of the tree.

Then she stood with the others, silently staring at this magnificent sight. They felt quite solemn. Then the tree slowly started to fall sideways. The family watched and followed, with their heads tipping along with the tree in slow motion. When it hit the floor with a loud thump, the family jumped, and Angelo laughed. His jovial laughter cheered the others, and they all hugged each other and laughed together.

After the laughter had stopped from the falling tree, there was a problem to solve.

"How do we keep the tree up? Okay, Cenza. What do we do?" Angelo asked.

Cenza thought. "That's easy. We will pour dirt in the bucket, and that should keep the tree straight and up."

"That sounds good!" Angelo said, still giggling, "Sweet children find something to carry the dirt. We need to hunt for dirt in a city that has no dirt."

Francesca took his hand, "Angelo, I just love dirt."

Anna laughed as her daughters dressed warmly in outerwear and left the apartment to venture outdoors to look for the dirt. Angelo had them all laughing as they went out, and they were still laughing as they marched back in several times with buckets of dirt.

Anna and Angie were shocked by how many buckets they brought inside. Soon, the tree bucket was filled with enough dirt to steady it.

Angie asked, "Angelo, would it be okay if I put an old towel under the tree instead of my good expensive linen tablecloth? I mean, to keep it away from the dirt in the bucket?"

Angelo winked at the daughters, making the little ones laugh, "Yes, that is a good idea, Angie."

Angie put several towels on top of the bucket then asked where they got the dirt. "Well... you see... Angie, since there is little dirt in this city, I had to take what I could. Excuse me, I mean, we took the dirt from the trees in front of each of the neighborhood buildings."

"Angelo, you can't do that. It's against the law. That is city property."

As Angie got up from under the tree, Angelo went over to her and put his arm around her. "It will be all right, Angie, it's a borrow. How can we get arrested for stealing if we only borrow it? We plan on putting it back after the holidays? Besides, who is going to complain? Some of our close neighbors saw us digging and asked what we were doing as we brought the dirt into the building. Those people came to help."

"Don't look so worried, Angie," Angelo giggled, "The neighbors promised to help get the children and me out of jail"! Angelo looked at the little ones laughing, "Oh, by the way, Angie, I promised our, sorry, we promised our neighbors that we would have a Christmas party. Mrs. Carney is bringing apple pies."

It amazed Anna that Angelo always found light in everything. She had come to love him dearly. He was wonderful. She reminded herself that she needed to do something special for him.

1949

The popular holiday film "Miracle on 34th Street" won 3 Academy Awards.

The New York Yankees defeat Brooklyn Dodgers.

Milton Berle hosts the first telethon, which benefits cancer research.

45 rpm records are sold in the United States for the first time.

Five

∾

The Gennusa family had been in the United States for one year and
four months.

> *March 3, 1949*
>
> *Dear Momma and Papa,*
>
> *It is amazing to me that I have been in this country for over
> a year. The snow is filled high through the streets. There are
> snowmen in front of the apartment buildings. Life in the city is
> slow at this time of the year.*
>
> *I feel fortunate that my daughters are all doing fine and are
> healthy. That is a big relief for me. Angie and Angelo are won-
> derful. They seem never to get tired of us. That, too, is also a big
> relief for me. Their love and support are bountiful.*
>
> *Spring is around the corner, and the city waits with antici-
> pation for it to come. The pale faces of the city's residents look at
> the sun to shine on them. I also wait patiently for the spring sun
> to shine again.*
>
> *Tell my sisters that I love them and miss them, especially Gi.*
>
> *Anna*

March 31, 1949, was a dark day, and the winter wind blew hard and cold. Anna, Angie, and Teresa came home from work and hurried upstairs and into their warm home, needing to get out of the wind and cold hallway. As they closed the door, they found Angelo waiting for them. Angie saw the disturbed look on his face and asked what the matter was.

Angelo looked at Anna, "My Enza... She is sick."

Anna quickly walked across the family room and found Enza lying across the couch, covered with blankets. Anna touched her head. Enza had a high fever. "How long has she been like this?" Anna asked.

"Momma," Pina replied, "She told me she did not feel well on her way home from school. When we got home, I put her on the couch, and she fell asleep. She just woke up a few minutes ago. She did not have a fever when I put her on the couch. Now she is burning up."

Teresa looked at her sister, and her face drained of color. She started crying, "No, Momma. Not again."

Enza had come down with pneumonia during the war. Even though Teresa tried to tell her father that Enza was very sick, Franco refused to listen. He was upset about Anna's difficult delivery.

He grew angry at her persistence and hit her. "Teresa, can't you handle the problem? Always wanting this and wanting that. Just for once, take care of your sister and stopping complaining."

Teresa put her hand to her face, haunted still by her father's attack.

Teresa went out into the cold night to the center of the village to the doctor's house. She remembered how scared she was as she held onto the baby. She looked in all directions before proceeding to the next corner, fearful of meeting German soldiers.

God had spared Enza, but Theresa's bitterness towards her father for hitting her never went away. She knew that her father loved her, but somehow, she could not forget that he was not there for her when she needed him. She alone decided to save her sister's life.

"Teresa, get me some cold, wet towels."

Teresa went to the sink. She put dishcloths beneath the faucet and soaked them in cold water before returning to her mother.

Anna reached for the towels and placed them on Enza's forehead and the back of her neck. Enza stirred at the cold towels' touch and told her mother it felt good on her head.

As the night progressed, Teresa sat at the kitchen table with Pina and Cenza praying.

Anna was anxious. "Enza had gotten worse."

Angelo said, "That's it. We are taking her to the hospital. She needs help right now! Angie, get me all the money we have in the house."

Angie and the older daughters searched. After they found all the money found, Angie, Anna, and the girls handed Angelo the money.

Angie hailed a cab.

Anna was upset, "We cannot take her to the hospital. We have no money to pay for her hospitalization care."

Angelo yelled to Teresa to get Enza's coat. After she got them, she announced she was going to the hospital as well. "I saved her life once. I need to be there with her again."

The ride to the hospital seemed endless. When the cab stopped at the hospital, Angelo quickly opened the door. The March wind blew mercilessly. As he covered the little girl's face, he realized that the child had stopped breathing.

"Anna, Enza has stopped breathing."

Angelo rushed Enza through the hospital door, shouting for help. Two nurses took Enza as soon as Angelo told them that she had just stopped breathing.

A doctor came running. They put Enza on a nearby table, and the doctor began examining her. He heard her throat gurgle from phlegm, grabbed a respirator from the nurse, put it into Enza's mouth, and hastily drew up the fluid from her throat. Enza started to breathe. A nurse put a mask over Enza's mouth, attached to an oxygen tank.

Several hours later, the doctor assured Anna that Enza was going to make it. They were advised to go home, but the three refused. They wanted to see Enza. The doctor told them that they could talk to her in the morning if she seemed strong enough. She had to stay calm. Her pneumonia was quite severe. He had already extracted fluid several times during the night, and she would have to stay in the hospital for at least ten days.

Angelo saw the frightened look on Anna's face when the doctor told her how long Enza would have to stay in the hospital.

"Don't worry, Anna, somehow we will manage."

"How are we going to do that, Angelo?" Anna asked. " It will be so much money."

Anna sat down and felt the moisture under her arms. She covered her head and bent between her knees, staying this way for a long time.

Angelo quietly said, "We will manage."

The sun rose, and its rays shone through the hospital window. Angelo stood beside the window, looking out at the bright, cold day. Angelo knew that God had answered his prayers. His Enza was going to be okay.

Teresa hugged Angelo, who was crying, "She will be fine. She has you, and she knows she needs to come back to you."

Anna, tired and stressed, prayed hard that her daughter would not die. When she was alone with Teresa, she asked what she meant about saving Enza's life before. After Teresa told her what happened to Enza during the war, she trembled at the thought. Now she understood why Franco had insisted that he take care of Enza during that time. Just one of his concerns during the war, and she now grasped why he drank so much.

The nurse came across the room and told Enza's family that they could see her for a few minutes and only one at a time.

Anna was standing by Enza's bed when a daytime nurse came and looked at the sleeping child, "She is unbelievably beautiful. How do you know her?"

"She is my daughter," Anna said, annoyed.

"Oh," the nurse was surprised that this young girl with her olive skin and dark hair looked like nothing of her mother. The nurse repeated herself about how lovely Enza was.

While the nurse was talking, Enza started to stir and opened her eyes. She struggled to smile at her mother, but she was fragile. She closed her eyes, "Momma, where am I?"

"You are in the hospital, Enza," Anna said softly.

"Why, Momma, what happened to me?"

"You came down with a high fever and developed pneumonia. You must stay still and not talk. You are very sick."

Enza groggily looked about the room and then focused on Anna and asked, "Where is Angelo? Momma, I need my Angelo!"

"He is outside of your room, waiting to see you," Anna said.

The nurse said that she could only have one family visitor because the hospital doesn't allow too many people to visit at the same time. Anna looked at the nurse, told her that the man out in the hall was Enza's father, and would not leave the hospital until he saw his daughter. The nurse was very adamant about not staying long and that her patient needed to sleep.

Angelo walked into the hospital ward and spotted Enza. Anna kissed Enza and told her she would be back to see her later that afternoon. Angelo stood beside Enza with a big smile, telling her that the nurse said that her prettiest patient in the hospital wanted to see him. "Of course, I knew it was you because you are the prettiest in this hospital," Angelo said with a big smile on his face.

Weakly, Enza said, "Angelo had you seen all the patients in this hospital?"

"No, Enza, I don't have to because wherever you are, you are always the prettiest," Angelo said in a low voice as he bent down and kissed her on the cheek.

Enza reached out and touched Angelo's cheek, "I love you."

"The nurse referred to me as your father, Enza. Do you know what that means?"

"Yes, you love me," Enza said.

"Of course, I love you, how could I not? I look into those beautiful hazel eyes of yours, with your thick eyelashes, and melt. No, what it means is now I can punish you like a father should when you get into trouble. Although, it's not much of a job for me because you never get into trouble unless I am the one getting you into trouble." Angelo giggled.

Enza, barely able to move, smiled at her Angelo.

The nurse came back to the side of the bed while Enza started to smile at Angelo's remark and told Angelo that it was time for him to leave. Enza needed sleep.

Angelo bent down to Enza and kissed her on her cheek. "Sleep, my sweet angel. Sleep so your small body can grow into your beautiful face." Angelo kissed her again.

"Momma," Cenza said, the night before Enza was to come home from the hospital. "We have a serious financial problem."

The family was sitting around the kitchen table, done with dinner, when Cenza continued talking, "But I have resolved part of it. When we pick up Enza, I will talk to the hospital office and give them some money. Then I will tell them that we will pay the bill every week until the bill is paid."

"Cenza, we have no money. Where are we going to get it?"

"I have taken out of my bank savings, which we will use to get Enza home," Cenza said. "We will also use the money that we have been saving for our own apartment."

Anna looking down, asked if it would be enough. Cenza said it would not be, but the hospital will have to take what we can give them.

Angelo said with a big smile on his face. "Well, that is settled. You will not be moving for some time."

Francesca started crying, went to Angelo, "Angelo, I am so glad we are not moving. I don't want to leave you either. You need me."

"Yes," Angelo said, "I do need you, my sweet child." As he held her tight, "We must get ready for our Enza to come home."

Angelo turned to Angie, "Angie, do we have any ice cream in this house?"

Weeks passed, and Angelo doted on Enza. Anna was concerned because Enza was becoming aware of her beauty, and Angelo was reinforcing her vanity. The hospital bill was being slowly paid. The hospital wanted more than the Gennusa family could spare.

Anna was becoming desperate, for she never seemed to catch up financially. She was feeling guilty for still living in Angie and Angelo's apartment. It became evident that the family needed more living space.

Several months later, Cenza saw her sisters Teresa and Pina walk into the grocery store. She walked over to them and told them to wait in the office at the store's rear. She said to them that she would be with them as soon as she could.

Several minutes later, Cenza walked into the small, cramped room. The office had no window, so the room was dark. Books and papers scattered on the floor, and a table leaned against a wall. A large file cabinet took up most of the room. Cenza came in and sat down on a chair by the desk. Her sisters stood beside each other close to the wall. Cenza asked, "Does Momma know you are here?"

"No," Teresa said, "Cenza, what is this was all about."

"It is about our finances," Cenza said seriously.

"What about them?"

"We need to pay off the hospital bill. This morning, they wanted either all their money or me to give twice as much. I don't know how much longer I can hold them off. They are becoming difficult about the bill."

Pina asked, "What should we do?"

Cenza said, "I have decided to quit school and work full time here. Mr. Brown has offered me a full-time job. He gave me a pledge for a raise. I'm telling you that I don't want to tell Momma until I quit school and start working. She has enough to worry about. I know she is feeling guilty for us still living with Angie and Angelo for so long."

Pina looked pensive, "No, Cenza, it should be me quitting school and working. Momma would be very unhappy if you were to let go of your education."

"I can't have you do that, Pina. Besides, I already have a job. I can make more money than you. We could get the hospital bill paid faster. What will you do?"

"I will go and work at the factory where Momma and Teresa work. I can get a job there."

Teresa leaning up against the wall, spoke up quickly, "No, Pina. It would not be a good idea. Momma would not be happy if you were there."

"Well, then I won't tell her until I start working," Pina said.

"NO! It will not work. Momma would be truly angry with me if you worked there." Teresa knew her mother was still serving DogFace and started feeling ill. Cenza and Pina were so upset about the situation and did not acknowledge Teresa's strong objection.

"Teresa, we have no choice. We need the money. One of us must work and help pay the hospital off."

Teresa asked, "Cenza is there another way?"

Cenza said, "Teresa, I don't know of any other way. One of us has got to go to work."

Pina touched Teresa's shoulder, "It will be fine. I will quit school and help pay off the hospital bill."

Slightly excited, Pina continued, "When the bill is paid, we will be able to save our money and go back to Sicily. We can go back home and work on the farm again. It will be fine. We can do that."

"Pina," Cenza exclaimed, "What are you talking about? Go back to Sicily? That will never happen. We have been here in this country for one year and a half, and we are still at the mercy of Angie and Angelo. How will we ever save money to go back to Sicily? You must stop being so naïve. We are here to stay, and you better get used to the fact. I see you moping all the time. What good does that do?" She wiped tears from her face, "You only make Momma feel bad. It is not her fault that we are here."

Teresa began crying. Pina, stared at Cenza as if she were a stranger, also shouted, "No... No... Momma told me we would be going back to Sicily as soon as we saved our money. . Momma would not lie to me. ."

"Don't be childish, Pina. There is no money to go back. Papa is not here with us. He is dead."

"Cenza," Teresa yelled, "Stop being so cruel."

"Teresa, I am not cruel. I am realistic." Tears flowed down her face. "Someone in this family has to be practical... I guess it will have to be me because the two of you have your heads in a cloud. A cloud that always is shining, and well, it is not shining for us right now."

Cenza wiped away more tears. "You both have to accept reality. Don't look at me like I am a monster, as if it's my fault. I want to be back in Sicily too. I want to see Grandma and all our Aunties. I want to feel the land beneath my feet. I want..." Cenza turned away, saying in a low voice, "One of us must stop going to school and go to work. I have no problem with quitting school!"

Pina wiped her nose with the sleeve of her shirt, "No, I will go to work, and we will go back to Sicily."

"Okay, Pina." Cenza ignored her remark. "Now, where are you going to get a job?"

Several days later, Pina entered the New York subway. She was to start her first day in a job at Simon and Simon. Anna had no idea that Pina was behind her. Pina stayed far enough not to let her mother see her.

However, Teresa was frightened of Anna finding out that Pina had quit school and worked at the factory. Teresa was terrified at the thought of DogFace seeing Pina. What would he do? *"She is so lovely and like me, so inexperienced."* Teresa thought. She always knew when her mother was in DogFaces' office. Sexually naïve herself, it still made Teresa sick every time Anna went in there. Now she had to worry about Pina too. Teresa felt old and tired. All she wanted to do was go back to Sicily, go back to school, and be with her friends. She missed her Mario and quietly mourned him every day.

Teresa left Pina on the same floor where she began. She checked up on her regularly. Pina managed to get to work without Anna ever knowing. After working for several weeks, she got paid and gave the money to Cenza to put toward the hospital bill. Working on the boring machine, Pina's mind wandered, remembering Cenza's harsh words. *"We are never going back to Sicily."* She felt lost in this part of the world. She needed the soil touching her bare feet, smelling sweet scents of the land and her island. Someday, she would return because that was where she belonged. Pina longed for Sicily and its striking rocky landscape. She missed her home.

Silently she hid her loss from her mother.

As summer approached, Cenza told Anna that the hospital bill was almost paid. Anna thought that was wonderful because it was time for a home of their own.

On a delightful, early summer morning, as they walked to the subway, Anna told Teresa how proud she was that Pina graduated from high school.

Anna said, "I think it will be all right if Francesca took care of the little ones during the summer. Then Pina can get a job," she paused.

"I know that you didn't have a chance to be educated in America. I am sure you are proud that Pina had this chance."

Teresa froze, not able to respond to her mother.

"Teresa, have you noticed how Pina has become quieter lately. Do you think she is not feeling well? She says so little to me. Almost like she is angry at me? Do you know what is troubling her?"

Teresa did not know what to say. Her stomach was in knots, and she had to avoid answering her mother. As they entered the subway, Teresa managed to sit far away from her mother. She prayed that Anna did not question her again. She hated lying and misleading her.

It was late on a hot Friday afternoon. Anna wondered why Dog-Face had not ordered her into his office. Closing time, near the weekend, or when the top management was away at lunch or meetings, were his favorite times for insisting on his gross sexual imposition. He had not ordered her on that day. She'd become numb to their sexual encounters, no longer getting sick after each one. She just did not care anymore. Anna returned to work with June and Sadie after a late afternoon break in the lunchroom when Teresa ran up to her, "Momma, It's Pina! Oh, Momma, I am sorry, but Pina is in the manager's office."

"Teresa, what are you talking about?"

"Momma, Pina has been working upstairs," Anna looked at Teresa, stunned. It took her several seconds with Teresa talking as the words swirled about her brain. Then she realized what Teresa had just said. "Pina quit school to help pay off the Enza's hospital bills."

"How long had Pina been in his office?"

Before Teresa answered her, Anna quickly walked over to a machine near her, grabbed a pair of enormous sharp scissors, and put them in her smock pocket. She then headed towards the manager's office.

Several women standing nearby overheard Anna's conversation

with Teresa. All the women stopped what they were doing as Anna entered DogFace's office.

Teresa was hysterical, and June held her. Sadie was having trouble breathing. Just then, Angie came out of the lunchroom and looked around. One of the women told her what was happening. Mrs. Barkowitz sat by her machine, feeling defeated, and bent closer to the floor.

As Anna opened the door, she spotted her daughter. The office seemed murkier and bleaker and smelled even more rancid than usual. Anna abruptly closed the door, and Pina automatically turned around and saw her mother. Pina bit her lip, knowing that her mother now knew that she was working at the factory. Anna looked at her daughter's large soft eyes and realized that this innocent child had a glow surrounding her.

Anna's heart raced as she scanned her daughter's body, gratefully acknowledging that Pina's clothes were intact. She knew that Dog-Face had not put his smell on her. DogFace sat behind the desk, and she knew that he was masturbating as he talked to her daughter. Anna was grateful that Pina did not understand what DogFace was doing. She yelled at Pina in Sicilian. Stunned by her mother's tone, she jumped up, scared.

"Leave this room."

Pina ran, frightened at her mother's harsh demand. She fled the office, closing the door behind her.

DogFace stumbled around his desk. His pants were down around his knees. His belly bulged, and he had a grotesque erection.

"What do you think you are doing? You whore, like your daughters. I will have the younger one. I don't care if she works on the third floor. She is gorgeous." DogFace was furious, "and I will have her. Now get out of my office!"

DogFace stood so close to Anna that his foul breath and disgusting body order washed over her.

"Get the fuck out of my office. Tell that pretty daughter of yours to come back in here. I love virgins. They are so stupid because they are naïve. Tell her I am going to give her a raise today." Laughing and shaking his head, "And I don't mean money!"

Anna glared at DogFace, who returned her stare and saw no fear in her. Boldly, he straightened up his body. This confrontation stimulated him, and he pressed his erection against her body. "Will this one be as good as you? Maybe better?"

DogFace smirked as he looked into Anna's dark unfeeling eyes. He became unsure of himself. His genitals shriveled, and he realized her strength. He stepped back from her, suddenly fearful.

She took one step toward him, putting her hand in her pocket and grabbing the scissors. With all her power, she plunged them as hard as she could into his loins. DogFace's blood squirted all over her hands. She let go of the scissors.

DogFace screamed, looked into her vacant eyes, and fell to his knees. The pain was excruciating. As he lay on the old filthy, worn carpet, his blood spilled from him in great gushing spurts. He raised his head for a few seconds and looked at the scissors stuck in his gut.

Anna watched him lie on the floor as he tried to control the pain. His ugly face distorted, making him look even uglier. Saliva ran from his mouth. He reached for the scissors, but the pain was too intense for him to grab them. His hands fell from his body and into a pool of blood. He raised his hands, and they were full of his thick red and sticky liquid. He stared at his blood as it dripped down on top of him.

Anna knelt beside him and looked into DogFace's tearful eyes. She grabbed the scissors as DogFace looked at this monster above him. Then he watched as she, with all her strength, twisted the scissors deeper into him. He screamed as his male organ detach from his body and watched it fall on the floor.

She then abruptly pulled the scissors out of him. He screamed again, from the severe pain. His howling echoed into the machine room.

Anna holding the scissors far above her head, squeezed and looked into the eyes of this blank empty person. As she was about to take his life, he cried for mercy, and out of fear, he had a bowel movement. He sat in his bodily waste and saw no empathy in her face. He screamed for the last time, and with all her might, plunged the scissors into his heart. His warm sticky red liquid spread out of him and landed all over her clothes and face. The silence that hovered in the room was eerie. He was dead.

Anna felt nothing as she stared at his lifeless body. No remorse as she pulled the scissors out of his body and stood up. She stood in a puddle of blood, then stepped away from him and turned to the door. She said no prayers for the person she was leaving. She did not ask for God's forgiveness. She put her bloody hand on the doorknob and opened it.

June ran to her and, looking into Anna's eyes, saw no emotion. Then June looked into the office. Her eyes lay upon the dead body on the floor, surrounded with blood, and she smiled, feeling deep personal satisfaction.

Anna stared at her hand. The giant scissors dripped blood onto the floor.

June took the scissors from Anna and held them down by her side.

Then Sadie grabbed the scissors from June.

Mrs. Barkowitz came behind Sadie and asked who the girl was beside Teresa. Sadie told her it was Anna's daughter, Pina. As she stood with Sadie, a small crowd of women walked over and surrounded Anna. They peered into DogFace's office while Mrs. Barkowitz took the scissors from Sadie.

Standing behind Mrs. Barkowitz, an anonymous woman took the scissors. Then from her, another unidentified person took the scissors. Then someone else behind her did the same. The shears traveled throughout the room, and then they were gone. The murder weapon disappeared into oblivion, never to be found.

Angie led Anna to the bathroom, passing Teresa and Pina standing frozen in fear. One woman went into the office with a rag in her hand and cleaned footprints off the floor. Others helped clean the blood wherever it appeared

Several women outside the office were on their hands and knees, wiping the blood that followed Anna and Angie into the restroom. When Anna and Angie emerged, Anna was clean.

Anna strode past her daughters, without any emotion, over to her sewing machine, where she sat down and started working.

Mrs. Barkowitz said, "Okay, ladies, let's get back to work. You have quotas to meet. It's almost the weekend."

She looked at June, and with her hand, indicated to her to get the Gennusa sisters back to work. Holding each other's hands with their heads bowed and crying, they finally separated, with Teresa stopping at her machine and Pina heading to the door. Mrs. Barkowitz limped to her machine and opened the drawer. She took out a pair of duplicate scissors, replacing the ones Anna used to kill DogFace.

The women in the factory obeyed Mrs. Barkowitz's demands. They returned to their machines with fear on their faces wondering about Anna's destiny. They at no time looked at Anna nor mentioned to her what she did.

At quitting time, everyone acted as usual. The women all started talking again. They chatted about their weekend plans, their families, their children - anything but what had happened here.

On Monday morning, Mrs. Barkowitz walked to the DogFace's office, opened the door, and stood in front of it. The stench that came out of the office was potent and repulsive. She stepped away, and with a straight back, she walked upstairs to the factory office. As she headed towards it, she walked a little faster than she had in a long time.

When she reached the office, she informed the owner, Abe Simon, that DogFace was dead in his office. She even used the nickname, which surprised Mr. Simon as Mrs. Barkowitz was always respectful of authority.

He accompanied her to the office, but the overwhelming stench left him little doubt the man was dead. He ordered all the windows in the factory opened, and then hurried back to his office and called the police.

Mrs. Barkowitz returned to the workers' floor, stopping every so often to catch her breath with a look of grim satisfaction on her face.

The police invaded the factory that early Monday morning, surrounding the office and blocking access to it for anyone but themselves and the medical examiner's officers.

As seasoned investigators supervised the crime scene, a rookie officer approached the lead detective to tell him that he had solved the murder. He stood as straight and as tall as he could in his newly pressed uniform with his buttons shined, so confident in himself. It was his first murder case, and with hard work, his ambition, and the will to work long hours, he hoped to be a detective someday soon.

"Sir, I have got a woman who has confessed to the murder of Dog-Face."

Lieutenant Miles Shane cleared his throat. "Really?" Shane, a medium tall, big-boned man with a reddish face, bright-red hair, ignored him and called out. "Has anyone found out this guy's name yet?"

"George Luffmann!" Someone near the dead man's office yelled.

Shane then looked at this new baby-faced officer in front of him, squinted his eyes, and read his badge. "Well, Officer J. J. Jones, congratulations, son, but don't be too pleased with yourself just yet because she is the third woman who confessed to the killing. I suspect there will be many more women coming forward with the same confession by the end of today,"

The rookie cop walked away from the dead man's office, feeling disappointed and embarrassed.

Another detective took the rookie's place. "Miles, another woman admitted to the murder. She gave the same reason that the other women gave as to why she killed him. Her name is June Hans. She told me...

"Yeah, Yeah," Shane said wearily, "I know, Scooter... DogFace made her have sex with him so that she could keep her job." He looked up from his notes, "Is she the tall blonde standing by the door?"

"Yes." Patrick "Scooter" McCarthy, a large bone, white-haired Irishman, had been on the Police Force for twenty years. Through the years, he had worked with Miles Shane regularly.

"All the women have given the same reason for murdering him. I will go to the owner of the company and tell him what we have found out. Has anyone found the murder weapon?" Lt. Shane yelled, "Was the murder weapon found?"

"Not yet." One of the forensics technicians called out.

"Miles, do you think a man could have done this? You know, like a jealous husband or...how about maybe...a group of women, together? God... I would hate to think that one of my daughters when older was capable of doing this, and yet if they are ever in that position, I would hope they would have enough courage to come to me for help."

"Well, it looks like most of these women are not fortunate enough to have someone to help them. When I got to the scene, I looked at the body, and I almost felt sorry for the guy. You know...I was thinking this guy was just being a guy and having fun. He was getting a little from that one and then a little for another. I thought to myself, what a great deal that he had with all these women." Shane's attitude changed, and his voice became cold and hard. "But this murder was vicious... The more I investigate this, the more he looks like he was a real bastard.

"The evidence doesn't show a jealous husband or a group of

women... No, I am sure it was one person... The way the weapon was stuck into his lower body points to a woman killing him. If it had been a man, the weapon would have been deeper, and if it had been a group of women, the wound would have been messier. It smells like this guy never bathed. The thought of that in and of itself is repulsive. No, I am sure it is a woman and one intent on revenge." Shane made additional notes. "Well, it looks like most of the pretty women on this floor have been sexually assaulted. These women got nothing back from him except keeping their jobs. It's going to be a long-drawn-out case. There are so many women here who hated him for what he made them do." Shane mumbled to himself, "This is one of those cases when I hate my job."

Shane could no longer stand the smell in the room, pulled out a handkerchief from his pocket, and put it to his nose. The combination of the dirty stuffy room and the body starting to decompose over three days was not pleasant. He bent over the corpse and looked at DogFace's ugly face, and noticed the saliva that had dried on the side of his mouth. It ran down his cheek and on the floor. He looked down at the victim's genitals sitting in a pool of dried blood on the dirty carpet and felt a pain in his groin area. He mumbled to himself, not wanting to acknowledge what he was looking at, and closed his eyes, "That must have really hurt."

Shane was still bent toward the floor while scanning the dead body as Scooter grimaced, showing his perfect white teeth, "Fuck... look at the dead bastard's genitals. Look at the trail of blood from them rolling off his body. That must have hurt! He is lying in his shit!"

He circled DogFace's body, "I've had some pretty ugly murder cases. Still, this one is on my top top-10 awful. Looking at those guy's balls on the floor stuck in his dried blood and shit! That almost makes me want to cry."

"Don't shed too many tears for this bastard. It looks like Luffmann got what he deserved." Shane removed his handkerchief from his mouth and commented, "The smell in this room is vile."

He looked around the room for activity, making sure that the many officers were doing their jobs. Cameras were flashing around the body. One of the forensic officers was measuring the wounds. He watched, reassured they were doing their jobs.

Shane and Scooter walked into the machine room, both writing notes. Shane stopped outside of DogFace's office door, "Make sure that you question everyone, especially the pretty young ones. It seems to me that those are the ones that DogFace targeted and sexually used."

"I hate these sex-murder cases. The women are the ones that will get the bad end of it all."

"Yeah," Miles agreed, "If we are lucky enough to find the murder weapon, we got a good chance to find the murderer. Without the weapon, we have nothing linking to the murdered body except all these women claiming to be the murderer. Are the police officers out in the ally looking for the weapon?"

"Yes," Scooter said, "Dennis is on it. He has at least ten men searching around the building, Miles." Scooter said, showing his half-crooked smile and shaking his head, "Office Jones just waved. It looks like we got another woman confessing."

After talking to Officer Jones, Miles and Scooter walked upstairs towards the owner's office. Miles was still writing. "I have never in all my years working homicide have had so many people come forward admitting to one murder. This killer is either feared or loved by all these women. If these women have that tremendous amount of loyalty to this murderer, this person, having that much power is scary, and this can prove fatal to this investigation. I wonder if the murderer knows how much control he or she, in this case, has."

Scooter was facing the large room with his back to the wall. As Miles talked, Scooter peered over Shane's shoulder and scanned the room. He spotted Anna with her head down, working busily. Scooter looked at the small, pretty woman with the long dark hair curly hair working as if nothing was happening around her. Miles turned and looked in the direction that Scooter was looking at and noticed Anna too.

"She is beautiful." Scooter said. "I wonder if anyone has interrogated her?"

Watching Anna, Scooter found enormous strength in her face. Anna looked up at Scooter for a moment, put her hand into her smock pocket, and put her hand around her white spool of thread, showing no fear.

"Should I interrogate her?"

"What?" Miles glanced at Anna. "Oh, no, she looks too old to me. DogFace liked the young ones. However, if you think we should, have Jones do it. You stay with the younger ones. Go back to the office and see if they found the murder weapon." He sighed, "Also, Scooter, there is a woman whose name is," He stopped and mumbled to himself, "Let me see." He flipped several pages of his pad, "Here it is, June Hans, she is one of the women who had admitted to the murder. She has already interrogated her. She's unbelievably beautiful, and somehow when I looked at her from a distance, she was extremely pleased with the victim's fate. I am sure June's one of the women he raped. She looks suspicious to me. Go talk to her first before you talk to anyone else."

Miles stopped midway and looked at the workers and studied some of them. They were all busily working, making their daily quota, not concerned, or showing any remorse with the matter at hand. He wondered as he stood in the middle of the stairs, who among them was capable, vicious, and dangerous enough to commit such a horrendous crime. He studied the room, not wanting to admit to himself that he admired the person who took control and ended her dreadful ordeal. He glanced in Anna's direction and saw that she was busily working. He was captivated by her beauty again. He forced himself to walk upstairs. His thoughts were spinning around in his head. He knew that this crime would become a cold case. With so many false confessions and no hard evidence, his experience told him that this crime was a cold case already.

Six

⌒

It was the fall of 1949, six months after the highly publicized, unsolved murder at Simon and Simon. Anna, Angie, and Angelo, along with the girls, were at the park enjoying an Indian summer early evening. The adults were watching the littlest ones run around the park and swing on the swings. Maria was running faster and more confident than the others. Slow, unenthusiastic Enza trailed behind Francesca. The three older daughters were walking toward the corner store for a soda.

Earlier that day, Anna and her family had moved their few belongings into the third-floor apartment where Mrs. Carney had lived. Reluctantly, Mrs. Carney moved to Chicago with her only son, wife, and grandchildren. The daughters were sad to see her go but happy about their moving into her apartment, except for Enza. She did not want to leave Angelo.

It was bright and sunny as the daughters excitedly brought their meager belongings into the upstairs apartment. The Supervisor of the building had no idea of the transfer occurring in the apartment. It didn't matter if he received his cash rent money from Mrs. Carney's apartment number, who paid it.

Anna sighed with contentment and looked towards the drug store where the daughters were walking, and then she turned to watch her younger daughters. Angelo rose from the bench and walked over to the little ones playing on the swings. Anna was sitting beside Angie and put her arms around her shoulders.

Angie returned the affection and put her head on Anna's arm. Angie said, "I had a son."

"What?"

"He died after birth..." Angie stopped talking, and then a few seconds said, "I never saw him." Anna stayed still. Angie moved slightly away from Anna, "The doctors told me I gave birth to a boy and that he was stillborn... I never quite understood that because I felt his movement up until I gave birth to him."

"Did you ever question the doctors?"

"Question... no, Anna. What was there to question?" Angie sadly said. "He had died."

Anna and Angie heard their names call out and together looked in the direction of the drug store. They saw June walking toward them, holding hands with Scooter McCarthy.

Angie smiled, "It's about time that they made themselves public."

"Angie! Why didn't you tell me?"

"Because... June is a very private person." Angie whispered, "After DogFace used her, she was afraid and angry at men. Scooter was so patient and understanding of what happened to her. He has helped her overcome herself and make her feel clean and worthy again. I think he is in love with her. The way he looks at her. It has to be love."

"Is he good to her?"

"I think so. June seems to be much happier... Yes, I think he is not only good to her but good for her."

June and Scooter approach the park bench, and everyone greeted each other. Angie and Anna slid over, and June and Scooter sat down.

"Mr. McCarthy, has there been any news about the murder at the factory?" Angie and June both stiffened, surprised at Anna's question.

"Call me "Scooter." "You have a strange name."

"Yes, my father gave me that name after he built me my first scooter. Boy, I loved that thing!" Scooter said with his half-smile. The sun was shining above his head, and it glistened on his white hair. "My father knew how much I loved that scooter and started calling me Scooter. That name," he continued, "stuck, and out of my great love and respect for my dad, I kept the name. My father was also on the force after many years. It just felt like it was the right thing to be called Scooter, as my father has done for so many years. I take great pleasure and love when the old-timers on the force would say, Hey, look, there is Scooter, that Jimmy McCarthy's boy."

Anna smiled. It was the first time she had ever talked to him. During the murder investigation, he never interrogated her. There were strength and gentleness in his large Irish eyes, and she instinctively liked him. She knew precisely from a few words that he just spoke to her that he would be good for June.

Scooter stared at Anna. She looked familiar to him. He realized that he remembered watching her at the factory as she worked during the day following the murder. He was comfortable in the presence of June's friends and relaxed with Anna. But in his experience and a sense of reading people, he found her mysterious. She was much stronger than her small petite self indicated. What was the truth behind her eyes?

"The murder investigation is still strongly underway. There are a few suspects, but without the murder weapon, it will be hard to solve. Her co-workers are doing well, protecting the woman who did it."

"Why do you say that?" Anna asked as Angie and June looked at each other uncomfortably.

"These women who confessed are trying to confuse this case, and in their way, they did commit the murder. The hate and contempt in these women for Luffmann was staggering."

Angie squirmed, trying not to show her uneasiness.

"They all tell the same story. But it will all work out, and we'll catch the murderer. There is no doubt about it, and we won't rest until we have her. Tell me, Anna," Scooter cleared his throat, "didn't your lovely daughters work at the factory at the time of DogFace's murder?" He shook his head. "I just love that name the women at the factory gave him."

"Yes, my oldest daughter worked on the same floor as I did, and my second daughter worked on the next floor right above us. I didn't know that my second oldest daughter at that time quit school and started working there. We had a large hospital bill to pay because one of my youngest daughters got sick a short time before. My daughter Pina took it upon herself to quit school and go to work and help pay for the bill without telling me."

"Did you have sex with George Luffmann?"

"Why would he want to have sex with me? I'm old. He had his pick of pretty young girls."

"Your oldest daughter is gorgeous. Did she have sex with him?" Scooter asked in a more professional cop manner.

"No, my daughter did not have sex with him. She was one of the fortunate ones he left alone."

Scooter frowned, "That makes me curious why he didn't at least try. Are you sure?"

"Yes."

"Tell me," Scooter keeping his momentum as a cop said, looking at Anna, "Would you murder to protect your daughters.

Anna stared into his eyes, "I would do anything to protect my daughters. And I would do it without remorse or thinking of the consequences."

"Even murder?"

Anna replied in a deep cold voice, still staring into Scooter's eyes, "Even murder."

June began weeping. She stopped the conversation by standing up and asked Scooter to stop talking about the case.

Scooter stood beside her and faced her. "I'm sorry. I'm sometimes too passionate and get carried away about my work." His half crooked smile eased her fears, and he put his large, securing arm around her shoulder as she shook. "I *am* sorry, June. I didn't mean to upset you."

"Okay, ladies, enough about my shop talk, let's gather the girls and go to the drug store and have ice cream. I just love ice cream."

As he was talking, he was watching Anna. Her expression never changed, even as she stared back at him. He realized she had skillfully evaded his direct question if she had sex with DogFace.

Later that evening, as Angie lay beside Angelo in their bed, she stared at the ceiling. She had to stop herself from going upstairs and checking on Anna and her children. She would miss them so much, even though they were only up a flight of stairs from her.

The lamp lights were out, but the light coming through the bedroom windows from the streetlights, the bright moon, and stars that shined brightly made the bedroom warm and cozy.

Angie felt a sense of calm that she had not felt since before giving birth to her son. She knew that talking to Anna about his death was soothing and helped her come to terms after all these years.

She was always troubled with his birth and death and never figured out why. The child would have been twenty-two years old, and for the first time, she wondered if he would have had his father's dark hair, dark eyes, and handsome looks.

Angie knew that when Anna came to her the night she arrived in America, the family needed her. What Anna didn't realize, though, was how much Angie needed her.

Angie wiped away a tear. She lay silent for a few moments and then turned her head towards Angelo. She could hear him softly snoring while he dreamed. She knew it was a soft dream because that was what he deserved. She took a deep breath and wondered why she never showed him how much she had grown to depend on him and how much she had come to love him.

She thought all those years that the love she felt for him was like a brother. But tonight, as she lay there under her warm sheet confronting the death of her son and setting that part of her life aside, she knew that her love for him was very deep. For the first time in her married life, she realized that she had not allowed herself to feel love towards this man because she never felt worthy of him. She always felt that if he were unhappy with their marriage, he could leave her without guilt. She was still pregnant when she and Angelo were married. He did not care. He was willing to raise this child as his own and love them both.

Tonight was different for Angie. She no longer felt unworthy of him. She no longer denied herself her true feelings because her past was gone. Angie listened to his sounds and longed to touch her husband. She hesitated to move toward him, thinking of her old soft aged body. She wished it were firm and young like it was when they first got married. She shook her thoughts and got her courage together. She slowly moved close to him. She could feel the heat coming from him. She took a second to absorb this heat and relished it. She slowly slid closer beside him and put her breast to his back and arm around his body. She held him softly and with care.

Angelo stirred and opened his eyes. Sleepily he half acknowledged to himself that he felt his wife holding him. He closed his eyes, not wanting to awake from a dream that he dreamed many times. This favorite dream was one that was his and his only.

The heaviness of his dream did not go away when out of alarm, he woke up. He felt Angie's arms across his chest and then realized his wife cuddled up to him. Startled, he slowly turned his whole body and lay on his back.

"Angie, what is the matter? Are you all right?"

Angelo started to get up when Angie, not letting go, said, "I am fine. I just want to be near you. I want you to know how much you mean to me. I want you to know that I love you."

Angie peered into Angelo's eyes and slowly kissed him warmly. He returned the long-awaited kiss. Angelo looked into his wife's loving eyes happily.

He reached his hand to her face and touched it affectionately, then stroked her soft hair. He took her head and slowly brought her lips to his. He kissed her tenderly, giggling, "Yes. I know how much you love me. I have always known."

"Why didn't you tell me about how I felt?"

"Because I felt you need to find out in your own time, and I have had all the time in the world to wait for you."

Angelo looked at his wife, whom he adored, and pulled her towards him.

"Angelo, stop giggling."

"I can't, Angie. You know I am my happiest when I giggle."

Angie was so delighted at Angelo's response that she started to giggle too.

"Angelo, giggling is not very romantic."

Angelo stopped giggling and looked in Angie's eyes lovingly. His heart melted for this long-awaited moment, and he ran his hand through her hair again. He put his hand behind her head and slowly brought it towards him. He kissed her lips gently. He took her close to him and snuggled his nose in her hair and kissed her ear. He kissed her neck in several places and kissed her other ear. Angie reposed to his touch, realizing it had been so long since she had felt this sensation. Angelo kissed each of Angie's eyes.

After the kisses, he looked at his wife, whom he adored, "I think I can handle romantic."

Angelo gently reached for Angie again.

1951

United States President Truman declares an official end to the war with Germany.

The film "African Queen" premieres in Hollywood starring Humphrey Bogart and Katharine Hepburn.

The first direct-dial coastal telephone call took place.

The popular television show "I Love Lucy" premieres on CBS.

The average car costs $1,500.00.

Advertising of women's clothing includes the description and price. The price of a corduroy shirt is $6.98.

March 6, 1951, the trial against Julius and Ethel Rosenberg began. The prosecution's primary witness, David Greenglass, stated that his sister Ethel gave nuclear secrets to the Russians. His testimony helped him escape the death penalty and received 10 years instead. When he was released in 1960, and again in 2001, he stated that he committed perjury about his sister's involvement to protect his wife and children.

Seven

～

J une waited for her friends in front of St. Patrick's Cathedral. She
wanted them all there before she went inside for her wedding to
Scooter. She wore an off-white suit that Anna had designed for her.
Her wedding suit jacket - made of white lace laid over off-white satin
with a knee-length white satin skirt – complemented her shiny blonde
hair, swept in an up-do and covered with an off-white pill-box satin
hat with a short lace veil attached. She held a bouquet of pink roses
with white baby's breath wrapped in a pink ribbon tied into a bow.

As Anna adjusted June's veil, she thought sadly of her own wedding dress that she and her mother had sewn for her wedding day. She
was proud of the gowns she designed, sewn, repaired, and enhanced
for her American friends and neighbors. Anna loved using her spool
of white thread and create her individual and unique designs. When
a bride came to her because she was unhappy with her dress, Anna
worked her magic and made the gown as personal as possible for its
owner. Although Anna made money working on wedding gowns, her
real reward was creating a dress that made a bride feel special on her
wedding day.

Anna's mind flashed back to Sicily and her youthful dream of
opening her bridal shop. This dream followed to her wedding day, and
the longing lingered even as she gave birth and raised her children. She

always imagined how the front window of a shop with one of her creations hanging in it would look. Because of the war and so many to feed in her family, her dream never came true. Today she slightly realized it as she helped June be the most beautiful and happiest of brides.

"June, are you ready?" Anna secured the veil in June's hair one last time.

"Yes, I am."

June's face was no longer sad, and the deep lines on her skin had vanished. She was genuinely happy.

"Anna, I can see you have a few worries about me," June said. "Is your concern about my wedding night?" June grinned, "Don't worry. Scooter and I have already had our wedding night. We have had many wedding nights." June sighed, "I had to be sure I would be a good wife to Scooter. I had to make sure that I was not afraid and that I could be a whole woman for him." She brushed aside a tear, "Anna, he has made me a whole woman again."

"I know. It shows on your face. You look radiant," Anna hugged her. "Well then, let get you married. Is it possible that maybe you and Scooter might have children?"

"Yes, my soon-to-be Irish Catholic husband wants half-dozen children, all daughters just like you."

"Daughters are good."

Anna and the bride turned toward the church door when it opened.

Maria ran to Anna and the bride, "I am ready!"

Maria looked quite grown up in the little pink knee-length dress that Anna had made for her and holding a basket full of pink rose pedals. Enza stood beside Maria in a matching dress, smiling and feeling very mature. In a darker pink dress, Sadie walked to June's side, took her arm, and flowed slowly down the church aisle behind the flower girl.

Everyone stood as Scooter and June were married.

The following week Anna received a letter from Lucia in Sicily. Everyone sat around their kitchen table, waiting impatiently for news from their home island. It was just before dinner, and as always, Angie and Angelo were there. Angie and Angelo had the little ones sitting on their laps. Pasta sauce was bubbling, with its sweet basil cooking making mouths water all over the community. The basil grew from pots sitting on the windowsill, lovely tended by Francesca during the winter months. Fresh baking bread showered its smell all over the kitchen while it baked in the oven.

Angelo said, "Hurry, Anna, read the letter. I am hungry."

All the girls laughed as Angie looked at him fondly, "Angelo, you are always hungry."

"Hurry, Momma!" Pina said. "What does she have to say? Did they.?"

"Pina," Anna said, "Stop and catch your breath, give me a chance to read the letter."

> *April 1, 1951*
> *Dear Anna and daughters,*
> *Today was an incredibly special day. We moved out of our rental house. We bought a place outside the city of Palermo and moved in. By the time you receive this letter, we will have opened our shoe store beside the shoe repair shop that we own. Vincenzo is thrilled that he is no longer repairing the shoes but selling them. He shines with the anticipation of customers coming through the door. A small bell hangs over the door. He may not be good at repairing shoes, but he knows quality shoes and knows how to sell them. I plan on spending my days in the shoe store, helping Vincenzo. Dino and Pepe are doing the repair business and are happy.*
> *My daughter is attending a private Catholic school. She*

complains a lot. Tell Francesca that she also has big tears exactly like hers. I know my daughter cries only to get her brothers' attention. They spoil her so.

It had been hard leaving the Monastery Muccune Di Pivire Farucco and the olive farm behind that we still worked, but we had no choice to leave. Our repair shop was so busy, and now we cannot handle both by opening our shoe store.

I dearly miss the nuns of the monastery, and my heart cries for them.

It has taken a long time to establish our lives again. I feel confident in our move to the new store. With the city healing itself by rebuilding, the War is becoming history to us.

My family sends their love. We miss all of you.

Lucia

Angelo yelled, "Let's eat!"

Anna folded Lucia's letter and put it in her apron pocket. She immediately thought of her parents and how the older they got, their letters were shorter, making Anna worry.

Pina walked to the window. The breeze was blowing through her long hair as she gazed at rows and rows of laundry hanging from building to building swirling through the breeze. There was no end to the laundry, and she could not see the sky. She felt suffocated. Pina closed her eyes, trying to erase the noise outside of the window. The sounds from people yelling, dogs barking, and cars blowing their horns were piercing to ears. In the distance, she heard a police siren. She wanted so much to shut out those awful noises, but she could not and knew she would never get used to those sounds.

"What is it, Pina?" Anna's standing beside her daughter and drew her closer to her. "Every time we get a letter from Sicily, you become more remote. It scares me that you are so sad all the time."

Pina turned to her, "It is nothing, Momma. I just wanted to feel the spring air coming through the window."

"Pina, are you troubled?"

"No, Momma, but I am hungry. Come, let's go eat dinner."

Pina turned, and Anna followed her daughter to the table. Anna did not understand why her daughter was so sad and so distant all the time. It troubled her that her daughter's mind was always somewhere else. She knew that Pina missed Sicily more than the other children and was having difficulty adjusting to their new life.

Eight

～

Cenza became obsessed with the trial of Julius and Ethel Rosenberg. Cenza thirst for past and present history increased as she avidly followed each part of the case. She read the newspaper every day, wanting to know about all the evidence presented during the trial. Her curiosity about the legal system absorbed all her spare time.

She knew everything about the couple, from how Julius Rosenberg was born to a Jewish family in New York to graduating from City College of New York with a degree in electrical engineering in 1939. In 1940, he joined the Army Signal Corps, working on radar. He met Ethel in 1936 at the Young Communist League

Cenza also read about Ethel Greenglass, Julius' wife. She was also from a Jewish family from New York and was a secretary after a failed attempt at acting. After joining the Young Communist League, she met Julius. They married in 1939 and had two sons, Robert and Michael.

The information found in Ethel's notes produced little that was relevant to the Soviet atomic bomb project. Still, there was enough evidence for the grand jury to indict her and convict her of espionage. Ethel's supporters felt that a capital charge of conspiracy to commit espionage was too extreme and not supported by the available evidence.

Ethel's indictment seemed as if it were leverage against Julius. The prosecution wanted to pressure Julius into giving up the name of others that were involved in the Communist Party.

Julius asserted his Fifth Amendment right not to incriminate himself whenever asked about his involvement in the Communist Party or with its members. Ethel did the same.

There was conflicting evidence that Julius ever had any dealing through an NKVD agent. However, in his attempt to escape the death penalty, David Greenglass testified against his sister and sealed her fate.

"Cenza, please stop reading about the trial," Anna said. "Go to bed!"

"Yes, Momma. I am almost done." Closing the newspaper and putting out her night light, Cenza came to her own conclusion to the trial. She felt that even if they were guilty, there was not enough evidence against either of them.

The Rosenbergs were convicted on March 29, 1951, and received the death penalty.

Cenza studied diligently for her final exams to graduate high school, which she did with top honors. Anna, Angie, and Angelo held a big party for her. Sadie helped with food preparation while June sat on the couch, unable to move because her baby would soon arrive. Scooter was running around, making sure that June wanted for nothing.

The day was chilly, so Cenza's party moved inside the Gennusa's apartment instead of the park. The kitchen table, loaded with Italian-Sicilian foods, included homemade cannoli for dessert and meat, potatoes, and pan gravy for the Irish guests.

Anna was so proud of Cenza, her first child, to get a high school education and diploma. Anna smiled at her newly graduated daughter, standing between Teresa and Pina, and wondered what was going through this daughter's very bright mind.

"Now that I have graduated from school, it is time that I go to work to help support this family the way I should."

"But you are. You already have a job." Anna reminded her.

Cenza was staring out into the room, thinking.

For many days after her graduation, Cenza spent her time off from the grocery store, diligently working out figures. She analyzed many situations and never seemed to be satisfied. She had piles of crinkled paper on the floor by the side of the table. Frustrated, she threw her pencil down on the table, picked up the paper she was working on, and threw it angrily to the floor with the rest of the trash

The family knew to stay away from Cenza. The tension was high around the apartment, and everyone felt it. The little ones were smart. They learned to survive Cenza's wrath. They would escape to Angie and Angelo's for lots of playtime and cookies.

"Cenza, what are you working on?" Anna asked.

"Please," Cenza said. "I need peace to think. There is so much noise here. Can't you all keep quiet?"

Anna looked at Teresa, who was now getting angry. Then she looked at Pina, who looked out of the window, ignoring them.

Cenza slammed her pencil down and said as she gathered her work, "I can't stand it here. I need to be where no one will bother me. I am going to the library." She put her work in a brown paper bag, grabbed her purse, and headed out, slamming the door. The three left behind took deep breaths.

Teresa said, "Thank God, Momma, I am ready to choke her."

A few weeks after Cenza's graduation, she stood in the outer office of Simon and Simon, facing two employees, "Good morning... I am Vincenza Gennusa. I am here to see Mr. Simon of Simon and Simon."

"Do you have an appointment, Miss....?" Mr. Simon's secretary asked, squinting her eyes, knowing that Mr. Simon did not have an appointment at this time.

Cenza stood straight with her beautiful blonde hair pulled back and tied in a low-neck ponytail, soft curls from the breeze outside, framing her face. Dressed in a very dark conservative suit, the young woman carried a package under her arm.

Cenza straightened her back and said, "No, but I have an important matter I need to present to him. Tell Mr. Simon that I have a proposal for him that I know will save him money. A lot of money."

"Please take a seat, and I will speak to Mr. Simon."

The plump, short middle-aged woman walked over to Mr. Simon's office and knocked. She heard Mr. Simon's voice and entered. She eventually returned and found the girl still waiting for her. Cenza was so focused on her mission. She never noticed the pretty young girl sitting across the entrance way desk, stop typing, and looked at her.

The older secretary told Cenza that Mr. Simon was busy and to make an appointment.

Cenza asked, "When will he be able to see me?"

"Several weeks."

"That is unacceptable." Cenza then stepped around the secretary, approached Mr. Simon's door, and knocked twice. Not waiting for a reply, she boldly opening the door and walking in.

Mr. Simon stopped at what he was doing and looked up from his desk. Through his round rim glasses, he saw a lovely young woman standing in front of him. Before he had a chance to show his annoyance, the girl introduced herself. She put out her right hand, and Mr. Simon rose and shook it. Abe Simon was a thin, middle-aged man with slightly balding fair hair. His face was soft with delicate lines, hinting at the handsome man he was once in his youth. His secretary, mortified at Cenza's ability to bypass her, followed her and began apologizing.

As Cenza shook Simon's hand, she introduced herself. "Good morning sir, my name is Vincenza Gennusa. I have a proposal for you to look at that will save your company a large amount of money."

Cenza walked around Mr. Simon's desk and handed him a stack of handwritten papers and, on top, a summary of the figures in the proposal. Shocked and intrigued at the boldness of this beautiful young woman, Mr. Simon told his secretary that the interruption was fine and that he would take care of the situation.

Simon looked down at the papers and looked at numbers.

After a short time examining what was in front of him, he asked. "Who did you say you are?"

"Excuse me for being so abrupt, Mr. Simon, but I have learned that in business, if a person is not direct, then that person gets nowhere. Let me start again. My name is Vincenza Gennusa. I have several connections here at your factory, and I know I can save you considerable money. My mother and two sisters work for you on the production line. I have studied your production, and I know that I can get more work done by your employees than you are already getting."

Mr. Simon looked at this pushy young woman standing beside him, impressed, and asked her to take a seat. Cenza sat down at the edge of a chair with her back straight facing him.

"Are you sure these figures are correct?"

"Yes, I am. I am also sure that with all these changes and with better treatment for your employees, you will never be without people hammering at your door for a job. I know many women willing to work at night and on weekends. Employing women at odd hours while their husbands stayed home with their children would be to your advantage and theirs. With my proposal, your factory will never stop operating. I know you are Jewish, and your day of rest is on Saturday. If you hired a non-Jewish person, like me, to run your factory, production doesn't stop, and you'd make more revenue. You would still observe your Sabbath day because you will not be in the office. Remember, you will be giving more people jobs. Your Synagogue should understand the need to employ during these aggressive times."

"Well. You are quite young to have such knowledge of business. Where did you obtain your education?"

"None... All it takes is a little common sense."

"Oh... A little common sense that is all it takes. I will look at this proposal and get back to you."

Cenza frowned, "Getting back to me will only waste time, and wasting time means losing money." She came around his desk. "So, let us get to my proposal now."

Anna was stunned that night when Cenza told her she had approached Mr. Simon about her proposal.

"What did you do?"

"I presented Mr. Simon with a proposal. How to increase his business, give more people jobs, and always have the machines working even when one person is out sick. He liked what he saw and hired me."

Anna was shocked to hear what Cenza had done. After she told her about the proposal, Anna understood what Cenza was doing so many late nights bent over the kitchen table. She knew her daughter was restless and needed to move more productively. She never thought that that restlessness would involve Simon and Simon

The following week Mr. Simon walked into his factory and found women scrubbing the bathroom and lunchroom. He was amazed to see so many of his employees on their hands and knees cleaning. Cenza had convinced him that if the building was clean and sanitized, it improved working conditions. That ensured employees would work harder with fewer sick days, especially during the winter.

He ran into Cenza and asked if she would come to his office the first chance. He was impressed already with her changes and her work ethic.

Anna was elated at her daughter as she watched her make her way to the factory owner's office as an essential manager-employee. She was in awe at her daughter's accomplishment. Teresa and Pina were just grateful that Cenza had made her mark somewhere, even at their factory, if only to have peace at home.

Cenza walked past Mr. Simon's secretary and smiled. "Good morning, Sarah."

Sarah grinned, "Good morning to you too, Cenza. It about time that this office had some sunshine, and I am not referring to the window. Abe is expecting you. Go right in."

"Thanks," Before she opened the door, she turned and waved at Alice.

Cenza entered Abe's office. He was reading papers on his desk and asked her to take a seat.

"When are we starting the new factory work structure and schedule?"

"I am already looking for someone to help run production on Saturday. I have someone in mind. She's from the third floor, so she knows the factory. I'll train and work with her until I feel she can run the operation herself."

Cenza paused. "Have you looked over the figures? What about operations on Sundays too? We are at such an advantage here. So many people want to work, and I know some people will work nonstop if you let them. These people want to make up for all the years being nonproductive because of the war. We could have the factory running to full capacity. We need to take advantage of the times and our potential. Clothing demands are going through the roof! Furthermore, have you looked over the meal program I have suggested?"

"Cenza! Please slow down and give me a chance to look into all that you have proposed?" Abe picked up the papers. "I know the time is money, and people are anxious to work. I promise by next week to have looked at all of your proposals."

Abe leaned back in his chair and said seriously, "Cenza... I want you to know I never knew what George Luffmann was doing to those women. I would have never had allowed that kind of treatment towards my employees."

"I know. You are just too kind of person." She hesitated, knowing somehow her family was involved in the entire mess. So, she changed the subject, "I've decided that Mrs. Barkowitz will no longer work on a machine. I made her my assistant. She knows so much about sewing clothes. She is more valuable to me in that area, and I want you to authorize a decent salary with overtime. She is worth a lot, and I want to use her full potential." She paused. "I don't know what our finances are. We need to hire mechanics, and if we can't, we'll have to consider a bank loan. Having our machine repairmen on staff at all times will save us time and money."

"Yes," Abe said, "I will get back to you on that. Is there anything else we need to discuss now?"

"Have you looked at the numbers since we took off the quota from the workers?"

"How did you know that if you removed the quotas and set up a system where they would be paid by how many bundles they produced that they would accomplish more?"

"Just common sense... If you remove the workers' pressure and allow them to make more money, they will work harder and longer hours. Our workers have no problem working. It makes them feel good that they can provide for their families and have a little money left for personal or family fun. I am now working on a plan for more incentives for our employees."

Abe smiled as he listened to Cenza, thinking that this young girl is the son I should have had. "Is there anything else?"

"You know Abe, you're emerging as a leader in the industry. With what you are achieving here, you'll be the first to demonstrate to other factories how to treat their employees better and increase productivity."

"Yes. I'm already getting credit for all your common-sense moves. Now before I compliment you more, you will ask for a raise, so out you go. Is there anything else?"

"Yes, one more thing. I ordered a shipment of paper towels. It will be here by Friday.

Cenza reached for the door handle, "Oh, by the way..." The door to the office opened.

There she saw a handsome man, an image of a younger Mr. Simon, enter.

"Hello."

Surprised at the encounter, Cenza stepped back, almost slamming into the office door with her back.

Abe looked up, annoyed, "Cenza, this is my son Matthew!"

Matt smiled, showing his perfectly straight white teeth. Cenza looked into dreamy eyes, smelled his seductive after shave lotion. "Cenza. It is nice to meet you finally. My father has told me so much about you."

Cenza her armful of papers. Matt caught them before they left her hands. She stared at him, this magnificent person, slowly walking past him, "Are you okay?"

She nodded.

After she left, Matt closed the door behind him.

She leaned against the closed door, flushed and breathless. Never in her whole life had she seen such a handsome man.

Sarah was watching her. "Matt is as nice as he looks too."

Cenza realized Sarah had seen her tremble. "Oh. Is he?"

Embarrassed, Cenza hurried out the office door, slamming it shut behind her. Alice giggled, knowing that Matt had that impact on every woman he encountered.

Cenza, still breathless at her encounter with Matt, went to her office on the second floor. Even though she was just eighteen and only had a high school diploma, her new ideas and drive assured her of a full-time, well-paying job and her own office. Once DogFace's domain, it was now hers painted clean, with new carpet and office furniture. She had vetoed Abe's desire to buy her more modern furnishings. Her common-sense convinced him it was unnecessary.

Walking into her office, Cenza didn't glance at the women fearing her visceral reaction to Matt would be too apparent. She did see Mrs. Barkowitz stroll around the machines, checking the women's work, her back straight, and walking spryly. She finally looked towards Mrs. Barkowitz and smiled.

She shut the door, walked to her desk, and sat down. For the first time in her entire life, she felt confused and out of control. She sat for a few minutes, thinking of Matt. *How silly can you be?* She thought to herself. She shook her head and focused on her desk, piled with paper, and started to work.

Now is not the time to obsess over the boss's incredibly handsome son.

Nine

～

In the early summer, June had her baby. Patrick Sean McCarthy III, named after Scooter, and his grandfather, was a big, beautiful boy and his father's "spitting image." His parents were thrilled that he was healthy and perfect.

Soon after the baby was born, Anna sat between Angie and Scooter on a park bench. Angelo listened to their laughter at the swings with Maria and Enza and swung them much too high. Francesca was playing stickball near the swings and beating all the boys.

June hung over the baby carriage, changing her infant's diaper. This infant was going to be big like his dad because of his broad chest. She never thought during her days of being raped by DogFace that she could feel so happy and fulfilled. She never thought she'd ever feel clean again, but Scooter had done that and more. He made her a mother. The day he was born, she held him in her arms for the first time and felt the most overwhelming love. She never thought that kind of love existed, but there it was, and Scooter had given it to her.

As June removed the baby's diaper, the air hit his soft bottom, and a stream of urine squirted up into the air and out of the side of the carriage. She jumped back and squealed.

Anna, Angie, and Scooter walked over to the newborn when the spray sailed up and over the carriage. All of them were delighted, proud, and laughing at what the baby had just done.

Anna was amazed at baby Patrick's performance. Never having a son, she never experienced this. For just a moment, Anna thought of Franco and never giving him a son.

She returned to the park bench and sat down. June, Scooter, and Angie stood by the carriage talking about the perfect child in the baby carriage, struggling to find his comfortable spot. All this little boy wanted was to fall asleep and not be disturbed. The three giggled as they watched him curl up his butt and scrunch his rosy-cheeked round face.

Scooter left the women and sat beside Anna. "It looks like my handsome son already has the attention of all my favorite women." Scooter sighed, "The murder at the factory still is a mystery to the police."

Anna turned her attention from watching Angelo playing with her little girls, looked into Scooter's soft big, puzzled eyes, "What did you say?"

"The murder at Simon and Simon is still a mystery to the police."

"What possessed you to bring that up now?"

"Well, we never seem to have time alone to talk."

"Why do you think you should talk to me about the murder and why privately?"

"It is still a mystery as to who the killer is. We don't have a suspect. That person, whoever she is, is protected and admired by her co-workers."

"Why do you think it was a woman? I heard he had many enemies, even outside the factory."

"How do you know that?"

"Just rumors that I heard at lunchtime."

"I didn't hear that during the investigation. What else do you hear at lunchtime?" Before Anna answered, Scooter continued, "I admire you, Anna. You and your girls are so attractive. It still dumbfounds me that DogFace...," Scooter sighed, "I just love that name..." He gave her a brief crooked smile., "I am surprised he never went after one of you? Many women hated him, but only a few had the motive to want to murder him. Whoever she was, she had an enormous motive to commit such an ugly, destructive crime. It could be that someone needed to protect others involved from his sexual demands. Maybe a mother protecting one or more of her daughters would fall within that category?".

Anna put her hand into her pocket, felt her white spool of thread, and held it firmly.

"I understand why someone murdered him. The bastard got what he desired. Being involved in death all the time, I'm indifferent to it because it has never involved me personally. I've always been tough; however, I see life differently these days. Under any other circumstances, it would never have occurred to me that I would be capable of such a heinous crime myself. Now that I am a father, I know that if anyone physically or emotionally touched my son, I could commit murder easily, without indecisiveness or repentance. The person who committed this crime is legally wrong by the law and morally wrong by God. Still, as a man who would do anything to protect his family, I find it understandable. I would be capable of such a crime and could do the same without any repentance."

Scooter got up, returned to June, put his thick arm around her, and looked with so much pride at his newborn son. Scooter never mentioned the murder at Simon and Simon to Anna, ever again.

Springtime and early summer frustrated her third-youngest child. Anna recalled how Francesca's skin took on such beauty at this time of the year when she was sweaty, dirty, digging in the dirt. She was at her happiest when planting seeds at the farm in Sicily.

There were pots all around the apartment of all the different herbs that Francesca had planted. She had tiny plants of tomatoes, peppers, and eggplants sprouting from seeds that she had saved from the last year's garden in a small pot. She even had a few stalks of corn. Mrs. Green living on the bottom floor of the apartment building, had a little backyard. Most of the ground floor apartments in the neighborhood had tiny rear yards. She not only allowed Francesca to use her backyard for her garden, but she helped her turn over the ground and fertilize it. Jointly they grew an enormous, bountiful feast of vegetables. With each other harvesting their pride garden, they gave their neighbors what the family did not use. The neighborhood helped pay for the fertilizer and cooked their favorite dishes to share with Mrs. Green and Francesca. Unbeknownst to the super of the building, Francesca sneaked into his backyard and planted a fig tree that one of the residents contributed. Whenever the tree needed care, Francesca and Mrs. Green would sneak into his garden while someone from the building would keep him busy. Of course, Francesca had her plants all over in Angie and Angelo's apartment too, and they loved just to spend time watching Francesca cared for them.

Anna saw that Mrs. Green, with Francesca at her side, the rooms were flooded with sunshine, and they were watering their small vegetable plants. Mrs. Green gave Francesca a bright smile, grateful for this lovely child with her turned-up nose and deep dimples. As she watered the plants, Mrs. Green thought how her life would be lonely without her. Anna willingly shared her child with a lonely woman and was grateful for all the vegetables they grew.

It was a Wednesday evening, and Teresa and Pina were in the kitchen cooking dinner. The little ones were at Angie and Angelo. Suddenly the door burst open, and Cenza ran into the room. She promptly tripped over one of Francesca's plants

"Momma, I need you! I need help! I need...!"

Anna saw her Cenza's flushed cheeks. "Calm down and tell me what it is that you need."

Teresa asked, "So what is today's disaster?"

"Does Francesca have to have all these pots on the floor?" Cenza yelled. "Momma, Abe has invited me to his home for dinner on Saturday night. He has invited some of his friends and business associates."

"Well, that's wonderful. You are so young to be involved with such respected people. I am proud of you."

Teresa asked, "So what is the problem?"

"Momma, you don't understand. These people are bankers and some lawyers." Cenza wailed.

"Cenza, you will do well with these people. Just be yourself. So. what *is* the problem?"

"Momma, you don't understand," Cenza said in a tizzy.

"Cenza, please calm down."

Teresa and Pina focused their attention on Cenza. They have never seen her so out of control. They stood by the kitchen table intrigued, trying not to laugh.

"Momma... I am not beautiful, like Pina... I not composed like Teresa, and I don't have that adorable turned-up nose that Francesca has... I don't have any of those attributes. And on top of that, I don't have a dress to wear! How am I ever going to wear high-heel shoes? I can barely walk in flats."

Anna, Teresa, and Pina finally started laughing.

Cenza became angry. "This isn't funny. You know how I hate to dress up and that I know nothing about clothes. You are all very mean. I need help, and all you can do is laugh at me?"

Teresa whispered loudly to Pina. "Bet Matthew Simon must be going to that dinner."

Annoyed, Cenza yelled, "What!"

While the older ones were teasing Cenza, Anna went to the rear of the apartment.

Teresa tried to be sensitive, "Pina and I see how you look at Matt. How you blush and practically fall on your face when he's around you."

Pina chimed in, with such pleasure. "It is obvious how he shakes you up."

"That is not true!"

Before Teresa and Pina commented further, Anna quietly returned to the kitchen, "Teresa, Pina, what do you think of this fabric for a dress?"

Anna unfolded an old cloth, and there in her hands was a lovely silk fabric. The pale blue fabric had big, bold yellow flowers with pink centers, soft green stems, and leaves.

Anna held out the fabric. Cenza stepped back, upset, "No, Momma!"

Teresa touched the material lightly. She brought it to her face and rubbed it gently against her skin. She got the fabric back down and looked at its vibrant colors, and said, "Momma, this is perfect. Do you still have that belt buckle with the white rhinestones? Wouldn't that look good if we cover fabric on a wide belt and attach the clasp to it?

"Momma, you can't give this to me. The Americans gave it to you at the end of the War. You spoke English to them. You carried this all away from Sicily. I know how much it means to you. I can't take it."

Cenza started crying.

"Yes... you can, and yes, you will take it. Yes... it is mine, and yes... I carried it from our homeland, but I have kept it for an exceptional occasion. This is it. You will look perfect for your dinner engagement."

Teresa hugged Cenza. "If I were Momma, I would give the fabric to you too. For all you have done for this family and all you have sacrificed, no one deserves it more."

"But the dinner party is Saturday. How will the dress be done?"

"Momma," Teresa said, "If you can cut out a pattern and cut the fabric Pina and I will sew it. We will need help with the belt. I have never done one like that."

Cenza cried again. Pina laughed, "You better stop crying. Your face is flushed enough already!"

Saturday night came, and Cenza left the apartment dressed in *haute couture*. A limousine waited for her at the front of the build. Her family and neighbors watched as the driver drove away. It was an event for a limo to be in their neighborhood, and the neighbors did not want to miss this fantastic occurrence.

The dress that Teresa and Pina had sewn for the night was perfect. The sleeveless dress had three pleats at the scooped neck that made the bust line look soft and showed enough cleavage to make it look feminine. It hugged Cenza down to the belt, and then the material flowed, reaching her knees. The skirt gently swayed as she walked. Anna covered the belt with the same fabric and added a sparkling rhinestone buckle. The vibrancy of the dress made her large eyes bluer. Carrying a handbag covered with the same material as the dress, and she had on dyed light-blue satin pumps. Her long curly hair hung over her shoulders while her flushed cheeks made her skin radiant.

A butler greeted Cenza as she entered the apartment that Abe and Debra Simon called home., Cenza looked around at the upscale and enormous Manhattan home filled with expensive furniture. She carefully made her way to an overstuffed chair, treading on shiny wood floors.

The gourmet dinner consisted of duck-a-l'orange, baked red potatoes with sour cream and grated cheese, and steamed green beans with creamy, thick butter sauce, served in the Simon's massive dining room. Even so, she did not eat the second piece of bread because it was not homemade and tasted less than fresh. The meal was cooked and served by male servants wearing white gloves and formal wear. Cenza thought to herself as she was given an after-dinner drink in a crystal glass from a gold tray. *This is not me. I will never get used to anyone who serves me.*

Cenza enjoyed the meal, especially the cherries jubilee dessert. The company was fascinating. The table talk was about business, politics, and of course, children. Cenza fit right in because she had read up on the latest magazines and listened to all the late-night newscasts. She read every newspaper she could find and felt confident in keeping up her end of the conversation.

Most of the guests were bankers and financial associates of the Simons. Cenza worried Matt would be one of the guests and was grateful that he was not at dinner. She did not want to feel inadequate and clumsy, as she always did whenever Matt was around her. She remembered her sisters' remark about how she became flustered when Matt was around and was irritated at herself because they were right.

The night was going well with the guests and Cenza on the veranda politely talking and enjoying the sweet smell of late spring. This charming young girl, with only a high school education from another country, impressed the bankers. Her knowledge of numbers and what was going on in the New York City political scene was remarkable.

Cenza's drink was strong, and she didn't want to finish it. She asked one of the servers for a glass of water. She handed the server her drink and thanked him. Then she heard her name called.

"Vincenza, my parents told me you were coming to the dinner party." Matt said in his deep, slow, naturally sexy voice, "I am glad I did not miss you."

She smelled his aftershave, took in his scent, and got weak knees. Slowly, she turned, catching her breath, hoping not to lose her composure and balance in her high-heel shoes.

"Hello... Matt."

"You look beautiful, Vincenza." Matt looked into her eyes. "Your eyes look bluer tonight, more than usual."

Cenza flushed. Matt gestured that they stroll to the end of the veranda. She led the way and stopped, her back against the rail. Matt came closer to her. The spring breeze flowed through Cenza's long hair and over the soft silk of her dress. Matt touched her gently, moved a piece of windblown hair out of her face.

Cenza stopped breathing at his touch. He then stepped aside, placed his elbow on the railing, and leaned slightly on it. He started to talk when his father called to Cenza. She was glad to get away from Matt because he made her extremely nervous, and she was beginning to sweat. She walked over to Abe, knowing that Matt watched her, and said a prayer that she would not trip.

On the way home in the Simon's limousine, Cenza was so glad to be going back home. She hated being off-guard, and Matt Simon always took her guard down. That night she tried to figure out why she was so uncomfortable around Matt. Or why he made her feel that way.

Ten

〰

Angelo waited impatiently one Saturday afternoon in the fall of 1951 as Anna and her older daughters entered their apartment. He was pacing the floor with Angie behind him.

"Angelo, what has gotten you so excited?"

"Anna, my sweet husband, has a surprise for you and your daughters," Angie said, excitedly.

Throughout the afternoon, Angelo and Angie teased the Gennusa family as to the nature of the surprise. Angelo had bought his extended family their first television set, and it was arriving soon. The older daughters went shopping, and of course, that was when the delivery arrived.

Finally, when there was a knock at the door, two men stood beside a large box. They asked Angelo if this was the Gennusa apartment. Angelo said yes, directed them into the living room, and pointed to a spot where the television would go.

Anna asked, "Okay, Angelo, what is it?"

"You will find out when all the children are home," Angelo answered with a giggle.

Once the daughters came home and put away their packages, Angelo could no longer contain his excitement. He directed them into the living room. With Angie standing proudly beside him, Angelo announced that they had a present for the Gennusas. He unwrapped the box, and a television set sat in front of the family.

Maria, standing beside it, asked, "Momma, what is it?"

Everyone laughed at her question as Maria looked puzzled. The others cheered with delight, hugging and kissing Angie and Angelo.

"Oh, Angelo, you can't afford this."

"Angie and I need an excuse to be with our family more. I hope you don't mind."

Anna went to Angelo and hugged him, her love showing in her eyes. "You don't need an excuse to be with us."

The RCA television tube was twelve inches wide. Although it was on, there were no shows on at that hour. Instead, the picture tube displayed a snowy screen and its irritating, annoying sound. Since viewing was new, there were only a few shows to watch. Nevertheless, they all marveled at the beauty of this television, with its fine-tuning and perfect black-and-white picture.

The family gathered on Saturday night to watch shows like "Your Show of Shows." Staring in this comedy show was Sid Caesar. Stars on his show were great comedians such as Imogene Coca and Carl Reiner. Or they took their bowls of ice cream and watched the Kukla, Fran & Ollie Show, a program famous for its entertainment with puppets. Adults, as well as children, watched what would become an Emmy award-winning show that that lasted ten years.

The leader of the troupe was Kukla, a sweet-natured gentle clown who was a worry-wart. Ollie, who was Maria's favorite, was a one-toothed dragon with a penchant for getting into trouble. As Angelo held Maria on his lap, with Enza beside him, they roared with laughter as Ollie got Kukla into trouble.

Angelo always woke up early on Saturday mornings. He sneaked into the apartment in his pajamas and slippers, wrapped in his night robe, to watch the kid shows with the little ones. The TV brought the

Gennusas and the Pertuccis even closer, and they spent more quality time together.

Even as the television became a great entertainment source and unity for the two families, Cenza headed in a different direction.

1952-1953

Highest Grossing Films were:
The Robe
From Here to Eternity
How to Marry a Millionaire
Roman Holiday
Gentlemen Prefer Blondes

Jacqueline Bouvier marries Senator John Fitzgerald Kennedy.
"The Diary of Anne Frank" is published.
The first successful surgical separation in "Siamese" or Conjoined Twins is conducted at Mount Sinai hospital in Cleveland, Ohio.
Dwight D. Eisenhower succeeds Harry S. Truman as President of the United States.
The first color television set goes on sale for $1,175.00.

Eleven

こ

Cenza hugged Angie and Angelo as they stood in the doorway to the Gennusa apartment one Saturday afternoon. She hurried them into the kitchen, where the Pertuccis noticed Anna and the sisters looked pensive. Angie and Angelo sat in the empty chairs around the kitchen table. Enza climbed into Angelo's lap while Maria went to Angie. Angelo thought this must be a big emergency because the little ones are not watching television. Cenza looked very eager and businesslike, which appeared so different from her reaction to the Rosenbergs' unlawful executions.

As the family gathered to listen to Cenza, inmate 1009054 at the New York State Correctional Facility sat alone in his cell contemplating the Rosenbergs' cruel and unjust executions.

"Okay, Cenza... we are all here. What is this all about?" Anna asked. Somehow, she knew that whatever Cenza had planned was going to shake all of them up.

Angie noticed that Anna had her hand in the pocket of her apron. She knew that she was feeling her spool of thread for strength and patience. *What is Cenza about to spring on us?*

Cenza took a deep breath and sat directly across the table from

Anna. "I have been doing much figuring, and I think it is time for us to move out of the apartment.

Angie and Angelo looked at each other, shocked.

"Now, before you get upset, hear me out, for it will make sense when I finish explaining my proposal."

"Cenza, what is in that head of yours now?"

Cenza looked at Pina. She saw her beginning to daydream. She felt terrible for starting her proposal the way she did and giving Pina the slightest hope that they would return to Sicily. Cenza put her arm around Pina and rub her back for a second. Then she removed her arm, looked down the papers filled with math calculations, and firmly gripped a pencil. "Pina,"

Pina looked at Cenza, "Yes?"

"I need you to focus on what I have to say. Do I have your attention?" Cenza asked sternly.

"Yes. Cenza."

Angelo sat pensively. His heart was breaking at the thoughts of losing his and Angie's extended family. He held on to Enza a little tighter.

Cenza announced, "I need everyone to listen to me with an open mind, not with a fearful heart." Everyone relaxed a little in their chairs. "This is a big decision to make, and we all have to make it together. This will undoubtedly be a struggle for us, but struggling is not new to this family. Now listen as I tell you what I have in mind."

Anna shook her head. "Cenza, what are you saying?"

"Momma, I have done a lot of research and feel it is time to make a move. The move will not be far, but it will change our lives enormously. I have found a large house. It is expensive, but we will make it affordable for us. This house will not be just for living but a place of business." Cenza paused. "We are going into business."

As Cenza explained, Anna now understood her daughter's pensiveness at the factory and home. She often found Cenza sitting at the kitchen table by herself wrapped up in figures, sipping coffee on many nights while the rest of her sisters slept. She assumed that her daughter's tension had to do with the factory, not connected to their family.

Cenza explained that she felt opening a business was the direction for them to go. When she finally had everyone's attention, she continued, "We are going to open up a bridal shop."

Anna said, surprised, "A what?"

"Momma, we are going to make your very secret dream a reality and open up a bridal shop. That spool of thread you carry in your pocket all these years is where our future lies. It's time to put it to good use. This shop is not just for you but for the whole family." Cenza said.

Anna's eyes went wide. Her hand curled around her spool of thread, needing reassurance that it was still there.

Enza started crying, putting her arms around Angelo, "No, I will not leave my Angelo." Angelo hugged her back, feeling his loss for her with a sick feeling in his stomach.

Angie looked hurt, "Well, we always knew there would be a day that you would have to leave us."

"Angelo and Angie, do you think we would leave you? You are our family. You are coming with us!" Cenza said, "We will never leave you behind. Besides, we can't do this without you both. The house is large, and we will share it jointly, and we are all going to work the shop together. Before the shop opens Teresa, and I will stay at Simon and Simon to bring in revenue. We will have to stay at the factory and bring in cash to keep us going for a while until we get established."

There was silence for a few minutes, and everyone thought about what Cenza said. Anna looked at her daughter. a little calmer holding on to her spool, "Cenza, what do you have in mind?"

"The house is large, and we can get it at a good price, but it needs work. A lot of repairs but with all our friends and giving back favors, we can make the house quite comfortable. Momma, you, Angie, and Pina will work in the bridal shop. You and Angie will design and sew the wedding gowns while Angelo works in the room that will be the warehouse. Angelo will also drive a small truck for home deliveries."

Angelo said, "I don't have a driver's license. I don't know how to drive."

"Well," Cenza said, "You will have to learn. The business will need you to learn." Angelo nodded his agreement. She continued, "I can get two old machines from Simon and Simon for nothing to start with. I can even get an old truck from Abe for a reasonable price too. All we need to start is the will to do it. I think it is time for us to move in a more financial direction. Angelo, we will have a legal contract written for your portion of the house.

Angelo started to object.

"It will be lawful or nothing. Momma will be responsible for one-third of the house and the business. My sisters and I will be accountable for one-third of the house. You and Angie will also be one-third owners, not only the company but the house too. I insist on it being legal because we all must be responsible for the project to all do the work. There will be no favoritism. This is not charity," Cenza said with conviction, "This will be our livelihood. This is business."

Pina, distraught her dream of Sicily had vanished, asked, "What will I do?"

"Pina, you will help with the sewing of the gowns, and after the shop is opened, you will have an essential job. You will be at the front of the store, taking care of customers, and showing the gowns. Entertain them with coffee and a sweet to eat while they look at our designs. You will make appointments and answer the phone." Cenza said, "It will not be an easy job, but with your looks and your personality, you are the best person for the job. I know you prefer casual clothes, but while in the shop, we will all be wearing high-fashion designs."

"And where will we get the clothes for Pina?" Anna asked.

"Momma, that is easy," Cenza said, "We will look into the newest fashion magazines, and you and Angie will sew them." Cenza paused,

"No, Momma... you will design them, and you and Angie will sew them. We will tell the customers as they come to the shop that you sewed Pina's outfits."

"Aye," Cenza said to herself, "you will design Pina's wardrobe. Teresa can help in her time off, and so can I."

"Why do you think we can make a go of it?"

"Momma, sometimes I think your head is in a cloud. Don't you ever acknowledge the compliments given to your work? Do you have any idea how good and creative you are with wedding gowns? The brides you've touched? Do you ever see how much they appreciate the extras you give to their gowns because of your personal touches? Those brides know no other bride will ever wear their gown. Do you have any idea what that makes a bride feel like on her wedding day?"

"We are intelligent, hard-working people, but we work for others. It is now the time that we work for ourselves and make a more comfortable future for us all."

Anna said, "It sounds to me like we will be working for the rich, not for our neighborhood people. Is that what you are thinking?"

"No, Momma," Cenza got excited that her mother was considering her proposal. "No, we will be working for ourselves, including our neighborhood people. We will never forget what they did to help us when we came to this country. When we are established, and I do not doubt our success, we will give back to our neighbor's needs and give back more than was given to us."

"I think we need some time to think over your proposal."

Angelo declared, "No, we need to discuss this and decide tonight. I think Cenza is right, and she has never let us down." Angelo looked at Cenza and said, "Thank you for including us! "

Cenza went to Angelo's side, kissed his forehead, and put her arm around his shoulder. Angelo reached up and touched her hand.

"Good," Cenza said, "Because I have made an appointment to see the house tomorrow afternoon after mass with the owners."

The family separated to contemplate Cenza's proposal. She knew it was the right direction for their family. She needed them all to accept her plans and work industriously and sacrifice for them to succeed.

After the noon mass the following day, the extended Gennusa-Pertucci family emerged from two cabs and stood in front of a large brownstone. The front of the house faced a huge playground three times the one on Greene Avenue, which Cenza knew was a big plus for the area and selling point. The park was clean, and the bushes and flower beds were well-trimmed. The little girls pointed at the many swings, giggling happily.

The older, childless couple who owned this corner house had inherited it from the wife's great aunt and wanted to get rid of this massive dwelling. They were aware that no one in their extended family was interested in this enormous house. As they were leaving for Europe in a few days, they wanted to sell the house and settle with their lawyers before leaving.

The couple greeted Cenza politely, hoping that she was their buyer but wondered how a young girl could afford to buy it. Cenza introduced the family and turned to the house. They were slightly envious of Anna's six daughters and surprised with Anna's second youngest, Enza's, dark-haired beauty. As they watched the family explore the place and listened to Cenza explaining her plans, they decided that they'd make the house affordable for them no matter what.

"The house has a full basement used for storage," Cenza explained to Anna. "If you look, these brick stairs lead to the front door and first floor. These bay windows are perfect for display, and the second floor has another four equally large windows. The third floor has that large multi-colored round stained-glass window between two smaller windows. It's bigger than our house in Sicily!"

The couple stepped aside as Cenza and Anna entered a grand foyer with a dusty crystal chandelier hanging from the ceiling. The rest soon joined them. The owners stepped back, letting explore the house but remained available for any questions they needed to answer.

Cenza quietly and privately showed her mother the location of the front desk. Pina's beauty would be the first thing customers saw as they came in. There was a large dark wooden staircase at their right, leading to the house's upper levels.

The floors were dark rich hardwood. They appeared to be in good shape but full of dust and dirt from many years of neglect.

The rest of the family separated to search the house's many rooms and its deep closets. The three little ones exercised their enormous amount of energy running through the many places. Their footsteps echoed from the second floor as they ran through each bedroom.

Angie and Angelo walked arm-in-arm as if strolling through the park on a sunny spring day. They examined every part of the house with care. Teresa and Pina explored the downstairs' rooms quietly.

Cenza stayed close to Anna, explaining her ideas. As they stood in the foyer, Cenza demonstrated how to utilize the space. She led her mother to a large walk-in closet on the right side of the entrance under the stairs and indicated it was a perfect spot for a bathroom for the customers.

"This will be our largest expense, but I have already talked to Angelo, and he said he has a friend who would do the job cheaper for us on weekends. He needed the extra money because his wife is having another baby. Angelo has seen some of his work, and he does a good job. I told Angelo if his friend gives us a good deal, we will recommend him to our customers."

"What will we do with coats during the winter?" Anna clutched her spool of thread for security.

"There is plenty of room here against the wall. We will have a coat rack installed. I thought we would use wooden hangers, have an umbrella stand, and a place to put rubber boots. We can even offer soft slippers for our customers to wear while browsing."

"Wooden hangers are too plain. How about if we take fabric and cover the hangers to make them more attractive?" Anna stopped for a moment and then said, "I think there should be a bench where the customer can sit with a fabric cover a soft cushion seat in the same fabric as the coat hangers. Maybe with a..."

"Momma, that's a great idea." ,

"Cenza, where did you get the idea for us to consider making this huge move?"

"Momma, working for Abe, gave me a glimpse into a new lifestyle, something foreign to how we've always lived. I've seen the most beautiful homes and dined in some of the best restaurants. I know how the rich live and what the rich want. They have plenty of money and are willing to pay for the best."

"Cenza, I hear what you are saying, but this is not us! We are farmers. We only know what the dirt will provide us. How will the rest of us fit in this world that you have experienced?"

"I will teach everyone how to fit in. I will teach my sisters how to sit, walk, and pose as if it comes naturally to them. " She laughed, "I will have problems with Francesca. She hates to put on dress shoes, let alone be taught how to walk in them!"

Cenza hugged her mother. "Momma, this is your dream. Your dream! It will finally come true. All I am asking is that you think about it." She led Anna towards the front. "Oh. Our home will be in the back rooms and upper floors. It's like with Pina. When the doors open, she'll dress in today's best fashion, but after hours and we lock up, she'll change and be her own comfortable self. When the shop closes, our lives will go on as always. I don't want our family life to change. We still need to teach the young ones our values. The money we make will not change us. The money will give us a little security."

"My dream was to own a small shop, not this." Anna looked

around, "I don't know how to take care of the rich. I am just a mother who only knows how to take care of her children."

"Momma, you have been waiting on people all your life. You already know how to take care of the rich. You take care of the rich like your family. That is your asset."

They moved into the main living room. "Momma, as I told you last night, the house has six bedrooms with a study that is attached to the master bedroom. I think Angie and Angelo should have that space. If they want, they could convert the study into a living room for themselves if they need privacy. There are two more large bathrooms, one in your bedroom and one main bath in the hall. There are also three bedrooms on that floor. The attic has another three large rooms in the attic that perhaps someday we could make into guests' bedrooms. Possibly one of our aunts will come from Sicily to visit us, and if she decides not to go back to Sicily, that will be okay because she will have her own bedroom."

"Wouldn't that be wonderful?" Anna instantly thought of her sister, Gi

Cenza opened hidden pocket doors. Anna marveled at these doors that disappeared into the wall. She had never seen doors do that before.

Anna was overwhelmed by the size of the room. After getting her bearings, Anna walked throughout the entire room. She looked out of the bay window and touched the luxurious, ivory satin drapes. Brocaded with dark and light mauve roses and green and golden leaves, they cascaded from the ceiling to the floor. A heavy matching swag at the top of the window with a golden fiber running through the fabric completed the look of elegance. A three-seat couch matching the drapes had green chairs flanking it, centered between the drapery folds. Anna visualized giant stuffed pillows in dark and light mauve with gold and green fringe, randomly placed on the chairs and sofa.

Anna's feet felt nestled into the high, plush, multicolored carpet. She had no idea that this was an original oriental. She had never seen anything like it before and was amazed. The carpet had several shades of rose and pink tones. A deep ivory swirl and a mint green touch make the roses' distinctive shades look even more luxurious. She felt slightly insecure, walking on its plush surface. All her life, she walked on either mountain terrain or hard stone floors.

Anna stood before two enormous high double windows that repeated the drapes on the bay window. Beside each window were two high-back chairs covered in one of the shades of green on the carpet. She ran her hand over the dusty fabric of a chair and felt the lush, heavy satin. She thought matching pillows would blend the chair nicely in the room. A high antique server in dark rich wood with brass knobs from lack of care stood along the wall. Above the server was a large mirror trimmed in a square gold frame, also dull from lack of dusting. Anna touched the edge wiping some dust and found the gold shone brightly. She imagined it clean and knew the mirror was elegant. There was a crystal chandler hanging from the ceiling, matching the larger one in the foyer.

Anna crossed to the other wall, avoiding the deep plush rug. There a massive fireplace dominated the side. On her left were two pocket-doors, and she wondered where they lead. She turned to the fireplace, touching the dusty Italian marble mantle, and marveled at the lavish scroll-work.

Cenza gave her mother plenty of time to look around the room. She knew that Anna was already decorating it in her mind making the room warmer and more lavish. She wanted her mother's approval because, without Anna, the business would never be.

"Momma, this room can serve as a waiting room for our customers. The former dining room is across the hall, and it's the same size as this room. We will show our gowns there."

"Come..." Cenza said, "Let me show you."

Cenza led Anna into the dining room, passing the owners. This room, decorated with the same drapes and carpet, had a large dining room table in the center and a huge China cabinet against the far wall. Another bay window faced the front of the house.

Anna inspected every inch of the room as Cenza demonstrated how the gowns could be displayed. She led Anna to another set of pocket doors leading to another large room. She explained that this third area seemed perfect as the storage room for other gowns not displayed around the fitting room.

"It is good for storage. It is a dark room and will not discolor the gowns."

Cenza grinned, "Yes, Momma."

"This is not good for sewing because it is dark, but it is good for storing fabric and white gowns," Anna said to herself. "Cenza. Where will we do our sewing?"

"There is another room across the hall we can use for sewing our gowns. We will install sufficient lighting in there."

Finally, Cenza led Anna through a pair of swinging doors into a huge kitchen. It was sizeable enough for everyone, including Angie and Angelo. They could still eat meals together as a family and with space to spare. What excited Cenza was that all the large pieces of furniture were part of the house sale.

Anna was entranced with the enormous kitchen. She never thought she'd have anything resembling her home kitchen in Sicily. Even though the appliances were old and filthy, they still worked — a large window brought in light from the backyard. Walls needed painting, but she liked the feel of the kitchen.

There was an open door leading into a family room to the right of the kitchen. Large windows lit up the room, making it feel comfortable and bright. Between the kitchen and family room, stairs led to the second floor.

"Momma, let me take you into the garden."

Anna raised her eyebrows at the word garden.

Cenza and Anna walked through the porch door that led to a stone patio. Leaves and debris built up from years of neglect filled the yard. Flanking the stairs leading down to the courtyard were ornate imported clay pots, also needing care. They stepped down several stone stairs and stood in a courtyard. The yard had a high wall surrounding it for privacy, and along the far wall was a wrought iron door leading the rest of the yard. Half-walls around the courtyard had one time been planters, needing care and new plants to come alive again.

More imported clay pots scattered about the yard. A massive wrought iron table and chair set that needed cleaning and repainting repainted. On the other side of the table and chair set sat was a two-seat wrought iron chair that matched the table and chair set.

Anna smiled as she imagined the backyard cleaned filled with beautiful fresh flowers grown from real dirt. It reminded her a little of her city home in Sicily with the beautiful flowers hanging from the balconies.

"Cenza, this is very overwhelming."

Cenza brushed off the leaves and tree branches from the table set and gestured for Anna to sit. Anna had been rubbing her spool of thread since entering the house with such force that her fingers became tender.

"Momma, I am not just thinking of us, but Angelo working down at the docks is taking a toll on him. What will become of Angie and Angelo if they need us later? We have nothing to give. We can barely get by now. What will happen to them?"

Cenza went on, "We need to do something for Angie and Angelo. They have given us everything. They saved our family. This is the only thing I can think of to be successful and bring in more money. I know with all my heart," Cenza paused, "that this will work and work very well... Momma, also, it is time we stop paying rent and put our money into a home that we will own someday. It is also time for us to work for ourselves."

"You think we can make a go of this?"

"Without a doubt!"

As Anna and Cenza sat talking, Francesca ran out into the yard. She ran up to her mother, then stopped and looked around. She walked over to the short stone wall and put her hands into the ground. She raised a handful of leaves and let them fall. She dug her hands into the wall, brought the contents to her nose took a deep breath. "Momma, look... It's dirt!"

She dug deeper and brought up a large amount of moist, dark soil. She lifted the dirt to her nose. She put the tip of her nose to the earth and smelled it. She rubbed the dirt with her hands until the soil left them. The falling rich dark land fell into small mounds on the ground. She turned to her mother and Cenza with a spot of earth on her nose. With tears in her big blue eyes and with her big dimples showing deep in her cheeks, and said very dramatically, "Oh Momma... I just love dirt."

Twelve

~~

Anna stood in front of her new home and looked up at the enormous, impressive building. She started to breathe a little harder. Angie and Angelo were getting out their things from a truck that Angelo had borrowed from a friend. As Anna stared at this house, her family scrambled past her. With the little ones running up and down the stairs getting their belongings from the truck, and running back into the house, their excitement was invigorating.

Anna's problem was that she felt unworthy of the house. She thought that she did not belong in this glorious dwelling. She hesitated, thinking of Cenza's words. visualizing what she said when Cenza described their new adventure, "Momma, the house would cost us."

"We will take two hundred and fifty dollars from our savings and use for paint, cleaners, and any emergency needs. Yes, the money will be tight." Cenza said, forestalling any protests, *"Think, Momma, it not the first time money has been tight for us. Think of the war and how much we suffered, and still, you found food and clothing for us and others. We will do this, and we will get through this and. We will come out ahead."*

Cenza took a large box from the truck, placed it into Anna's hands, grabbed another box, and headed up the steps.

Teresa walked up to Anna, put her arm around her, and hugged her. "It's okay, Momma. We will make it. We have each other just like in the past. We have always survived and will do so again."

"This is bigger than anything we have ever done."

"No, Momma, the biggest thing we did is surviving coming to this country. I agree with Cenza. We will make it work, and we need to take care of Angie and Angelo. So come, Momma, let's go into our new home."

Together Anna and Teresa walked into their new home, their new life, and what adventure lay ahead for them and their family. Anna felt so much better with her oldest daughter's encouraging words and walking jointly with her. Teresa always made her feel secure. She never had to hold her spool of thread while this daughter stood beside her, at least for right now.

The grand old corner brownstone stood beside other brownstones, much more magnificent and cleaner than two months earlier when its new occupants entered it. Its tired old facade almost smiled at you proudly with its fresh white paint around the windowsills. The door to the house was sanded to its bare wood and stained in vibrant dark color. The original brass doorknocker was polished to its highest shine. The cleaning of the door took much thought by its new owners. It had to be exactly right for when customers entered through it into its foyer.

Everyone, except Cenza – the family accountant and not a fashion coordinator - discussed the entryway at great length. Meanwhile, Anna, Teresa, and Angie designed the windows at the front of the house. Using rose-colored tulle under the cream-colored purses and pearl necklaces gave the display a luxurious, dreamy look. Behind the presentation was deep rose-colored tulle. Anna decided to display the bridesmaid dress in a lighter rose shade because it was creamy and not a standard color used in the house's right bay window. The left bay window showed Anna's original designs in wedding gowns with veils and headpieces. Anna felt the contrast of the deep rose against both types of dresses would receive positive reviews.

Flowing up the steps on either side were pink flowers in the ornate planters that Francesca brought from the backyard.

A dark rose-colored sign with painted pink writing read, *"Anna's Bridal Design."* Small pots of pink flower placed around its legs that Francesca planted strategically placed in front of the house.

Everyone was ready for their grand opening event. They were all exhausted and cranky, getting prepared for this unforgettable day. Everyone wore clothes that Anna created. The women also wore lace gloves to hide their scratched hands and broken fingernails from the labor that the house demanded of them.

A high society florist knocked at the door at 11 am and presented Vincenza Gennusa with magnificent dark roses and soft pink flowers. They were set in gold table bowls and larger containers for the waiting room and the bridal room.

To Cenza's surprise, the arrangements were a gift from Abe Simon and his wife Debra with a very affectionate note. The florists had instructions to place the pots and the arrangements where they thought looked best.

Teresa stood beside Cenza as she stood speechless. "I will show the decorators to the bridal room, and you take them to the sitting room."

Francesca was miserable having to dress up and put on dress shoes. She came ready to complain to Cenza when she stopped in the foyer. She watched the decorators by looking in the dressing room and then entered the sitting room.

"Francesca! Don't even think of touching those flowers or the dirt." Francesca stood looking at all the abundance of beautiful flowers in awe when Cenza added, "Yes... I know you love dirt! Yes... you can have them after the show is over, and you can plant them behind the house! But don't you dare touch them before... are you listening to me, Francesca?"

When Anna removed the heavy drapes, shook out the dust, and only put the valences back onto the windows, she transformed the sitting room. Instead, soft, delicate lace drapes with an open weave allowed the sunshine to make everything bright flanked the windows.

Anna reused the heavy drapery to make large throw pillows trimmed in gold thread. She covered the credenza between the two windows in the living room because there were scratches on the wood that was too expensive to repair. The chairs between the server were covered in green fabric. The material on the coffee table had heavy gold tassels hanging down the sides. Some pillows also had tassels at the corners, while others had gold-covered buttons pinched at the center. Anna also made pillows to accent the green in the rug placed on the couch and end chairs. Green cushions and pillows made from the drapery fabric were also placed on the sofa.

Cenza scrutinized the room and did not believe how attractive the room looked with all the fresh flowers around it. Francesca went to Cenza and said, standing beside her so entranced, "The flowers are "sooooo" beautiful. Can I bring some flowers to Mrs. Green? She just loves flowers."

"Of course, you can."

The white marble fireplace shined brightly, and with the touch of color from the flowers placed on it, looked dazzling. Cenza arranged the gold candlestick holders that Debra Simons lent her. She had inserted dark rose-colored candles to match the flower arrangements.

Then Cenza passed through the foyer, saw the enormous flower arrangement situated before the reception desk. The dressing room was filled with flowers placed by the decorators. Somehow, she had managed to get the three youngest girls into pretty dresses that Anna designed. Maria wore a light rose dress. Enza was in a light pink dress, and Francesca, with considerable protest, had on a dark rose grown-up style dress. The little girls were excited by the activities, and Angie tried to herd them into the kitchen.

Anna had repurposed the drapes in the dressing room as well. The fabric now covered the cushions of the chair sets found in the basement. The chairs were placed before the bay window for customers to sit on while drinking coffee. Anna matched more green throw pillows as she had in the living room and put them on each chair. When they had explored the cellar, they found old picture frames that they cleaned and filled with some prints that Cenza found. These adorned the bridal shop walls.

Anna was straightening one of her wedding gown's skirts. Most of the dresses were on display—some on hangers, the remaining ones on a rack – next to the dressing room door.

The tension was very apparent. The family had worked long and hard for this day. When the little bell over the door rang, Cenza nodded to Pina to answer it. Nervously, Pina walked to the door in her original Anna's couture of pink lace and opened it. There stood June and Scooter, and everyone relaxed. June was very pregnant, again, and slowly entered with Scooter walking behind her. Everyone embraced and giggled. Scooter lifted Maria and gave her an enormous hug.

Maria whispered to Scooter, "You can eat all the cookies you want. There are a ton more in the kitchen. Don't tell Momma that I told you."

Scooter smiled his crooked smile and said, "How about I meet you later in the kitchen?"

Maria swayed around gently in her party dress at their secret with a smirk on her face.

Anna escorted June and Scooter into the sitting room and served them coffee and Scooter's favorite cookies. Soon a stream of guests arrived for the open house. Everyone was greeted, served tea or coffee, and shown around the shop.

Pina and Cenza were in the foyer when the Simons arrived. Cenza embraced them, thanked them for all the beautiful flowers, and thanked Debra for the candlesticks' loan.

Debra Simon took Cenza's hand, and they walked into the sitting room. Debra commented on how beautiful the room looked and was delighted with the flowers she and Abe sent. As Cenza poured coffee, Debra realizing that Abe couldn't hear her said, "It would give me great pleasure if you kept those candlesticks."

"Oh no, I could not do that. They are too expensive."

Debra looked at the candlesticks. "They are beautiful, but they were given to me by my mother-in-law, who hated them. She gave them to me because she did not like me, either. She felt I was never good enough for Abe. They look exquisite there. Please keep them. You are doing me a favor because while I love those candlesticks, they are a constant reminder of how much my mother-in-law disliked me."

Before Cenza could argue, Debra added, "At least let us talk about you keeping them until later." Debra then changed the subject. "Who is that pretty little girl in the pink dress, the one with the darker complexion than the other little girls?"

Cenza smiled, "That is my sister, Innocenza."

"What a beautiful name. What does it mean?"

Cenza said, "Yes, she is lovely and not shy at all about her looks. Her name means innocence."

By now, the house had started to fill up with other guests. Cenza excused herself and mingled, greeting these hopefully future customers, checking that Pina was greeting everyone as they entered. Abe and Debra Simon even joined in by welcoming some of the friends and associates they had invited to Anna's Bridal Shop's grand opening. Cenza had feared wealthier potential clientele would not come, but there they were. She wondered if Abe had bribed them to give up their free afternoon and come. She did not want to think about it because she needed these people to be here.

Anna, Angie, and Teresa worked the room, socializing with the neighborhood friends. Sadie arrived with her oldest daughter and Mrs. Barkowitz, just as Mrs. Green was getting out of a cab.

Cenza spoke to each guest about her mother's designs. She explained that they were all wearing Anna's creations. Every dress and gown in the shop was an original design from drawing to the final product pattern. Cenza's feet were killing because of her high-heels, but the suffering was worth it. As she circulated, she heard comments about the clothes and was delighted. When she returned to Pina, she learned that she had already scheduled two appointments, with several promises to make later appointments.

Cenza entered the sitting room and crossed to the server that held the coffee and cups. She was pleased with the dishes that she and Teresa had picked out at antique stores. Each bowl used for the cookies, and each coffee cup and plate were different. It was her idea to have distinctive dishes for serving. She arranged a few spoons, pleased she had found a treasure-trove of them in the cellar. When she cleaned them, she realized they were solid silver. She contacted the previous owners of the house and told them about the spoons. They thanked her but told her that they did not want anything found inside the home. It was all theirs, even if very costly.

Cenza poured herself a half-cup of coffee and started to pour fresh cream when she realized that someone was standing behind her. She recognized the scent of his aftershave, and her knees began to buckle. She flushed hotly and realized that the only time she sweated was when she was around this person.

She looked up at Matthew Simon.

"Hello, Vincenza. I hope you don't mind my stopping by. My parents told me about your open-house. I know I am not a candidate for a wedding gown, but I could not resist your homemade cookies. Though," Matt looked at her eyes and said softly, "I didn't really come for the cookies, but to see you."

Cenza swallowed hard, "You did?"

"Yes... I had hoped to talk to you longer the night of my parent's business party." He reached over to the cookies on a tray beside Cenza, brushing her arm.

Cenza shivered at Matt's touch. He stepped closer to her, and she stepped one step back from him. Matt said, "I see your open-house is a big success. You must be enormously proud."

"Yes, I am delighted... there are so many more people here than I expected," Cenza said slowly, looking into Matt's captivating bright blue eyes. "Please excuse me... Matt... and please forgive me, but my mother is looking this way for me."

With difficulty, Cenza backed away from Matt, and he watched as she moved away from him. He noticed that Anna was not in sight as she slipped through the crowd of guests. Matt smiled to himself, liking the fact that he could shake her confidence.

Cenza knew Matt was watching her walk through the crowd. She felt as if she were going to faint. She hurried into the kitchen and got herself a large glass of cold water, gulping it down, then she straightened her back and composed herself.

Cenza returned to the front desk, where Anna was talking to Pina when the door opened.

Anna looked up to see gentlemen walk through the door and came up to her. "Mrs. Anna Gennusa?"

Anna saw a man about her age. He was medium height, his face had a few wrinkles, but still young, with a full head of brown hair spotted with a little gray at the temples. He was Italian.

"Yes," She looked into his familiar eyes. She thought to herself, *I knew this person. Who is he?*

He handed her a card, "I am Joseph Stevens. I sell jewelry, and I would like an appointment to show you some of my goods." The gentleman glanced at the crowd of people. "May I make an appointment and come back when you are less busy? Please read my card. I did not get an invitation to your open house, but I am familiar with your work. If you don't mind, I would like to look and browse your creations."

Anna looked at the card. The man reached and took the card from Anna's grip and flipped it over. It read---*Please meet me at Portobella's on Thursday*. Anna looked at the man and told him yes by nodding her head. The gentleman said that his car would pick her up at 6:30.

Anna stopped, "Osc...?"

"Yes, that is right." He continued slowly and precisely, repeating his name, "Joseph Stevens."

Joseph Stevens stood before Pina, amazed at what a stunning adult she had become. Pina was too busy to notice the man standing in front of her to recognize him.

Anna watched "Mr. Stevens" make an appointment with Pina and then walk into the sitting room with no more comment. Joseph spotted each daughter and smiled in remembrance, making sure that the older ones did not see him. He looked at the second youngest and remembered thinking that she would grow to be the most beautiful girl in the family when he last saw her.

"Momma," Pina said, "I heard what that man said."

Anna looked at Pina and wondered if she should be worried at Pina listening to her conversation with this very private person that just made an appointment.

"I heard the man," Pina looked at her registration book. She found the man's name and said, "Mr. Stevens had said he did not get an invitation to our open house. It is so surprising how many people came to our open-house without an invitation. I hope we have enough cookies to serve."

Anna, half-listening to her daughter, watched Mr. Stevens standing by the coffee buffet. "I will go to the kitchen and get more cookies."

By 6:00 p.m., when their open house was over, the Gennusa and

Pertuccis gathered in the kitchen. Pina complained about her feet hurting and kicked her new shoes in the kitchen corner one by one.

Anna quietly said, "I think all went well today."

Cenza put her head down on the table to cover her flushed face and mumbled, thinking about Matt Simons, "It went very well."

Angie stretched her back and said, "I am so glad today is over with. I am so tired, and the tips of my fingers hurt. Pina, how did we do?"

"We have twelve appointments." Pina looked at Cenza, "Cenza is that good?"

"I was hoping for a few more appointments," Cenza said without lifting her head, reluctant to let her family see how flushed she was over her thoughts of Matt.

Teresa said, "Cenza, I was in the dressing room most of the time, and the women were impressed with the gowns. I answered so many questions about them. These women were richly dressed with large diamonds that asked if Momma would design evening gowns for them."

"I hope you said yes."

"Of course."

"Good, because we will design evening gowns for our customers if that is what they want,"

"There was a man who came in," Anna looked at Pina, concerned she had recognized Mr. Stevens. "He gave me a card."

Pina took out a card in her dress pocket and read it, "The card read the New York Local News."

"What!"

Pina started to repeat herself when Cenza grabbed the card out of her hand. She knew that Pina would not have left her desk under any circumstances to go find her, to tell her. Cenza paced, looking at the card, acutely aware of the New York Local News. It was a small, newly owned newspaper struggling to get started, but still a paper. She didn't want to complain since Pina was doing her job at the desk but was frustrated at missing free publicity.

Angelo said as he had Enza curled in his lap, "Is anyone hungry?"

They all yelled, "No!"

"Good," in his very tired but irrepressible personality, "Let's have ice cream!"

Maria sitting on Angie's lap, perked up and yelled, "I just love ice cream. I want chocolate."

Enza jumped off Angelo's lap and ran to the refrigerator.

Cenza still paced, "Angelo, I hate chocolate, but I will take a large bowl of vanilla."

Francesca was about to disturb Cenza when her sister cut her off. "Yes, you can have the flowers, and yes, you can plant them out in the patio in the backyard, and yes, you can give some to Mrs. Green... Stop being a pest."

Anna asked, "Do we have any strawberry ice cream?"

The tired family all got up from the table, scurrying around the kitchen. They were happy to get their tired bodies up from their chairs to help with their favorite dessert.

Angelo asked, "Are there any cookies left?"

"No."

Disappointed, Angelo said, "I guess that's good, right?"

No one answered.

Thursday evening, Anna headed to Portobella Restaurant, located on the other side of the city. It was a chilly evening around six-thirty. Joseph's driver picked her up in a long black magnificent limousine. He was a very gentle large man with broad shoulders and thick arms, who had knocked on her door and introduced himself as Manny. He wore a black uniform with a flat black cap with gold trim on it, looking more like a bodyguard than a driver. He opened the back door and let her take her seat on the lavish burgundy velvet seats.

She snuggled into her seat, grateful to be in a comfortable car but feeling a little out of place while wondering about the person she was about to meet.

Anna thought about the day after the open house and the enormous strain that no longer surrounded her. The family anxiously read an article about the shop in the New York Local News. It was one column, but a piece nonetheless. The reporter wrote favorably about the shop, stating that the gowns were beautiful, unique, and original designs. The news was spreading, and the telephone started to ring all day.

The limousine reached the restaurant five minutes before seven because the road traffic was light. Anna thanked Manny as he opened the door for her.

Anna was escorted to Mr. Steven's table. She looked anxiously around the room for Joseph as she followed the owner in his restaurant decorated in an Italian café style. She could smell the warm bread baking as she was led to a booth at the restaurant's rear

When she reached the booth, Joseph stood. The owner placed two menus on the table and left. Joseph refrained from hugging her. "Please sit, Anna. I hope you don't mind, but I ordered a bottle of Chianti before dinner. I hear it is a good year..."

Joseph choked back his tears, "I didn't come to pick you up for fear I would cry and not stop. I would have held you and never have let you go. You are as dear to me today as you were years ago."

On the table were a bottle of wine and two glasses. Joseph poured Anna and himself wine as she got herself comfortable in the booth.

Anna looked at Joseph puzzled, "Oscar?"

He interrupted her, "It is safer if you call me Joseph."

"I don't understand?" Anna asked.

Joseph lifted his glass and drank. "After my sons and I left your home in Bisacquino, we returned to Palermo. We found a great part of our city in ruins from the shelling, and our home was almost gone.

We hid in what was left of the house, away from the war. I had hidden money and jewelry in the house, so we had plenty to live on until the war was over."

Anna took a large drink from her wine, trying hard to not cry. When Franco was in their country house harvesting the olive trees, several Jewish families were out in the woods hiding from the islands' enemies. They had come to Bisacquino asking for shelter until they could return to their homes in the cities. They need accommodation from the Italian Communists and the Germans.

Joseph Stevens (Oscar Stein) and his family were one of these families looking for refuge. She was distantly related to his late wife, so Anna and Franco had taken them into her village home because they needed help. They had money to give her. It helped them feed their children during a horrible time.

When Franco returned from the farm, Anna had convinced him that the family was harmless, and the money was needed. They resided in the attic. The young boys had to stay quiet, which was a big challenge. Between her little ones and the boys, keeping them quiet was not easy. Somehow, they got through. When they left, they were very much missed and never heard of again until now.

Anna stayed quiet as Joseph continued to talk in their Sicilian Dialect. Anna enjoyed responding to him in their native tongue.

"When we returned from one of our supply trips, we heard a noise and went into hiding. Lena did not make it. She was killed by the Germans.

"Finally, that night, I wedged the trap door open. When I felt it was safe, we came out of our hiding place. My sons and I found Lena stiff and cold. We buried her in our backyard. We spent a long time in the house, moving about only at night when we needed supplies. We, of course, were devastated. Staying quiet and shut up in our house for months was fine because we needed to grieve, besides staying safe and out of harm's way.

"One day, when I felt the boys were safe to leave, I left them. I went to the Underground and asked for help. Because I was an Italian Jew, they were more than eager to risk their lives to help me and my sons escape Sicily. Any Jew, regardless of nationality, was helped to escape the wrath of the Germans. The large amount of money that I gave them was more than enough to get us on a boat transfer with papers that got us safely to Italy's mainland. The underground was so grateful for the extra money I left them. I hoped that the money I gave helped other Jews escape. Once on the mainland, we traveled undercover through Europe. We reached Switzerland, where we set up residence. My sons and I had Italian papers indicating that we were Catholic, given to us by the resistance. I placed my sons in a Catholic boarding school as the safest place for them. After the war, I set up my import-export business here. The nuns still protected them as I traveled to get my company started. I still have a home in Switzerland and an apartment in the city."

"Where are your sons now?"

"My sons are still in Switzerland. They love it there. My oldest is married to a beautiful blond Norwegian woman and has honored me with a grandson. He works with me in my business there in that country. My youngest is what you would call a 'ski bum.'"

Anna looked puzzled, not understanding the phrase when Joseph smiled and explained that he lived to ski in the Swiss Alps with his friends. Joseph laughed, "My oldest son says I have nothing to worry about. He knows his baby brother will settle down and join the family business someday. With all the playing he does, he is still at the top of his class. I am proud of them. My only regret is that Lena did not live to see what remarkable sons she had given birth to."

"Do you and your sons practice Judaism?"

"Only in private," Joseph said, "But someday we will practice openly when we feel safe. Even now, after the holocaust, Jews in Europe, and even in some parts of this country, are still persecuted." He paused. "Anna, what happened to Franco?"

Anna looked anxious.

"When I heard about your bridal shop opening, I recognized the name. One of my colleagues at my bank complained about being forced to attend the opening by a business associate I asked about the invitation. I got your address, hoping it was your family. I even hired a detective to find out. I know you came to this country with Franco and I know that you have been in this country without him. I know how much you both loved each other... where is he?"

Joseph poured more wine, and Anna took a sip. Then she explained that Franco's drinking had worsened while in Sicily. How he insisted that they emigrate, even though they did not want to leave their homeland. She knew that once in the States, they would never go back. She described Franco's death on the ship and what the ship's doctor did to bury him. She explained how God was with her the night they arrived and described her journey and how she brought her daughters to the Pertuccis. "We were penniless and destitute. These wonderful people took us into their modest home with no hesitation and have given us unconditional love. These people, now my family, saved our lives."

They talked for hours. Anna spoke about her current life - the factory (leaving DogFace out), her daughters' progress in school, and adjusting to their new society. She bragged about Vincenza and her accomplishments at Simon and Simon. Anna showed her pride for all her daughters but also had concerns for Pina. Again, she told Joseph how wonderful Angie and Angelo had been with them, and as little as they had, they made room in their lives for her and her daughters.

Finally, dinner had come. They ate heartily. During dinner, both reminisced about how much they loved Sicily, and both missed their homeland. Joseph asked her about the ruby ring he had given Franco, hoping that it had helped them survive the war or even paid for their passage to the United States. Anna was surprised to learn this and that Franco had refused more jewelry from Oscar, now Joseph.

After Manny drove them to Anna's house, she asked, "Will I see you again, Joseph? It has been such a long time since I talked to another adult about my home and life in Sicily. Especially with someone who shared my life there. Is it safe for us to remain friends?"

"Yes, I would like that very much. If my identity is not talked about, I think it will be safe for us to continue our friendship."

"Joseph, would you come to Sunday dinner? We eat at noon."

"Yes, I would love to, but only if you make me pasta," Joseph said.

"I know my older girls will remember you. I will explain to them about your new name. I will tell the younger ones that you are an old friend from the village so that we can converse in our native tongue." Anna stepped from the curb and gave Joseph a hug. "I will see you on Sunday."

Joseph drove away, longing for the past but happy to be with his old friend.

On her way back to her bedroom, Anna thought about her friend. She still felt the shock in finding out that Joseph had given Franco a ring of great value. Once again, she was disappointed in Franco for not telling her about it. Now she understood where the money came from to buy their transportation to this country. She felt angry again, as she had felt many times whenever she found out the secrets that Franco kept from her. If she had known about the ring, maybe that could have been put towards their daughters' dowries, and they could have stayed in Sicily.

After spending the evening with Joseph, Anna buried herself under her blankets and longed for her home. She thought of her sister Gi and felt empty. As Anna weighted her body down into her bed, she felt sad for her past but pleased to see Joseph again.

She felt very delighted knowing that since her bridal shop open house, the phone had been ringing, and many appointments were made. She was pleased to live in a beautiful place that was now her home and where she finally felt comfortable.

She was also happier now that her Cenza was a lot easier to live with because she was less tense since the open house. Anna thought to herself, *thank God. I don't think I could have handled her moody attitude for too much longer.*

Before Anna got to her bedroom after leaving Joseph, she checked on her daughters, all tucked in bed. When she got to Maria and Enza's room, she peeked in. Of course, they were not there.

Anna walked over to Angie and Angelo's master suite, knocked softly, and entered. Angie and Angelo's bedroom was warm with all their personal belongings hanging on the walls and with blankets that Anna crocheted for their bed. Anna walked past the bed and the dresser and entered the sitting room, finding her girls cuddled in their arms, in front of a blank television screen. They were sound asleep, snuggled in heavy blankets.

Anna shook her head, knowing this was normal for her little girls to be there. They enjoyed complaining to the Pertuccis how scared they were because of the monsters under their beds and needed protection. Anna knew it was all an act, but Angie and Angelo enjoyed comforting them. There were bowls of leftover melted ice cream on their coffee table.

Anna woke them all up gently, picked up Maria, and took Enza's hand, taking them to their bedrooms. Anna put Maria into her bed without a stir. Enza yawned, slipped into her cover, and curled up without a word.

Joseph came to Sunday afternoon dinner and was welcomed by everyone. As soon as he walked into the homey kitchen, he felt like he was back in Sicily. The pasta sauce was bubbling. The bread was baking, and the wine was room temperature. Homemade cookies were on the sideboard beside a bowl of fruit and nuts. June, Scooter, and their son were there. From that day forward, whenever Joseph was in New York, he came to the Gennusa's Sunday dinner.

After introductions, Joseph announced that he brought ice cream. The group all looked at him and hollered, "We love ice cream!"

Thirteen

〜∾〜

After one of their weekly Thursday evening dinners, Joseph's limousine stopped in front of the shop. Joseph took Anna's hand as she got out of the car. In his other hand, he had a bottle of wine and two glasses. "Come, Anna, let us go to the park. I need to talk to you."

"Joseph, it is not safe in the park at this time of the night."

"Don't worry. Manny will not be far away from us. He will make sure we are safe."

They settled down on one of the benches facing the house. Anna looked across the park and noticed only one older person sitting there, far away from them. Manny sat near them but out of earshot. Anna took her glass of wine and sipped it while Joseph poured one for himself.

"I have felt all night that you are troubled about something. Is everything all right with your sons?"

"Yes... I am troubled about something, but it not my boys." Joseph took a drink from his glass and then sighed. "It's about the Pertuccis..."

Joseph hesitated and said, "I hope you will not be upset with me, but I have been troubled about some information I found out about them. I kept this information for a long time before deciding to tell you what I have found out. I am telling you this because it is very hurtful, and I think it would be best they found out from you. I know if I were them, I would want to know. Now that I have gotten to know them, I know they would want to know."

"Joseph… you are scaring me. What is it?"

"I had a detective look into their background. I needed to know that these were good people. I know that they are well-liked in their neighborhood and that they are hard workers. However, I found out something about them that I think they should be aware of."

"You are going to tell me something about their lives that they don't know about?"

"Yes. But it is extremely complicated."

Joseph lifted a large brown envelope.

"What is that? "

"My detective went back into the individual histories of the Pertuccis. Angelo led a simple life. So did Angie until she gave birth to a baby whom the records showed died. Anna, did you know that?"

"Yes. Angie told me that she was going to have a baby when she married Angelo."

"Did Angelo know that the baby was not his?"

"Yes, but it did not matter to him. He planned to help Angie raise the child as his own."

"Since I met Angelo, I could see him raising a child who was not his."

"Joseph, what is this about? "

"What I am trying to tell you is that the child Angie gave birth to did not die."

"No, that can't be true. How can that be?"

"Anna, there is no doubt," Joseph started his story. "Apparently, Angie's son was born perfect. He was sold on the black market to a childless couple in New Jersey who paid a handsome price. They were Catholic and gave the child a good life. When the child turned twelve years old, his parents were killed in an automobile accident.

The boy, since he had no extended family, was put into foster care. He ran away several times, not wanting to be there. Finally, from lack of a home, the state put him into a juvenile detention center. He barely survived there. He was beaten and raped several times, got blamed for the fights, and was in solitary confinement many times. By the time he was eighteen and was able to leave the system, he had no education and had no way to get a job. He began robbing grocery stores. When he was nineteen, he and his accomplices were caught, tried, convicted, and sent to prison. He has been there for a couple of years. He has two or three more years to serve. I am sorry I am the one to tell you this, but I think Angie should know. She has the right to know that her son is alive."

Anna tried to comprehend how something like this could happen. She could not contemplate losing one of her daughters, let alone anything like this. Anna shook as she lifted her wine glass and asked Joseph, "How does someone steal a child from a hospital?"

"According to my sources, when Angie gave birth, a doctor and nurse working at the hospital told parents that their children were stillborn. This went on for ten years. It was during a war, so no one thought about questioning a doctor's ethics. The doctor has since died, and the nurse lives at a privately owned, expensive home for the elderly. She is half crazy. My detective went to see her, and he found out that she brags to all the nurses about how many babies she helped steal and sell. This nurse is now giving out her records to people willing to pay for them because she runs out of money. She feels she has the right to stay in that very exclusive home, so agrees to sell her information on the baby-selling ring to anyone willing to pay for it."

"How much did you pay for the information on Angie's baby?" Anna asked.

"The money is not important, but the information is... Angie needs to know... She has the right to know.

"Can you tell me how the boy is doing in prison?" Anna asked.

"I have been told that he is doing well. The first few months were awfully hard for him. His anger was intense, but after a while, he calmed down. He is doing his time quietly, studied, got his GED, and some college work. He has no friends, which is good. That will keep him out of trouble. I can tell you that before his parents died, he was doing well in school. He was at the top of his class. I also know that he plays the piano. I have been told that he plays brilliantly. Sometimes during rest periods, he can play for the inmates."

"How do I tell Angie this?"

Joseph handed her some paperwork with the information about the child, he said. "These papers will help you prove to Angie that my finding is right. I am glad I am not the one who will tell her. It will not be pleasant.".

Anna and Joseph parted for the evening

"Anna," Joseph said. "Be brave and be strong. Your best friend is going to need you."

Anna wiped her tears and hugged Joseph again, needing encouragement.

Anna returned home with a heavy heart. She took a glass from the upper cabinet, opened the faucet, and let the cold water run for a long time, hoping it would be cold and refreshing.

Then she took the envelope, her purse, and the water and proceeded upstairs, reluctantly. When she got to the second floor, she peeked into each bedroom. She noticed that all her girls were asleep except for Vincenza. She was reading one of her many books scattered over the room. Anna did not disturb her because she needed to talk to Angie and Angelo alone.

Anna just wanted to go to bed. However, she passed by the main staircase on her left and turned the corner. She stopped at Angie and Angelo's and heard their television and Angelo laughing. Anna was grateful that tonight her younger daughters were asleep in their own room.

Anna felt immense sadness about ending their laughter. She waited patiently for the laughter to subside and softly knocked on the wall in the doorway.

Angie and Angelo were in their nightclothes, looking warm and comfortable. Angelo rose from the couch turned the sound down on the television set.

Angie said. "You had a late night with Joseph tonight. You are missing the "I Love Lucy Show. If you hurry and sit down, you will be able to see the ending. This is the funniest epodes yet. Lucy is working at a chocolate factory. She is stuffing chocolates into her mouth because she can't pack the candy fast enough. If she doesn't pack the chocolate, she will lose her job."

Angie started to get up from the couch when she stopped and asked, "What is the matter? Anna... you look pale. Are you all right?"

Anna shut off the TV. She went to the couch and sat down beside Angie. "No, Angie, I am not all right."

Angelo became concerned. "What is it?"

"I am not sure how to tell you this, so I think the best way is to give this envelope to you. Angie, before you read the documents in it, I want you to know that it is true. There is no doubt about it. Here, drink this water. It will be good for you. Please, try to comprehend, and I will answer as many of your questions that I can."

Anna handed the envelope to her. Angie opened it up.

It took her only a few minutes of intense reading when she put the papers down on the coffee table. "This is not true."

"What is it?" Angelo started reading

"Yes... Angie, it is true."

Angie rose from the couch, stood in the middle of the room, and started to scream. It was loud and bloodcurdling.

Seconds later, Cenza and the little ones were at the bedroom door. Anna stopped them from entering. She told Cenza to take the girls back to bed and stay with them. "I'll explain all this later."

She returned to the bedroom and found Angie curled into a fetal position on the bed. In the sitting-room, she found Angelo.

"Is this true?" Angelo asked.

"Yes."

"How did you find out?" Angelo asked.

Anna told him what Joseph had told her. She explained why Joseph inquired about him and Angie.

"So, you are saying that this son of ours is alive and in prison?"

"Yes."

The next morning Anna brought coffee to Angie and Angelo's room and waited for them in their sitting room. Angelo got up, came to Anna, and sat beside her on the couch. He took the coffee and drank it willingly.

"Did you get any sleep?"

"No. Angie cried all night."

Then Angie came into the sitting room and sat in a high-backed wing chair by the couch. She looked out of the window. "Anna, what is my son's name?"

"Thomas James Walters."

"Does he know about me?"

"No, I don't think so. He thinks his parents died when he was twelve. I don't even think he knows that he was adopted, Angie," Anna said. "The report states he plays the piano and plays beautifully – almost professionally."

"Just like my father." Angie had tears running down her face. "I want to see my son." She turned to her husband, sobbing, "Angelo, I need to see him...today!"

Angelo held Angie close.

"Joseph arranged for you and Angelo to see him at two o'clock today. Joseph's driver, Manny, will take you and Angelo. Joseph and I think it best if we go with you."

"What about the shop?"

"The shop can wait. Today, family comes firsts."

At one forty-five, the limousine arrived at the New York State Correctional Facility on the city's outskirts.

The four entered the facility with apprehension. The grounds were surrounded by a barbed-wire fence with guarded towers. There were guards in the towers in between, slowly pacing back and forth with rifles in hand, scanning the ground.

The visitors walked through a long hallway on the first floor of the prison. The authorities led then by many rooms, went up several flights of stairs, and walked down very grim gloomy cold hallways. They were met by guards at every entrance point of the building. Every time the metal door closed behind them, there was a dull echo. After each entry, it was closed and locked. At each stop, the guard would use a walkie-talkie to contact the next guard to expect visitors.

Angie walked deeper and deeper into this dungeon that had been her son's home for several years. Her mouth became dry, and her throat tightened. Her head ached, and her eyes were swollen from crying. The prison's air was still and stale. Angie was having trouble breathing

They were led into a room and were told to make themselves comfortable and that the Warden would be with them shortly. This room was also gloomy, even with the sunshine shining through the two high large windows.

As the visitors sat quietly beside each other, Angie and Angelo sat close together, holding hands. Several minutes passed when a large, broad heavy-set man in an old tired navy-blue pin-stripe suit entered the room. He was around fifty.

"Welcome," Warden Whitter said in a deep, penetrating voice. "I see you are here to see prisoner *1009054*." The Warden sat down as Angie cringed at her son being called a number instead of his name.

"I am here to brief you before you see Thomas. I was told of the circumstance of your visit. Someone has a significant influence on our Mayor Impellitteri? I am not sure how the prisoner will react to who you are and why you want to see him. I will have a guard in the room with you while you visit. If there are any signs of aggression, he will be handcuffed, and he will be brought back to his cell immediately."

Angie cringed.

"When inmates are imprisoned, it is difficult to say how they will react to family. It is very tough to predict what they will do when they find out after a long time that they have a family and are not alone."

Warden Whitter continued, "This is a prison. Remember and keep in mind how important it is not to have any physical contact with the prisoner. Only his parents can visit with him. Since this is a usual situation, I am allowing you to visit even though it is not a visiting day. I suggest that you follow the rules unconditionally. "

Now," the Warden looked at each of the visitors, "Who are his parents?"

Angie and Angelo stood.

"Well then, let me escort you both to our private view room. As you go into the room, notice that there are cameras on the corner of the walls. You are not allowed to hand the prisoner any articles, hard or soft of any kind. You are not allowed to bring in your handbag. You will always be watched. If all goes well, you can return on a normal visiting day if the prisoner agrees to see you. If not, you will not be able to enter the prison another time. Once again, let me state that this is very unusual. Like I said, someone here has good connections to the Governor. I will be in the next room monitoring your visit through a two-way window. You will only have twenty minutes with inmate *1009054*. Good Luck!"

Angie handed her purse to Anna as she and Angelo followed the Warden to the next room. Angelo looked up at the ceiling in the corner of the room and spotted the cameras. The door shut behind them, and Angelo led Angie to a chair. She sat down and put her hands on the table and folded them.

Angelo and Angie waited for five minutes. The door opened, and a young man handcuffed, wearing a gray jumpsuit, entered. His head was bowed, and his back was to his visitors as his handcuffs were unlocked. The guard stepped away and stood by the door, and the prisoner turned to stare at his visitors. Angelo held Angie's icy hands tightly.

The prisoner sat down, facing the strangers. No one spoke for a few minutes. Angie looked at her son and noted that his dark hair and dark eyes were like his biological father's. She was shocked to realize that this very handsome young man resembled her brother.

Angie tried to control her tears. "I know you must be surprised to get visitors. I found out yesterday that you existed. They told us before meeting you that we just have twenty minutes of your time. I need you to be patient with me and to listen to what I have to tell you."

The young man said flippantly, "What is this about? Did I win a million dollars?"

"No, Thomas." Angie said slowly, "I wish it were that simple. Please don't leave us until you hear what I have to say. It will be difficult for you to know who we are, but keep in mind that it was just as difficult for my husband and me to learn about you. Last night, a good friend told me that you existed. My first thought was that it was crazy."

"Are you a friend of my parents?"

"No, I wish I had known them. I was told that your parents loved you very much and had a wonderful life with them. I was also told that you were a happy child and that you did well in school before your parent's death."

"I don't know what this is all about, and I don't care. You are talking about my parents, and you don't even know them. What right do you have to come here and feel you can get personal with me? I loved my parents, and you have no right to stir up my feeling about them," Thomas called, "Guard, I want to go back to my cell. I don't care what these people want. I want out!"

The Warden stopped the guard standing beside him from going into the visiting room. "Let's give them a few more minutes. I think Thomas and his parents have earned at least that much after what they have been through."

Angelo rose from and stood beside Thomas. Angelo said without touching him, "Please, son, please sit and let my wife finish. It has been an awfully long day for her. Please let her tell you who she is, who I am, and why we are here."

It was hard for Thomas to refuse Angelo's gentle request looking into his tender eyes. He sat down in the chair but did not slide it closer to the table. He sat tensely, ready to escape at any moment.

"Thank you, Thomas. When Angelo and I were married, I was carrying a child. The child was not Angelo's. He knew I was pregnant, and it did not matter to him. He wanted both of us. When the child was born, I was told by the doctor that the child was born dead. Last night, I found out that the child was not stillborn but was taken from me. How I found out about my child still being alive is a long story, and if you ever want to hear it, I will tell you, but not today, because I don't have the luxury of time. I found out that the son I gave birth to was stolen from me and sold." Tears ran down Angie's face. "Yesterday, Thomas, I found out that that baby I was told was stillborn did not die, and it was you."

Thomas said nothing.

"I have proof you are my son. I have documents, and I have the word of the nurse who helped the doctor who stole you away from me."

"You are both crazy." Thomas got up from his chair and continued to talk, "I know who my parents are. I know who I am."

He turned toward the door and headed to it, not waiting for the guard to handcuff him."

Angie jumped up, ran to him, and grabbed his arm. "I love you, Thomas. Even when I thought you died, I loved you."

He turned from her and walked out of the room.

On the way home from the prison, the atmosphere was solemn. There were many tears shed by all four of the passengers. Even Manny felt a tear or two slid down his cheek.

Two and one-half years before his sentence was over, Thomas James Walter, aged 22, walked out of prison a free man. He held his few possessions under an arm. He never knew that his fellow prisons would miss him for his soft, gentle demeanor and for his piano playing. Especially his piano playing that brought peace to hardened criminal hearts.

He walked through several prison doors, with the guards shutting and locking each door behind him with loud metal clanks. He stood contemplating each step before the guard standing beside him forced him to move to his next station.

Thomas was finally greeted by the last guard. He escorted him out on the open grounds towards the exit door. This guard led Thomas through the grounds through a thick, high wrought-iron fence. That too was shut behind him and locked, making a loud clanking sound, but this sound did not echo behind him.

Thomas looked up to the vast sky, which calmed him momentarily. The fragrant spring air and his freedom were sweet and refreshing. He felt light, no longer subject to cramped accommodation. Strangely, as he tried to adjust to this feeling of enormity surrounding him, it did not come easily or quickly to him.

He took his first step of freedom away from the prison gate into the open world, not knowing what to do after that step. Restrictions, structures, and limitations were no longer a factor in his life, but compulsion and exercising his alternatives were.

Thomas noticed a man standing across the street watching him. The man walked across the street smoothly and approached him. "Mr. Walters?" He held out an envelope.

Thomas jerked at the mention of his name by this stranger. "Yes?"

"Sir, I was told to take you anywhere you wanted to go."

Thomas took the note and read his name on the envelope. He turned the envelope to its back and gently peeled open the seal. Thomas had difficulty focusing on the print in the sun's glare, so he turned away and read:

June 1, 1953

My Dearest Thomas,

It has been a long six months since I have met you. When I first set my eyes on you, I was thrilled you were alive. Still, I feel angry that I was robbed of you all this time. When I can control my anger, I think of you, and I see your father's eyes. I am so proud that I gave birth to you. I know I have no right to you anymore because you are of age and have the right to live your life as you see fit. Angelo and I have a beautiful home and would love to share it with you. We do not live alone, but you will understand when you see it and meet our other family.

If you feel you would prefer not to be part of our lives, I will understand and give you your privacy. If you can find it in your heart to spend your first day of freedom with us, it would make Angelo and me incredibly happy.

Remember, when deciding what to do that, Angelo and I love you very much. We want to share in your life. You will never be alone again. Please search your heart.

Angie Pertucci

Manny watched as Thomas read his note. "Where to, sir?"

The driver turned to his vehicle, and Thomas, not knowing why, followed him. Thomas looked at the driver and asked while walking to the limousine. Again, not understanding, instinctively answered, "Can you drive me into New York City?"

"Yes, sir," Manny opened the door for Thomas.

Thomas hesitated when the car door was open for him. It had been a long time since anyone had waited on him. He wasn't sure how to respond. He clumsily stumbled into the car, feeling ill at ease. After years of hard seats and benches, Thomas had trouble adjusting to the lush car seat. He wiggled himself, sinking deeper into its rich dark-red velvet material.

Thomas wondered if these "real parents" owned the car. He tried to relax but instead felt more stressed and emptier. Thinking of the only parents he'd ever known, he wanted to cry for his loss. He remembered being a child and the security they had as a family. He recalled all the games they attended, the vacations they spent together, and Sunday mass. He wondered if his parents would have someday told him that he had been adopted. Thomas thought they would have eventually when he was older because they never lied to him or kept secrets from him.

After they died, Thomas felt lost and afraid. Whenever he ran away from the foster home those many times, he ran to his old house. He stood in the front yard and cried. He needed to see his old house, to feel close to his parents again. Every time he left a foster home, the authorities knew where to find him.

Thomas politely asked the driver if it was too late to drive him to Hoboken, New Jersey. The driver headed towards the New Jersey Turnpike. It took two hours, giving Thomas plenty of time to think. As he relaxed in his seat, he sank deeper into it. Although thinking was hard, his mind wandered to his not-so-good past. Spending all those years in prison was not what he wanted to do again.

Even though he had obtained his GED and studied music in his cell, he was still uncertain about adjusting to his new reality. Thomas looked out the window at the houses passing and wondered about the people that lived there. He pondered if their lives were as simple as his was once. Passing many backyards, he saw swings and swimming pools. He saw lawn chairs, lawn tables, and barbecue cookers. He looked at the trees and noticed them beginning to show their spring colors. His heart ached for the life he once had.

When the limousine arrived in Hoboken, Thomas took a deep breath and wondered if he should keep going. He knew that in the end, there would only be his loneliness and sadness for the only parents he had ever known. Still heartsick, he decided to continue when he told the driver where to turn. Manny turned with Thomas's every direction.

Thomas was pleased and yet sad that his hometown had not changed much. They drove down one street, and Thomas looked at a small two-story house, thinking of its former owner, Frank Sinatra. Unconsciously he hummed one of Old Blue Eye's songs.

Thomas asked Manny to turn down several other streets and drive slowly. Thomas looked at all the houses in his old neighborhood. He longed to know what happened to his friends. The driver drove by a small park where Thomas spent many hours playing ball with his friends. After playing hard, he and his friends would go inside his house. There, his mother always greeted them with a plate of sweet homemade sugar cookies and glasses of ice-cold fresh whole milk. Half-way down the street, Thomas asked the limousine driver to stop at the house with number sixty-two just before the driveway on the right-hand side of the vehicle. There was a large bush obscuring the driveway.

Thomas looked out the car window said a prayer. Feeling ill, he told Manny to pull into the driveway that was past the bush. The driver drove into the driveway and stopped in front of a one-car detached garage painted mustard yellow. The car stopped, and Thomas looked at the house. For some reason, unknown to him, Thomas was not surprised that the house was not occupied. He was not sure why he felt the house would be empty, but he knew.

Before Thomas got out of the car, he asked Manny when he had to return to his employer. The driver said not until Thomas reached his destination whenever and wherever that was. Thomas was surprised by the answer and told the driver to wait for him. He opened the door, got out of the car, and started walking towards the house.

Thomas stopped in the middle of the small yard and could not help noticing that the ranch house looked shabby and unattended. Faded dirty yellow with white window trim made the place look sad. The flower beds had not been tended for a long time. He visualized his mother lovingly working at them. He walked up to the front door, stretched up to a diamond shape window, and looked in. He saw nothing because the window was dirty. He walked over to the front bay window, stepping on low-growing bushes covered with leaves and debris, and looked in. He saw nothing because the drapes were shut tight.

Disappointed, Thomas walked to the side of the house, over to the garage. He checked out the two small windows at the top of the door. He put one of his hands up to his forehead and leaned up against the window. The garage was empty. It was as empty as his heart. He stepped away from the garage, put his hands together, and wiped the cob's webs off them.

Thomas then walked into the backyard. He saw his red and blue swing set. It was rusting and needed a fresh coat of paint badly. He moved to it slowly, his thoughts wandering in all sorts of directions, and then he sat on one of the swings. He swung slowly, listening to all its creaks. Not wanting to break the swing because it was too small for him, he still gently squeezed himself into it.

"Dad, where do I go from here? Mom, please help me find my

way." He got up from the swing and walked to the back of the house to the small back porch. He saw something lying up against the porch, almost camouflaged with leaves covering it. He walked over to the item and picked it up. To his amazement, it was his old baseball bat, which he was nicknamed Hitter, because of his many home runs at the playground. Most of the finish and wording on the bat was gone, but he knew it was his bat. The wood was still intact. He was so pleased to have it back that he placed the bat next to his heart. He held on to it as he came around the house and walked over to Manny, standing by the limousine.

"Where to, sir?"

Thomas said nothing for a few minutes, thinking, then turned to his house and looked at it, rubbing his childhood bat. He stared for a few minutes, and then he turned to the driver. He said, "Please bring me to Anna's Bridal Design on..."

"I know where that is, sir."

The limousine headed away from Hoboken towards New York City. Thomas wondered if he was doing the right thing. He knew nothing about these people, except that they were very persistent. After meeting Angie and Angelo, he did not believe what they had told him. It took several days and sessions with the prison psychiatrist to sink into his head that he was adopted. He received letters from Angie every day. He never opened them and returned them unread.

Thomas felt by opening those letters meant betraying the only parents he had ever known. He needed to hang on to their memory. He looked at their picture every night, wondering why they never told him he was adopted. Then when he started to forgive his parents for not telling him that he was adopted, he missed them more

Thomas was staring out the window, not seeing the people, street signs, or the buildings flying by. He was still in a trance over getting out of prison and going to his old home. Before Tom realized it, the limousine started to slow. He gazed at an old huge stately, corner brownstone house with beautiful flowers on the steps with a sign that said "Anna's Bridal Design." Across the street was a large park, alive with children's laughter. It had been a long time since he heard children laugh.

Manny turned off the engine, got out of the car, went around the other side of the vehicle, and opened the back door for Thomas. As Thomas slid over to get out of the limousine, he grabbed his paper bag and the baseball bat. He held on to it, looking inside the bag for security. He touched his baseball bat, hoping it would give him the courage to go up the stairs and knock on the door.

After getting out of the limousine, the driver asked if this was his last stop. Thomas looked at Manny, surprised at his words, and said no. The driver told Thomas that he would wait for him there until he was ready to travel again.

While Thomas walked up the front steps to the house, Maria and Enza looked out the window. Thomas has spotted the little daughters watching him. He wondered who they were.

Maria left the window, ran to Angie, and yelled, "Angie, he is coming."

Everyone in the house rushed around the first floor, hoping that he would come, and anxiously waited for the door knocker to sound. Once it did, Anna ordered all her daughters to go into the kitchen and give Angie and Angelo privacy.

Angie fretfully waited for Thomas to come. It had been hours since Thomas was let out of prison, and Angie was convinced that he would not come. She thought that she had lost her son for the second time. She was trying to prepare herself for a huge disappointment when Maria ran up to her.

Thomas knocked on the heavy door, scared, feeling the warm sun on his back, and waited only a few seconds before the front door quickly swung open.

Angie, with Angelo standing by her side, smiled at Thomas

"Thomas," Angie said, holding back her tears and wanting so badly to hold her son, said, "Welcome to our home. As you can see, this is a Bridal Shop. Our living quarters are in the back."

Thomas looked around him and was impressed and intimidated at the same time by the beautiful rooms that surrounded the foyer. He could not help but smell the fantastic aroma coming from the kitchen of dinner cooking.

"Come, Thomas, Angelo, and I have cookies and coffee. I hope you will enjoy the cookies. They are homemade."

Thomas walked into the sitting room and was amazed by how beautiful the place was. He sat on the edge of the couch, not knowing how to sit on a luxurious seat. Angie handed him the cookie tray, and he took one. He took one small bite as he scanned the room. It was delicious, so he popped the whole cookie into his mouth. Angie handed him the tray again. Thomas took several cookies, not realizing how hungry he was and how good the cookies tasted.

"I hope you had a good trip."

Thomas said, "How did you manage to get me out? I was shocked when I was told last week that I was being released."

Angelo said, "We have a friend, who is like family to us, who knows the Mayor and the Governor. Because of your birth's usual circumstances, the Governor was more than willing to listen to our plea to let you out. Angie signed documents stating that her son was stolen from her, which helped put the nurse who stole you in prison for the rest of her life."

Thomas thought to himself, someone had a lot of pull with the Governor and probably paid a lot of money. "Thank you," he said, "It was very magnanimous of you both and your friend to do that for me. I will somehow pay you and your friend back for your kindness. I am not sure how I feel to be out of prison yet... I have been incarcerated for a long time." Thomas continued to talk, not realizing that his words were so hurtful.

"Do you have any plans to where you will be going from here?"

"No," Thomas said.

"I hope you don't mind, but we have a big dinner planned for you. We would love you to meet our extended family. The mother of the family was Angie's friend many years ago. When she and her daughters come into this country, they had no place to go and came to us. We have lived together as a family ever since. The house is filled with all women, and then there is me. There are a lot of advantages to living in a house full of women." Angelo started to giggle, "There are always lots of fresh homemade cookies."

Angelo laughed again, "Thank God, there are plenty of bathrooms in this house. In our last house, there was only one bathroom for the whole floor of apartments that had to share."

Angelo had hoped to get a smile out of Thomas but did not.

"Will you have dinner with us?"

"Yes," Thomas said.

Angie got up from the couch and asked Thomas to follow her to meet their family. As Angie turned away from Thomas, she put her hands together and thanked God for her blessing to have her son stay for dinner.

They led Thomas past the bridal shop rooms and into the enormous kitchen.

The kitchen activity stopped. When the door opened, everyone turned. The room was filled with women, cooking, setting the table, washing dishes.

"Thomas," Angie said, "This is the Gennusa family. These beautiful children and their mother belong to Angelo and me."

Thomas was shocked to see so many people. He looked at each daughter and was surprised to see so much beauty. There were so many of them. He was spellbound when he looked at Pina. He looked at each face and felt nervous about being watched by so many women.

Anna walked over to Thomas and said she was glad he decided to stay for dinner. Thomas said it was hard to refuse since when he entered the house, the cooking smelled terrific.

Anna introduced herself and then her daughters. With each handshake, Thomas could not believe how each girl was prettier than the last. When he came to Francesca, she smiled and showed her deep dimples. When introduced to Teresa, he paused, not wanting to stop looking at her. He took a deep breath while looking into Teresa's blue eyes.

As Anna led him away, he kept looking at her and was then introduced to Enza. Thomas's eyes widened again at being presented to another beautiful child. He noticed she was different looked from the others with her olive skin and hazel eyes.

When he came to the youngest, he bent down. "Hi... my name is Tom. I think I saw you and your sister looking out the front window watching me walk up to the door."

Maria turned to Angie and said. "Oh, Angie, he is so handsome. He reminds me of Sal Mineo. I just 'looooove'... Sal Mineo."

"Maria, I thought you were in love with Frank Sinatra," Angelo said.

Maria looked at Angelo wide-eyed and said, "Him too!"

The room broke into laughter. Tom laughed so hard and put his arms around Maria and hugged her. She hugged him back.

Dinner was delicious. It had been years since Tom had a home cook meal. He ate heartily, taking seconds that were offered to him and eating almost a whole loaf of hot homemade bread. The laughter soared, and the daughters all chattered as they ate. The most moving part of the meal was the prayer said before the food was served, thanking God for Tom having dinner with them. It was years since he said grace before a meal. Tom got a little choked up, reminding him of his childhood days when his family prayed together before a meal.

After dinner was over, Maria sat on Tom's lap. He was surprised. He helped her scoot herself close to him.

Maria whispered, "Did you know that today is special for us because you are here? We have ice cream for dessert. We always have ice cream on special occasions. I love chocolate."

Tom's eyes got large. "I just love ice cream."

Everyone stopped and looked at Tom. The silence was obviously making him uneasy since the first time he came into the house. His shoulders and stomach tightened. They all yelled, "I love ice cream!"

The ice cream was served and eaten fast. The older daughters got up from the table and started to pick up the ice cream bowls. They put the dishes in the sink.

Maria said, "Angie, we are done with the ice cream. Now can we show Tom his present?"

Anna was annoyed with her youngest child and said, "Maria, it was not for you to tell."

"That is okay. Tom, come into the family room." Angie said.

They all escorted Tom into their family room.

Tom appreciated the warmth and hominess of the room with the open curtains allowing the sunshine through. He turned to his left, and there sat a grand piano. Tom stood still.

Angie said, "I hope you like it. It is not new, as you can see. The wood varnish has peeled off, but it is in tune. I was told that you play well. My father loved and played the piano well too. Would you play for us?"

Tom slowly walked and sat at the piano. He looked at the keyboard, closed his eyes, and ran his hands gently across its keys. He placed his hands on the keyboard and began to play. Even the little ones paid attention to the magnificent sound of George Gershwin's Rhapsody in Blue.

Tom's eyes glazed, and he was almost in a trance as he played. Angie and Angelo stood arm and arm near Tom as the rest of the family spread out sat on the couch and the chairs about the room. The little ones occupied the fireplace hearth with their mother. Angie had tears running down her face as she listened to her son play, reminding her of her father. Not wanting Tom to see her tears, she turned her face and wiped her tears from her face with the back of her hand.

As Cenza listened to Tom play her favorite solo piano piece, which had classical shades with a jazzy touch, tears ran down her eyes. Never hearing the music played with such accuracy and precision, she was enthralled. She listened, not believing that such majestic sounds came for that old piano and that Tom could make such vibrant tones come alive.

Tom played, lost in his own emotional existences with each press of the keys, and played for a long time. When he stopped, he was physically drained. Once done, he arose from the piano and walked over to Angie.

"Tom, you look exhausted. Anna, the girls, and I have made up a bedroom for you. Would you like to stay tonight? I cannot promise you peace and quiet because there is none here, but I can offer you clean sheets to sleep on."

"Yes. But I have to take care of the limo driver."

"I'll do that," Angelo chirped, "I will bring Manny some cookies and ice cream.

The night came to an end, and the house was quiet. Tom had a low light lit beside his bed. He could not believe how homey and warm the room was that he was in. He was on the third floor in a vast chamber. So different from his cramped prison cell.

Angie had quilted a bedspread in different shades of bright green, with red and blue patches and a splash of yellow trim. Anna suggested this because she felt that yellow would brighten Thomas's spirits after being in prison for such a long time. Angie agreed. She worked on the bedspread, not knowing if it was ever going to be used. The project helped her keep up her spirits. Otherwise, she would have just cried for months until she saw her son again.

Tom sat down, feeling relaxed yet very sleepy. He enjoyed the rich, clean air swirling around him as it touched his face. He had taken a long private shower. Taking a shower alone was a luxury. He hoped that he was not taking advantage of being a guest, but the hot steamy long shower felt so good. The hot water warmed and rested on his stiff muscles. In prison, whether it was day or night, his muscles were always tight.

Tom put on the bottom of a pair of pajamas that Angie had given him. He could feel that they were new and freshly washed. He slipped under white cotton sheets, smelling of the fresh outdoor air. He took a pillow, fluffed it, and put it down behind him. He took a second pillow, fluffed it too, placed it on the first pillow, and laid his weary head down. The crisp white cotton pillowcases also smelled like fresh air hanging outside to dry for some time. The smell of the pillow was sweet. After getting comfortable, his muscles loosened up again. He stared into the air for some time, feeling the pungent night air circulating around him. He curled up into a ball, and then he cried. He fell asleep that night in complete solitude with a puddle of his tears soaking into his clean pillowcase.

The next day close to noon Angie went to the third floor to check on her son. She walked into the bright bedroom and placed his clean clothes on the only chair in the room. The sunshine shone across the room, making the room feel cozy. She put a hot cup of freshly brewed coffee on the nightstand beside Tom's bed. Tom stirred. He opened his eyes and saw Angie. Forgetting who she was and where he was for a second, his body tightened.

Angie gently touched her son's shoulder, urging him to ease off and unbend. She felt her son's soft skin and his warm body for the first time. After realizing where he was and who was touching his shoulder, Tom loosened his muscles and stretched. He asked Angie what time it was.

"It's close to noon."

Tom started to jump up when Angie put her hand at his shoulder again. She looked at her handsome son and told him he needed to rest. He put his head down on the pillow.

"It is hard to sleep in prison. Someone is always praying, crying because that person is lonely or just been raped. I did not realize how tired I was until last night. I hope I have not imposed on your hospitably by sleeping late?"

Angie's heart ached when she listened to Tom speaking about his experience in prison.

"Not at all."

She sat on his bed, looking at him, and noticed the old, crumbled picture of his parents on the nightstand. With a pain in her heart, she raised the image and looked at it closely. Trying not to sound deprived of having her son's young life stolen from her, she said, "I was told that these people were very good to you and gave you a good home."

"Yes, they were wonderful to me. They never told me that I was adopted. I think they would have when I was older."

"I don't blame them for wanting a child. I don't blame them for taking you away from me. They were used just as I was. Foolishly I believed what I was told about your birth. How could I question a credible doctor in a reputable hospital? I can understand how they loved you. I wish I had known sooner I would have spared you from your misguided teenager's years. If it had not been for Joseph, we would not have ever known you existed. Angelo and I are indebted to him." Angie said.

"Who is Joseph?"

"He is a good friend to the family. When he was in Sicily, he and his family stayed with the Gennusa family, hiding from the Germans.

172 - Mary B. Patterson

Anna and her family fed them and protected them until they felt safe to go back to their home in Palermo."

"It's not your fault. I was stupid. I did many stupid things after my parents died."

Angelo knocked on the door and peeked his head into the room. "Get up sleep-head. I have a truck full of gowns that I must deliver, and I could use the help. Do you know how to drive a car?" Angelo said.

Tom jumped out of bed and said enthusiastically. "I would love to help you! I do know how to drive, but I don't have a license anymore." Quietly he said, "The courts took it away from me."

"Well, we will have to do something about that."

Fourteen

～～

Tom never asked to leave his new home. How could he? So much warmth and acceptance from his new family gave him a sense of peace he'd been missing for years. His first day was spent with Angelo. He was having a hard time accepting that Angie as his mother, although he could sense the pain she carried. Whenever she looked at him, there was in her face, and he realized that she wanted to protect him and feared that she would lose him again. Angelo was much easier to be around. Working with Angelo that day was not work at all. His giggles were contagious.

The entire Gennusa family took Tom under their wings. They never criticized him or looked down on him but accepted him whole-heartedly as a new member of their extended family. The youngest, Maria, never left his side when they were at home, and he fell in love with the sweet little girl. The older daughters took him shopping. Maria insisted that he get a black leather jacket since that was what Sal Mineo wore. They even bought Tom grease for his hair and showed him how to comb his hair into a duck-tail.

Tom really didn't like the tight black jeans and the tight tee-shirts. He preferred a more conservative look, but he didn't want to disap-point the sisters. He tolerated the clothes and loved the leather boots but was not crazy about the cigarettes rolled up in his shirt's sleeve, mostly because he didn't smoke.

Angie was unsure about Tom's new look, but the girls were adamant about it, and if Tom was nearby, she was happy.

The movies that the girls took Tom were the most fun. The arguing they did before any show was comical to watch. Cenza, always the serious one, wanted to see movies of a historical nature like "The Robe" or "Julius Caesar." Teresa and Pina always wanted to see romance, preferring "From Here to Eternity or "Roman Holiday." That first night "From Here to Eternity" won the toss.

After the movies and a stop for ice cream that night, the girls came home dreamy-eyed. Even Tom had some dreams about waves breaking on a hot Hawaiian beach.

On Sundays, the girls took Tom to museums and concerts. While he was thrilled to attend these events, the concerts somehow left him feeling unfulfilled and somewhat empty.

Every day the Gennusa girls discussed current events to make sure he was aware of what was happening globally. Although he was on top of current events while he was in prison, Tom still let the daughters discussed and debate problems. He listened, even though he did not always agree and never gave his opinion. Although Tom had fallen into this comfortable life as if it were meant to be, he didn't want to disagree with his new family in any way. He knew within his heart that his parents in heaven were watching over him and led him here and that he needed to make sure he was a successful member of the family.

Joseph watched Tom become a member of his new family. He adjusted beautifully to his new home. He noticed that the children fussed over him like he was their own brother. Tom grew to love his new family.

Three or four weeks after Tom arrived, Joseph, June, Scooter, and their two boys were over having their weekly Sunday dinner. June's little boy was held, tossed in the air, and kissed many times while the baby was cuddled and passed around. Someone always had him as he slept peacefully through all the noise. June was amazed, thinking that her little one felt comfortable in all the commotion surrounding him, just napping.

Joseph and Scooter especially enjoyed the pasta dinner, and the fresh bread with butter melted. The conversation was lively and happy as the littlest was being spoiled by everyone. After dinner, ice cream was served, but not until the dishes were washed and put away. Tom played the piano for everyone, and the toddler, usually noisy and active, sat quietly listening to him play. He was fascinated by Tom's fingers gliding over the piano keys. June's baby, snuggled this time in Teresa's arms, was toasty warm, never to stir and dreaming peacefully.

Once Tom finished playing, Joseph sat on the bench with him. The family had scattered, except for the little one who sat in front of the television.

"Tom, I need some private time with you. I have some papers that came to my possession, and they belong to you."

"What papers are you talking about? Is the law after me for something?" Tom felt panicked.

"No, nothing like that. Apparently, before your parents died, they made a will stating that you are their sole beneficiary to their estate."

"I don't understand. What does that mean?"

"You have inherited your parent's house and some stock that they owned."

"You are telling me that I own my parent's home?"

"Yes, Tom, you do, and apparently everything that is in the house.".

That evening while in bed, Tom lay awake. He heard a soft knock at his bedroom door.

Angie peeked into the room and looked at her son lovingly. "Tom," she said, "May I come in."

"Yes, of course."

Tom sat up in his bed. He arranged and placed his back against his pillow. He had the legal papers that Joseph had given him on his nightstand.

"I noticed after dinner that you looked troubled. I am concerned. Is there anything I can do to make whatever is troubling you easier to handle?"

"Joseph told me that he came across some legal papers of mine." Tom picked up the papers. "He told me that my parents ... adopted parents...left me their house and all their belongings with it. Joseph also told me that they left me stocks. He explained to me what the stocks were, but I didn't understand what he said."

"How do you feel about that?"

"Confused? Joseph told me that I was never informed because I was underage, and the state took care of my affairs. After I came of age, the information was lost through the cracks of the system. Mostly, I guess I'm upset with myself. I was robbed and served jail time because I had no money. I stole because I did not know how to make money. I did not realize that my parents left me money to make my life easier in case they died."

"It's not your fault that you did not know about the inheritance. How do you feel about owning your parents' home now?"

"How do I feel? I am not sure? One thing I know, I can't go back to that house the way I feel... the day I left prison, I had Manny drive me to my house. The house needs painting badly, and the yard needs tending. Now I understand why no one lives inside the house." He grew upset. "I felt so lost after I left there. I thought I never wanted to go back again."

"So... that is where you went the day you got out of prison?" Angie touched Tom's hand. "I wondered where you had gone that day. I was so relieved that you decided to come here. You gave Angelo and me so much that day that you rang the doorbell. Thank you, Tom."

She frowned slightly. "It seems to me that you need to go back there. There is nothing wrong with feeling the love that was given to you in the past. All children deserve to be loved. If your parents left you everything they owned, maybe it was because you gave them more than they felt they could ever give you. The love of a child can make a person feel very wealthy. It's okay, don't be so hard on yourself, Tom. You were just a child. What did you know?"

"I knew enough. My mind was jumbled. I was alone. I did not trust anyone. There were times I did not believe that my parents were dead. I thought the authorities were lying to me. I rebelled every time I was brought back to one of the foster homes. I thought that if I stayed in my house, my parents would come home to me. I felt so misplaced."

Tom felt Angie's warm, caring hand, rubbing his gently as he talked. He gently wrapped his fingers around her hand. Angie tried not to cry as she felt her son's hand around hers. "When you are ready to go, would you like Angelo and me to go with you?"

"Yes... thank you." He squeezed her hand gently again.

Angie kissed his cheek. It was the first time she had done so. She felt that her son had come home to her. He smiled at her and kissed her hand.

After Angie closed the door to Tom's bedroom, she turned toward the stairs, put her head to the wall, and cried. It was the first genuine affection that she had received from Tom since they first met. In her bedroom a moment later, listening to Angelo's gentle snore, she pulled his covers over his shoulder to keep him warm. She kissed his cheek and felt like God could not make her life any better than this.

1954

Elvis Presley made his recording debut.
Senator John F. Kennedy was on Meet the Press.
Judy Garland appears with James Mason in a "Star is Born."
Marilyn Monroe marries Joe Di Maggio.
Texas Instruments announce the world's first transistor radio.

Fifteen

⌒⌒

It was the spring of 1954 before Tom came to terms with his inheritance. He was thoroughly happy with his new family and reluctant to face his past. Everyone was prospering, and he wanted to enjoy his freedom and prosperity in peace – at least for the time being

The sacrifices and rationing after WWII were a memory. People bought small homes in the suburbs, their first car, and even had money to spend or save for their future. For many families, women were returned to their pre-war occupations of tending their children and homes. At the same time, men spent their days working to provide for his family. The New York Subway was filled with men dressed in business suits going to the city for their jobs.

The Gennusa and Pertucci family recalled that Jackie Bouvier's wedding gown was designed by an African American, Anne Lowe. Considered one of the most iconic, if not best, wedding gowns of that time, the family discussed the dress on countless occasions and found nothing to complain about. Anna agreed it was one of the most beautiful wedding gowns she had ever seen. The silk flowers in Jackie's dress reminded her of her own wedding gown that she and her mother designed with its lace roses.

Finally, one Sunday during that summer, Tom, Angie, and Angelo headed to Hoboken, New Jersey. The ride was quiet because Tom was tense. Angelo drove the van, while Tom had the key to his house in his hand, rubbing it, turning it, and staring at it. He recalled the information that Joseph had given him regarding his estate the day before in the kitchen. If he sold the stocks that he inherited, he could pay the back taxes. There was a little left to pay for a few more years of taxes if he did not want to sell the house right away. Tom was grateful and relieved to hear that he did not have that worry.

Now Tom, Angie, and Angelo drove through Tom's childhood neighborhood. To distract them, and himself, Tom told Angie and Angelo about the movies the night before and how much fun he had with the girls. They decided after many minutes of debate to go see "On the Waterfront" with Marlon Brando. However, Tom preferred "20,000 Leagues Under the Sea" with Kirk Douglas.

Tom nervously kept talking. He even told them about the famous singer that lived in the house they just passed. Angie's eyes got wide at the sound of Frank Sinatra's name.

Angelo giggled, "Angie, stop with those dreamy eyes of yours. He would never look at you. Besides, Frankie is not as cute as I am. If you had a choice, you would see me and my cute face and chose me."

That cut the tension, and Tom relaxed slightly as they approached his old house.

Angelo realized that Angie was crying when they stopped in the driveway of the home. "Tom... Son... I think you should go to the house. When you are comfortable with us to see it, you come and get Angie and me."

Tom nodded. He walked to the front door, taking a deep breath. He unlocked it, shocked that is opened so easily. Tom walked in. He smelled the stuffiness of the house for having been closed for so many years. He stepped into the living room and looked at the familiar furniture. To his surprise, the place looked much smaller than he remembered. The side table near the couch still had a lamp, an ashtray, and a picture of his adopted parents and him when he was around two. He raised the picture and held it tightly as tears fell down his cheeks.

Ten minutes later, Tom brought Angie and Angelo into his house. "This house is exactly like I remember it. I don't think anything's been touched."

Angie clung to her son as he led her into the house. The door was open, and Angie saw landscape pictures on the walls and above the couch in the entrance-way. Two chairs flanked the small picture window that was across from the sofa. A television set sat on a stand with a black shiny leopard porcelain figure beneath it. The animal was a lamp that was turned on when Tom and his parents went out. On the empty wall adjacent to the couch and the picture window was a credenza with a beautiful, tarnished silver tea set on it. Above on the wall was a large clock. On either side around the clock were two light gold shade sconces.

Tom handed her the picture. Angie saw her son at two years old and cried. She looked up at Tom, and he took her into his arms for the first time, and he wept with her. He told her how sorry he was that she had to endure this pain, but he needed her there for support to get closure to his past.

Tom led Angie toward the kitchen with Angelo tagging behind them. The kitchen walls were dull with a one-time soft white paint with a white lace curtain at the window, now gray. The window was above the sink that looked over the backyard. Angie smiled, thinking it was her house looking out at her son playing in the backyard. She walked over to the window, put her hands on the counter, and closed her eyes. She swore that she heard her son and his friends laughing in the backyard as they threw a ball at each other.

Tom retook Angie's hand, and they made their way to Tom's tiny bedroom. The walls were painted a light blue. His single bed had a faded bedspread on it with red and blue trains designed in the fabric. The curtains on the two windows were the same material as the

182 - *Mary B. Patterson*

bedspread. Tom explained that his mother had sewn them. Angie felt a twinge of jealousy and sadness that another woman had sewn her son's bedroom bed and curtain set.

Tom walked to a small closet that still held clothes, books, and a few toys. He picked up two books and recalled how his father read them to him every Christmas Eve. He tucked them under his arm.

Tom led the way back to the living room. Angie was not comfortable going into the master bedroom, and Tom felt her resistance. As they walked to the front door, there was a flight of stairs. Tom explained that that was the attic and told the Pertuccis that his parents had promised to convert it to a new bedroom when he was a teen if he was a good boy.

Tom smiled proudly, no longer crying. "I think it's time to go."

They left with Tom, who was content to go back into his past and come to terms with it. He realized his adopted parents were to be remembered and loved. He held his books and his family picture when he got to the van.

"Angelo, can we stop and get ice cream? I need chocolate."

At that happy moment, Angie and Angelo and giggled together.

"There is an ice cream parlor near the movie theater where we go after the movies."

Angie said, "Let's go to our old neighborhood and show Tom where we used to live. Let's show him the park and the ice cream store where I met his dad."

"Let me tell you about what I know about him."

Angie and Angelo told Tom about their lives as they sat in the old neighborhood, in the park, eating ice cream.

"I met your dad at the corner where we bought our ice cream. He was so dreamy. I was shocked to see that he was interested in me. Your father was Puerto Rican - you have his dark eyes and hair. I fell in love with him the first time I saw him. All my girls' friends were so jealous.

My parents would never approve of him because of his nationality, so I crept out of the house to meet him. When I got pregnant, he was seeing another girl. She was rich and got him a job in her father's meat factory. They married and have been married since. I know little about him now except that he took over his father-in-law's business and is successful. If you want to meet him, I can tell you where the business is. I never told him that I was told that you died after birth. I never spoke to him or saw him again."

Angie waited patiently for Tom's reaction. "I don't want to know about him."

He looked at Angelo. "I have my father right here."

That Saturday night, after the bridal shop was closed, Tom and the older girls went to the movies. Cenza and Teresa argued over what film to seem while Tom and Pina did not care. They all agreed that going to the movies in Joseph's limousine was the best part of the evening. Manny opened the door for them at the theater and waited for them after the film was over. He drove them to a parlor known to be the best ice cream parlor in the city named "The Ice Cream Parlor."

"Tom, what are you thinking about?"

"What?"

Teresa asked again, "What are you thinking about? You look so far away."

"Oh... I was just thinking about what Angie told me about my real father, and if I want to know more about him."

Tom looked around at his sisters. He was so grateful that he was here with his fantastic family, eating the best ice cream that the city had to offer with all the turmoil in his life now over. Why worry about a man who didn't even know he existed?

Manny drove them back home as they discussed the movie and the different ice cream flavors they tasted. They never realized that Anna, Angelo, Angie, and Joseph relaxed, knowing their children were protected by Manny from a dangerous city's outside elements. They were all thrilled too that Tom and the girls considered themselves family.

1956-1957

Elvis Presley's big record hit was Blue Suede Shoes. He made music history appearing on The Ed Sullivan Show and entered the United States music chart for the first time for "Heartbreak Hotel" and at 22-years old, he buys Graceland for $100,000.00.

Norma Jean Mortenson legally changes her name to Marilyn Monroe. The same year she marries playwright Arthur Miller.

American Bandstand makes its national television debut.

Sixteen

ℳ

Days, then months passed until the harsh winter of 1956 arrived. Polar conditions were seen throughout Europe and even in North Africa. Sicily rarely had snow throughout its history. However, this winter, it not only had snow but frigid cold as well.

It was nine years since the Gennusa family had arrived in the United States. Vincenzo wrote from Palermo, Sicily, that since Elvis Presley's single about his "Blue Suede Shoes" came out, he was having trouble keeping up with customer demands.

Even the Gennusa girls got into the fad when the older ones bought Tom a pair of blue suede shoes and made him wear them. Maria thought they were perfect and very dreamy. Tom smiled and accepted them.

"What do you mean you had the right? Who gave you the right?" Anna shouted as she angrily paced the kitchen.

Six months earlier, Angie and Angelo knew what Cenza had done and how angry it would make Anna. On this night, they took Tom and the two younger sisters to their suite to watch Elvis make music history. They managed to escape the loud and unpleasant confrontation between mother and older daughters.

"Momma," Cenza said in a determined voice, "I do have the right."

The older girls seated at the table watched their mother anxiously.

Anna took a bowl of fruit, sitting on the table, and in her fury, threw the bowl against the far wall. The crash made the girls jump. The bowl shattered, and pieces fell to the floor with the ripe banana's smashing and the oranges and apples rolling all over the kitchen.

"You explain to me why you feel you have the right?" Anna's voice cracked with rage.

"He is my Papa, Momma. I have every right." Cenza answered calmly.

"Because he was your Papa, you feel that gives you the right?"

"Momma...! Please sit down and let me explain."

Cenza calmly sat and waited until Anna sat across from her.

"Momma, the day that Papa died aboard the ship when I found out we could not afford to bury him, I made a promise to myself that someday and somehow, I would give him a proper burial. I saved all my money. I went to Joseph and asked him for directions on how to get Papa un-buried. He told me money would do the job."

Anna snapped, "You did not ask Joseph for money. Did you?"

"No, Momma, I would never do that. Just for help. Joseph contacted the city and gave them the information on where Papa was. It was straightforward. They had a Franco Gennusa death record from the Maria Perch for the day we arrived here. After obtaining Papa's burial number, it was easy to find him in Potter's Field. Joseph pulled in some favors, and they exhumed Papa's body."

"You know it is a sin to un-bury the dead," Anna snarled.

Cenza replied with conviction. "Momma, it is a sin to leave the dead alone and where they do not belong. Especially Papa! He has a family. He should be with them and in his own country to rest."

"Cenza, what are you saying to me? Are you telling me.? Are you saying that you are sending Papa's body back to Sicily?"

"Yes, Momma, I am saying that Papa's body is on a ship right now on his way back to Sicily. His coffin will be met by men in Palermo. I hired them to take him to Bisacquino. He will be buried at our home in our village in our backyard. I purchased an appropriate gravestone. That is where he belongs, Momma." Cenza repeated, tears streaming down her face, "That is where he belongs."

Anna sat down, shocked. Her pulse was racing, and she was having trouble breathing. She saw that Francesca, sitting had tears running down her cheeks. She looked at Teresa and Pina. "Did either of you know Cenza's plan to send your father back to Sicily?"

Both daughters, frightened at their mother's reaction, stared at the table, afraid to make further eye contact with her, shook their heads no.

"I don't know what happened between you and Papa when we were children," Cenza was relentless, "There was so much love between you. Then, there was so much hate in your eyes for my Papa on our way to this country. I love you, Momma, and I am not insensitive to you. I just feel that it was the right thing to do. What happened between you and my Papa is between you and my Papa. It has nothing to do with the rest of us. It has nothing to do with where he should lie. Try to understand."

"Your father brought us here with no thought to what was good for us. He did not care about what this country held for us. He died and left us destitute. You felt during that time that he deserved this? After all our struggling, you still feel he deserves this?" Anna asked furiously.

"Yes."

Teresa walked around the table and sat by Anna. Teresa put her arms around her mother and held her close.

Anna pushed her away. "No, Teresa, this time you being beside me will not make what I just heard easier. I cannot condone what Cenza has done without my permission, and I will never forgive her for doing what she has done."

Anna pushing her chair abruptly, scratching the hardwood floor, and leaving a screeching sound in the room, jumped to her feet. "No, you don't know what happened to your father and me. All I can say is that your Papa's love for me changed."

She stormed from the room, thinking, *I don't even know.*

The three girls stared after her.

"Cenza, did you have any idea that Momma would be so mad at what you have done?"

"I knew she would not be happy for what I did, but no, I never expected her to be this irate, Teresa."

Pina got up and went to the window, tears streaming down her cheeks. "Cenza, I think you did the right thing. Momma is angry now, but she will understand why you did what you did. She knows how much time you spent with Papa selling vegetables. She knows the love and respect you had for Papa and how he felt about you. Papa never had those feeling for the rest of us. He would have loved us more if we had been sons. Maybe he was angry at Momma for not giving him a son. You were the son he never had."

Pina took out a handkerchief from her pocket and blew hard. She looked at Cenza with tears streaming down her cheeks and said, "Papa should be in Sicily." She hesitated and then said. "That is where he belongs. That is where we all belong." Pina turned to the window again after stating her opinion and cried harder, thinking to herself. "*That is where I belong.*"

When Anna reached her bedroom, she slammed her door and went to bed. She lay looking toward the ceiling for a long time. Her head was pounding, and her ears were ringing. She was appalled. She was unreasonably upset. She stared at the ceiling, "*Why God? Why does Franco have the right to be back in Sicily, and we are trapped here?*

"*I should cry. When was the last time that I cried?* She could not remember. Was it the day that she said goodbye to her family in Palermo, the day she and her family left for the New World? *Well, even if I could cry, it would not be for Franco. He doesn't deserve my tears or my love. He deserves nothing from me."*

Then, reluctantly she wondered what she did to him to lose his love. *What did I do? Why was he so guilt-ridden, so much so that he moved us here? Will I ever know?"* But deep in her heart and in the pit of her stomach, the agonizing question was, *Do I really want to know?"*

On the day after Cenza told Anna about sending Franco's body to Sicily, Maria was at school waiting for Enza to meet her. They walked home from school every day together. While waiting, she looked down at her skirt and decided not to wear it again because it made her look babyish. She didn't like her blouse because the buttons at the back of it hurt when she leaned against the classroom's wooden chair. Her pure white starched stuffed shirt with its short puffy sleeves with a ruffle around them and the ruffle around the round collar was for a younger unsophisticated person, not someone aged ten-and-a-half.

That morning Pina made her put on that outfit because wash day was a few days away, and clean clothes were sparse.

"Hi," said a boy Maria had seen at school. "You are waiting for your sister?"

"Yes," Maria said.

"She asked me to come and get you and bring you to her."

Maria looked at this cute boy who was around sixteen. He was well built, average size, and muscular. He had piercing blue eyes with blond curly hair with a wide bright warm smile, and straight white teeth. He was dressed in expensive, fashionable clothes and was the captain of the football team. His name was Samuel Vaughn. He was extremely popular in school. The teachers loved his intellectual ability, whereas his coach praised his athleticism. His friends called him Sam. The girls, giggling when he was around, called him Sammy.

Feeling very grown-up by his attention to her, Maria got up and, holding her books, followed him.

"Your sister is in the back of the building."

Maria said nothing as the boy took out two lollipops from his pocket and handed her one. She removed the paper from a bright, cherry-flavored candy and put the pop into her mouth the same time Sam put his in his. They sucked on their lollipops. Sam strolled casually, leading her towards an old empty warehouse building beside the school. Kids sometimes gathered when they felt they could get away with smoking cigarettes and hang out. Sometimes they vandalized it by breaking windows.

"Where are we going?"

"We're going to meet your sister there." He was pointing toward the back of the warehouse.

They passed two large dumpsters. Sam turned to Maria and smiled gently again. She felt so grown up that this handsome upperclassman was paying attention to her. He moved closer.

Maria looked deep into his eyes and was mesmerized.

He touched her arms deftly, rubbing them tenderly. "This, you will remember forever." He bent and kissed her sweetly on her lips.

Maria, surprised, looked up at him.

Suddenly, Sam grabbed her ruthlessly. Shocked at Sam's painful hold on her, Maria stiffened and started to pull back from him. His face came close to hers, and she could smell his cherry breath from his lollipop. He smiled his unbelievable beauteous smile at her and then, with all his strength, threw her on the ground. Maria hit her head on the hard pavement with her books flying up into the air. Her books fell to the ground and scattered all around her. She dropped her lollipop that was in her hand, and it fell on the dirty near her.

Maria was half-unconscious when she realized that Sam was on top of her. He was pulling up her skirt. She lay confused for several seconds and then realized what was happening. Terrified, she tried to struggle but could not. He tugged at her panties and tore them off. Frightened, she sought to scream, but no sounds came from her throat. Sam's weighty body on her was keeping her from moving as he forced her legs open.

Sam struggled to get his belt unbuckled. Frustrated, he made a fist and hit her pubic bone with all his might. The impact of the force that Maria felt made her mind go out of control. She closed her eyes, feeling the excruciating pain, and it took her breath away. No longer able to resist, she stopped fighting, and her body lay limp.

Sam spread Maria's legs as he got his pants down and forcefully stretched out his penis. He pulled on his flaccid genitals until it was large and hard. He looked at his member in his hand and became appalled at its sight. His loathing and repulsive consciousness made his male organ grow harder until it brought him tormented pain. With all his strength, rage, and cursing, he rammed it into Maria as hard and as violently as he could. Maria did not feel his penis plunging into her because her vagina was in excruciating pain from his punch.

Sam continued thrusting into Maria many times with all his force, inflicting enormous pain. Maria gagged, trying not to choke on her vomit. She tried to think but could not. Maria struggled to move but could not. She tried to scream but could not.

After Sam had ripped Maria's virgin body apart, he was entirely pleased with himself and engorged with his climax. He pulled out of her before his sperm exploded into her. Kneeling beside his victim, Sam stroked his wilting male part with satisfaction and pleasure. He was content when he looked at Maria and laughed at her, not seeing her face but his father's. In his state of mind, he was raping his father instead of his father raping him.

Sam felt the warm liquid sperm on his finger and admired it. He smelled its scent and then took his wet finger and rubbed it across

Maria's lips. Then he savagely whispered, "You are just a stupid fucking cunt. You got what you deserved. If you liked it, I could do it again and again and again, anytime. Just let me know. Watch your step because I will be watching you."

Laughing, he stood up, enjoying Maria's pain, and pulled up his pants. He looked at the young bleeding girl and laughed harder. "If you tell anyone about this, I will find you and do it again whether you want it or not." He giggled, "And I will do the same to your very long-legged olive-skinned pretty sister of yours." Then he took his fist, with all his might hit Maria in the vagina again. Maria was in so much pain; she did not feel her pubic bone crack from his punch. Sam said, "MMMM, that was fun. I really enjoyed that."

Sam walked away from Maria, feeling relieved. He was pleased and flexed his masculine body feeling superior in his encounter. He never looked back to see Maria move her tormented body onto its side and curl into a ball.

Maria lay on the cold concrete and stared straight ahead. The pain in her vagina was agonizing, but the rest of her body felt numb. She rubbed herself gently, trying to ease its pain. She shook her head, trying to get her thoughts to think straight. She lay motionless for some time, and then she gently moved her body. She threw up several times, unable to catch her breath between vomiting.

Eventually, she rose and sat on the cold, hard asphalt for only a few seconds. Sitting made the pain worse. She struggled to get up. Carefully bending, she gathered her books and scattered papers. She picked up her underwear and put the torn pieces in her skirt pocket. She looked at her torn bloody blouse and straightened it out. She took her free hand and ran her fingers through her hair. Slowly and uncertain how she got to the school building's front, she looked and did not see her sister. Only a few students were standing in front of the school holding their musical instruments. She knew they were part of the band. They were waiting for their parents to pick them up and take them home, never looking her way.

Maria walked away from the small crowd and headed slowly in the direction of her home. She wiped her mouth several times. Her lips felt burnt. She finally arrived at the front of her house. She hesitated for a few seconds, looked at it, and felt emptiness. She slowly climbed each step with care, hoping she could get to the next level without screaming. She reached the door, and with what little strength she had left, she opened it and stepped inside the house. Without caring who might be there, she looked into the bridal shop dressing room and saw Pina with a customer.

Enza came down the stairs telling Maria she had to stay after school because she needed math help. Maria heard Enza's muffled voice as she walked up the stairs, not acknowledging her sister. Enza didn't notice anything wrong with Maria and headed out of the front door to the park.

Maria climbed the stairs, firmly holding on to the stair rail. Enduring her physical pain, she climbed slowly, one step at a time.

By the time Maria reached the top of the stairs, she was shattered. She took a deep breath and found the bathroom. She shut the bathroom door behind her, locking it.

She asked herself, *should I cry?*

"No," she answered herself. "I won't cry."

She walked over to the tub and plugged it. She kept rubbing her pubic bone to ease the pain. She felt the scorching hot water rise over the top of her hand. She took the torn underwear, dropped it into the steaming water, and removed her ripped skirt and blouse. They fell to the floor. She looked at her naked body and saw her bruises. Her pubic bone was swollen black and blue, and blood was dripping from her vagina. The insides of her legs were also black and blue. Her buttocks were sore, scraped, bruised, and blood was seeping from the skin that had was torn against the asphalt during the rape.

She got into the tub, feeling the heat, and gently submerged her body into the water. When the hot water hit her vagina, she stopped and controlling herself from screaming from the burning sensation. After managing her pain, she slowly immersed her body waist-high into the water. She shut the hot water off, and after getting used to the scorching water, she slipped her body into it until it reached her neck. Immersed in the blistering water, she settled herself into a comfortable spot and stayed there.

Maria stayed until the water got cold. She sat up gradually and reached for her underwear. With a bar of soap, she slowly started scrubbed the dirt off them. She painstakingly put the underwear back into the water, not wanting to do any more damage to the fabric, and watched it release its soap, dirt, and grime. As the water and soap dissolved, Maria watched in slow motion the evidence emerging to the top of the water as it separated and dissolved.

She carefully brought the wet underwear up, squeezed the water gently out of them, and brought it to her lips. She scrubbed her lips slow and hard. They burned, and she did not respond to her inflamed lips. She lifted her underwear at eye level and looked at it for a while. She placed them back into the water. She watched her underwear drifting in slow motion away from her. Floating in the now icy water, making her shiver, and wondering what made them float. She got out of the tub, let out the cold water, and filled the tub with hot water again. She repeated her ritual several times.

Later that evening, when dinner was ready, Enza come to get Maria for dinner. Maria was lying on her bed, not moving, and curled up into a ball. When Enza went to bed, Maria closed her eyes. Enza thought she was asleep.

When Enza closed the bedroom quietly, Maria opened her eyes and stared. She was holding on to her torn bloody clothes that she wrapped with a towel from the bathroom. She took another old towel that she knew would not be missed and put it between her legs, hop-

196 - Mary B. Patterson

ing that the blood coming from her vagina would not leak onto her sheets. She had in her hands her torn underwear, holding them tightly under the covers. She was afraid that if someone saw her underwear, they would know what happened to her. She knew that she never wanted anyone to know what happened, for she felt dirty and worthless.

Several days went by. The house was extremely quiet, and Anna said little to her daughters. She became reclusive and immersed herself in the sewing room, working long hours, avoiding everyone. She needed solitude. She needed time to heal her aching heart from Franco's betrayal, but mostly from the rage she felt towards Cenza. She did not sense the needs of her youngest daughter, who desperately needed her.

During this time, while the daughters crept through the house, staying away from their mother, Tom felt unsettled living in such a quiet place. He loved listening to the sounds of the little ones running up and down the back stairs. Tom loved listening to their laughter and giggling to himself at their joyous noise. He enjoyed even the constant bickering among the girls as to who was going to wear what. It made it worth getting up in the morning.

But the quiet of the house made the house feel eerie. The few sounds echoing through the place reminded him of prison at night isolated and when he heard someone crying down the hall. He played the piano as much as he could in hopes it would fill up the emptiness of the house. He stayed close to Angie because she made him feel loved and less exposed to the outside world. He knew that he was vulnerable to life outside and could not survive without his new family.

Anna spent most of her time working through her anger by being alone. She knew it was so unlike her, but she could not control how she felt. She enjoyed Tom's piano playing immensely. It calmed her aching heart and soothed her mind. She was mending again from

Franco's rejection of her, but it was slow and painful. She thought that that part of her life was solved, but unbeknownst to her, hidden deep in her heart, hurt and confusion were still there. When Franco died, unanswered questions left her with so many doubts about the love they felt for each other.

Anna suffered and was unemotionally detached from her family. She went to Maria's room to check on her. She felt her daughter's head to make sure that she did not have a fever and left her youngest daughter's room as dispassionately as she entered. If she didn't have a fever, Anna presumed everything was fine.

Maria closed her eyes whenever her mother came to check on her. She did not want to talk to her or anyone else. When Anna went to Maria's bed, she bent and touched her forehead. After Anna left the room, Maria would open her eyes, clutching the towel, trembling, holding on to her torn clothes in it, and squeezed as tight as she could. After touching her clothes, she raised a hand, and with the back of it, rubbed her lips hard, wanting the burning sensation of Sam's sperm to go away. She stared for many hours in the room, focusing on nothing, occasionally rubbing her lips as hard as possible.

His voice always echoed in her head. *"Tell anyone, and I will do the same to your sister Enza!"* The vision of the boy touching Enza made her vomit several times. She learned to bury that image, but never her hate for what he did to her.

Several days after Maria was raped, she got up for school. She rose from her bed and felt a sharp pain in one area of her pelvis again. She touched the spot and felt a break in the bone. She straightened her body out. As she moved to her dresser and closet to get fresh, clean clothes, the pain was excruciating. Halfway back to her bed, she doubled over. She sat, and then refusing to give in to her agony, she dressed for school.

Maria put on her torn underwear and then put on a regular pair. Under her school clothes, she wore her torn clothes and the bloody towel from the rape. She walked to the kitchen. Her back was straight as she entered the kitchen to eat her breakfast. There was no sign that she was in pain or distress.

The kitchen was filled with activity, with everyone in the house getting ready for their day. She went to her mother, kissed her, and went and sat in a chair. It hurt to sit down, but she smiled if anyone watched her, wanting to feel the pain and never wanting to forget what happened to her. She ate little of her breakfast that morning, but she ate it like nothing was wrong. Although her body and spirit were irreparably damaged, she left for school with Enza as if nothing had happened.

"Remember, girls, the dangers out there!" Anna said as Maria looked back at her mother with a cold, unfeeling look. Anna also reminded Enza to walk her sister home from school. Maria walked out of her house and to school with torn clothes under her school clothes from the rape. She never let on she was in excruciating pain, refusing to let Enza know that she was in dire discomfort. Her backside was still raw, and the rubbing of her clothes made that area burn more. When they got to the school building, both girls separated, each going to their different floors for class. Enza reminded Maria to wait for her after school.

Maria waited until Enza was out of sight. Then she left the building through the front door at a normal pace. She walked down the stairs and around the school building and to the warehouse. She went to the dumpster where she had been trapped several days before, refusing to endure her pain.

Maria opened the dumpster. The smell that came out from the trash was rotten and moldy. She took out the bloody towel from under her clothes and threw it into the dumpster leaving her torn bloody clothes on from the rape.

She turned and looked on the ground where the rape had taken place. She spotted a small splatter of dried blood, bent, and touched it gently to protect it. She noticed her dried vomit on the ground nearby. When she started to rise, she spotted the lollipop wrapper on the ground close to the blood spot. She got up, put the wrapper into her pocket, put her hand on her underwear, and rubbed it. She then headed for the school building. She did not cry. She did not feel weak or in pain. She only felt numb

When Maria returned to the school, before she took her first step, she looked up. She saw Samuel Vaughn at the top of the steps. The pain from her broken pubic bone was evident. Refusing to accept and recognize her pain, she smiled. He turned just as she smiled and spotted her.

He was standing with two of his friends laughing. She brought the back of her hand to her lips and slowly rubbed them hard. She straightened her back, picked up her head, carried her books closer to her damaged undeveloped breasts, and walked up the stairs. If Maria was in pain from her cracked bone, she refused to let it show. She stared at him, never taking her eyes off him, and walked up the stairs. She went past him, unafraid, without acknowledging her apparent broken condition.

Sam moved near her and gently touched her arm. She felt a sharp pain in her broken bone as he pulled her gently toward him. Her stomach churned, and she knew she would never forget his sweet, sickening scent.

He whispered, "Just remember you tell, and I will do the same to your pretty sister Enza. That would be more of a pleasure to me than you. She is so pretty and those long legs of hers. I just love those long legs of hers. It would be fun to get them to spread open."

Sammy looked down at Maria's skirt. "I love that poodle skirt you are wearing. That pretty coat surrounding your thighs makes me want to feel them. I am surprised you're here in school. I notice you're walking straight... next time I mess you up, I will make sure that you are off your feet longer."

Still smiling, Sam let her go, and she stared at him. She reached up to her burning lips and rubbed them hard. While rubbing her lips, Maria thought of her best friend, her sister Enza, protectively. She took her hands away from her red, burnt lips, not feeling their rawness, and put her hand into her pocket. She grabbed the lollipop wrapper and rubbed it. She continued walking up the last stairs in great pain, still not accepting it, and stared back at him. She stepped inside the building, and her pain from her broken bone was gone. She walked down the corridor to the school building and up to a flight of stairs. She walked into her day, feeling no physical pain, but felt emotionally cold.

That evening Teresa was roaming about the house looking for her mother.

"Pina, have you seen Momma. I have searched the whole house, and I can't find her." Teresa asked as she stood in the kitchen while Pina and Cenza were preparing dinner. Cenza did not look at her sister as she cut lettuce for the salad.

"No," Pina said, stirring the pot.

Teresa left the kitchen and stood in the foyer, wondering where her mother was. She thought for a few seconds and then walked over to the closet, taking out a sweater. She headed out the front door.

The air was crisp, and the smell of the late spring flowers was evident. It was early evening, and the sun was setting. She stood on the top of the stairs, looked across the park, and saw her mother's silhouette. She walked over to the park bench where her mother was and sat down close beside her.

Anna smiled when she saw her oldest and slid closer to her.

"Mamma," Teresa said," I knew this is where you would be when I couldn't find you in the house. I notice that occasionally, you sneak out of the house. I watch you from the window sitting here on this bench. You love it here, don't you?"

"Yes," Anna said, "I love coming and watching the children play. I especially love to hear their laughter."

"Like you don't have enough noise in your own house?"

"It's different," Anna said. "I can enjoy this noise because I am not responsible for their laughter after these children go home. I can tell that you are worried about me."

"Yes, Momma, I am. Are you all right? You have been so pensive. Do not be angry at Cenza because of Papa. You know how emotional and passionate she is. She did what she felt was right."

"I am not... Teresa." Anna said, "I was first when she first told me what she did with Papa's body, but I am not mad at her now. I am enormously proud of her and proud of her love for her father. I truly hope you all loved him. He adored all of you. You were his life. I hope Pina someday will forgive him for bringing her here to this country. But I think only a miracle will do that. Tell me, my sweet daughter, you seem not to be bitter at your father for making you come to this country. You seem to have adjusted well. Do you ever feel deprived of not going to school in Italy and becoming a medical doctor like you wanted to so badly?"

"No, Momma," Teresa said, "and I cannot tell you why. I just feel that this is where I am supposed to be. Here, with you and my sisters. I don't know why I feel that way. I think about it sometimes, and I wonder. I guess someday, God will show me." She paused. "What happened between you and Papa?"

Anna kissed the back of Teresa's hand. "That is a good question. I was sitting here thinking about that. It spins around in my head repeatedly. When your father and I first met, I was shocked to see this handsome man standing in my parent's kitchen, asking for my hand. I was surprised and wondered why he would want me. I fell in love with this stranger the first time I saw him. I knew he would always protect me. Yes, the war was hard, but we got through. There was a

202 - *Mary B. Patterson*

time we did not know how we would feed you and your sisters, but somehow, we managed. I know the war was difficult for your father, and the pressure of survival weighed heavily on him. The responsibility for helping to feed others like my parents and my sisters plus feeding the poor at the monastery was hard on him too."

"Do you think the war drove him away for you, Momma?"

"I try to blame the war for our problems, but I keep thinking that was not it. I know the death of Saverno, Papa's very dear friend, and his son Mario was such a loss for your father. He carried their deaths with such pain in his heart. My dear friend Lucia and her family also were a big concern for your father. I know he wanted to do more for them but could not. Several of the nuns died right after the war because no food was available to them. After the war, life got better for us, and we helped them, but what we were able to give was still not enough."

Anna sighed, "I always felt that Papa kept secrets from me during the war, but I never found out what they were. He never told me about the near-death of Enza. That must have made him feel guilty for not being more sensitive about our home circumstances. I suppose that the near-death of Maria and me when I was giving birth didn't help either. Your father must have been so distracted that he didn't realize that Enza was so sick. He would have carried that guilt for many years. He must have been so proud of you."

"Yes," Teresa said, "Papa was and showed me how much he was grateful for my saving Enza's life. We had our problem sometimes but now. I am grateful for all he did for me. Now that I am older, I pray to him in heaven and thank him for being my father."

"Your father became so dependent on his wine. It was not my place to tell him that his drinking was ruining him. I know feeding another child would have been difficult for all of us. Having another child was out of the question." Anna was not used to talking about sex so freely to her daughters. "I know there was something else that drove your father. I know after the war, we were working awfully hard, but I don't think he minded. Everyone in the village struggled during that time. Everyone in the world struggled during that time. No, there was something else." Anna sighed and said," He is dead now, and I guess I will never know what it was."

"Momma, I know I was too young to understand, but I know one thing, Papa loved you. I used to think that someday I want someone to love me like that. Could I ever be loved like that?"

"You are young, and someday it will happen to you. Why is it that when you are around me, you make me feel so much better? Come, let's go inside the house and help with dinner. I need to give Cenza a big hug and tell her how proud of her; I am."

Anna and Teresa walked arm-in-arm towards their home, feeling a richness of love and respect for one another.

1958 - 1959

1958

In 1958, Senator John F. Kennedy was re-elected for his second term
in the Senate.
The best films of the year are "Gigi" and "South Pacific."
The best singers are Ricky Nelson and Frank Sinatra.
The United States launches the first Explorer satellite.
United States creates the National Aeronautics and Space
Administration (NASA).
Milwaukee Braves loses the world series to New York Yankees.

1959

Elvis Presley, King of Rock-and-Roll, becomes United States Army
private #5331061.
Top singers Buddy Holly, Richie Valens, and the Big Bopper were
killed in an airplane crash.
Walt Disney releases "Sleeping Beauty."
The Barbie Doll, created by United States businesswoman Ruth
Handler, debuts at the American International Toy Fair.
New York Yankees finished 3rd in the American League.

Seventeen

ᨒ

It still took several months before Anna felt less hurt and betrayed over Franco's reburial in Sicily. However, she tried to behave as if nothing was wrong

Maria was healing physically but not emotionally. She buried her feeling as well as her anger and memory of the rape. Her broken pubic bone healed but not correctly. It was evident when she touched it that her pain from the fracture had dissipated but was never forgotten. She put her lollipop wrapper in her favorite book and placed that book under her bed, never forgetting that it was there. The book remained beneath the bed, never reread, and only touched when cleaning around the area. Maria grew quiet and withdrawn, which was lost in the chaos of family life.

Tom thrived from the attention the girls lavished on him. The adoration from Angie and Angelo made him so happy. Whenever he glanced into the sewing room, he was always amazed at how hard Angie and Anna worked. Whenever he met his mother's eyes, she always gave him an enormous loving smile, and Tom held her love and smile close to his heart.

"Tom," Cenza said, "Your clean clothes are on the table in the kitchen." Having all the love and his clothes properly washed was great. Laundry was not his forte.

Cenza and Teresa were doing delicate hand sewing on wedding gowns that need to be finished that day. Cenza never raised her head as she worked. She said, "Hey, big brother, all those clothes on the kitchen table? You'd better take them to your room, or you will find them on your bedroom floor." She looked up then and grinned. "By the way, my sisters and I are sick of picking up after you in the bathroom. I'm tired of hearing them complain, so next weekend bright and early, there will be two men on the third-floor building you a full bathroom. I don't want to hear any complaints from you on Saturday when the workmen start early." Then she looked down at her sewing again, not seeing the tears fill his eyes.

Tom wondered how much more this family would do for him. He was so careful that he did not stay long when he used the bathroom, especially when taking a shower. He cleaned up after himself, making sure that the bathroom was spotless after every use. He realized Cenza was teasing him, to announce their newest gift to make him feel even more welcome.

He looked at Teresa, who said nothing as she worked on her task. She was so sweet, gentle, and stunning. He loved her blue eyes. He adored every one of his new family and was devoted to them.

Pina was in the bridal shop showing gowns, answering the phone, and pinning dresses on customers for alterations. Pina peeked her head in the sewing room, going around Tom, not disturbing him, and asked Cenza for help. The phone rang, and a new customer came into the shop. Anna got up from her sewing machine, watched what Cenza was doing, and took over her job. Cenza returned to the front with Pina.

Teresa called after them, "Cenza, I am almost done. I will come and help you in just a minute."

"Tom," Anna said, "There are some cookies on the kitchen table for you. At least, there should be. I told Maria and Enza to save you some."

"Thanks, Anna."

Tom started to turn into the kitchen when Anna asked, "Would you check on my little ones? I am worried about Maria. She seems to be so quiet these days."

"Sure, I'll check on the girls and make sure they stay out of trouble," Tom said.

Angie said, "Enjoy the cookies, Tom."

Tom smiled at his mother and headed for the kitchen. He entered the kitchen to find it empty. He spotted a large plate of chocolate chip cookies on the table, took one, and popped it into his mouth. The girls knew he loved cookies, and when they had time, they always baked for him. He decided that this cookie was the best so far. They were still warm and so good. He grabbed the plate and took them to the family room. The television set on, and he knew that was where the little ones were.

Tom stood in the doorway across the family room, observed the girls. He stepped past his piano and looked out to see Francesca digging in a flower bed in the backyard. She was covered in dirt and radiantly happy.

He sat down on the sofa with Maria while Enza was on the floor, her eyes glued to the set. Maria smiled, scooted over, and sat beside him. She reached for a cookie and started to nibble on it.

Tom found it very strange that Maria did not sit on his lap. As big as she was getting, she regularly sat on his lap. Tom took a cookie and started eating it, thinking of Anna saying that Maria was acting too quiet. Tom agreed with Anna and found Maria was doing things she never did before, like sitting beside him instead of his lap. He also noticed that Maria was tense whenever she was with him. Maria snuggled beside Tom, and he put his arm around her. He watched as Maria took the back to her hand, brought it to her lips, and rubbed them until they became red. He wondered why she did this, never having done this before and now doing it often. He worried about Maria's personality change as they both reached for another cookie.

Life was good. The bridal shop was busier than expected, and orders were continually coming in. Cenza decided it was time for Teresa to stop working in the factory. The bridal shop needed her more and was making a nice profit. She was happy running Simon and Simon. Her improvements and work ethics made people want to stay. She had a long waiting list of people wanting jobs at the factory.

Cenza finished scanning the floor, and all workers seemed to be working effectively. She headed for her office. She had filing and bookkeeping to do. Just as she opened the accounting ledger, she heard a knock at the door.

A young girl out of breath exclaimed, "Quick, Cenza, it's Mrs. Barkowitz."

Cenza raced out of her office. She found Mrs. Barkowitz on the floor by her machine, having trouble breathing. Cenza screamed for a taxi. Several of the men from the warehouse came and helped Mrs. Barkowitz into the cab.

Cenza ordered the cab driver to head to St. Aquinas hospital.

As soon as the cab pulled up to the emergency room, Cenza jumped out and ran into the hospital. Seconds later, nurses and orderlies came flying towards the taxi. They put Mrs. Barkowitz on and gurney and rushed her into the emergency room.

Twenty minutes later, a doctor came to Cenza, sitting in the waiting room. He introduced himself and gave his apologies. "I am so sorry, but Mrs. Barkowitz has died. She died of a massive heart attack. She felt no pain."

After the doctor made his condolences, a woman dressed in a business suit approached and asked to speak to Cenza. She told Cenza that she was from the billing office. She wondered who would be paying off the hospital bill and where the hospital should send the body.

"I'll pay the fees," Cenza said coldly. "I'll also be sending a mortuary to get Mrs. Barkowitz."

After leaving the hospital, Cenza went home, into the kitchen, and poured herself a needed cup of coffee. When Anna saw her daughter go by the sewing room, she did not stop to say hello. She knew something was wrong.

She followed her into the kitchen. "Cenza, what is the matter?"

"Mrs. Barkowitz died today. She had a heart attack. I did not know that she was not feeling well. I should have known."

Anna hugged her daughter, and they cried for their old friend.

Mrs. Barkowitz was buried in the George Washington Memorial Park on a cold and windy morning. The cemetery was named for America's first president because from 1785 to 1790, New York City was the United States' capital.

Cenza had purchased an extravagant grave plot with a large dark rich shiny marble headstone. Cenza knew it was an appropriate memorial for a woman who gave her life to protecting and helping many women who needed jobs and security.

Mrs. Barkowitz hid the pain that she carried for the women at the mercy of DogFace and comforted them as best she could. She encouraged these women to continue working, including June, and endure their shame. She showed these women how to maintain their self-respect while working. She saved many women from destitution because if they lost their jobs, they would have not another way to provide for themselves and their families.

Cenza knew about her mother and DogFace. She loved her mother more after realizing what happened, but out of respect never said a word. As an inexperienced virgin, she did not fully understand the ramifications of her mother's sacrifice. Still, she always felt guilty. She made Pina get a job at the factory as it was necessary. She was beholden to her mother for saving her sister and her from an experience that would have devastated them forever. She would never mention her murdering DogFace.

After the burial, everyone returned to the bridal shop for refreshments. Mrs. Barkowitz had no family, but the house was filled with many friends from the factory and her neighborhood. Scooter and June were there without their active boys. June's face was white as Scooter held her, thinking about all the times Mrs. Barkowitz consoled her because of DogFace. Sadie was in the corner beside the fireplace with Anna. Sadie was crying hysterically. Abe and Debra Simons stayed the whole afternoon, not wanting to leave Cenza. Debra helped serve coffee and pick up dishes. Abe and Joseph spent a long-time talking business. They were becoming good friends.

Teresa and Pina were putting the food on the table when Pina said to Teresa, "I hate this country. There are so much death and despair here."

"Pina," Teresa said sadly, "There are death and despair in Sicily too. I wish you would acknowledge that."

"No," Pina said, "Not like here."

In Teresa's heart, she knew Pina was right. There were so many dangers to living in this massive city. Much more dangerous here in this city than their small home village.

Francesca, Enza, and Maria were serving cookies after the meal had ended. The meal consisted of baked pasta, a cheese tray, an olive plate, and several salad varieties. Anna rose early that morning and baked bread. Each one of the guests insisted on bringing the food. Cenza accepted the food gratefully, realizing they wanted to share in honoring Mrs. Barkowitz.

Angelo, Angie, and Tom circulated around the rooms, talking to the company. Their conversations were quiet, and words of love were shared by all about Mrs. Barkowitz.

Cenza was making more coffee when Joseph came to her and said, "Your mother told me that you paid for Mrs. Barkowitz's hospital and funeral costs." He hugged her. "I have so much money. I could never spend it in my lifetime. I would like to pay for Mrs. Barkowitz's burial. May I?"

"No, that is not necessary."

"Cenza... you should save your money for yourself."

"Money means nothing to me, Joseph."

"I know... You are the most unselfish person I have ever met."

"You give me too much credit. Thank you, Joseph." Cenza kissed his cheek.

She took a hot cup of coffee and walked over to where her mother and Sadie were standing. She handed Sadie the coffee.

Sadie kept crying over the loss of a good friend and for herself because she had no one in her life and wondered who would take care of her if she got ill. She was the same age as Mrs. Barkowitz and felt very vulnerable.

"Sadie," Cenza said, "I want to talk to you about leaving the factory and coming to work for us here in the bridal shop. We need your help." Sadie wiped her eyes and smiled. Anna met Cenza's eyes and nodded.

Tom went to his piano at the sound of his playing made all the conversations stop. The guests all gathered around Tom. There was no dry eye in that room as Tom played for Mrs. Barkowitz, giving her a last loving tribute.

Eighteen

～

Francesca was out in the back courtyard digging her dirt as Anna approached her, "Will the basil be larger and sweeter this year?"

"Yes," Francesca said, "They will be ready this summer for the sauce. I can just smell the sauce simmering."

Anna looked around the backyard and the flower beds and admired how clean and trim it was. There were no leaves or twigs on the patio and no weeds of any size growing in the flower beds. Francesca painted the furniture white and kept it spotless. She also cared for all the plants around the house and in the shop with love and pride.

"Momma, can you come and sit with me? I want to talk to you."

Anna sat opposite her. She looked at Francesca and giggled to herself, seeing her face streaked with dirt that she wiped off with the back of her hand. The soil on her face sank deep into her dimples. Her beautiful blue eyes shone even brighter with the dirt circling them from rubbing the sweat away from them.

"Momma," Francesca said gravely, "I have decided to go to college when I get out of High School this June."

"What!" Anna exclaimed.

"I want to go to college, and this summer, I want to go to Connecticut and work at a tobacco farm. I want to start saving my money for school."

"College! Tobacco farm! Where is this all coming from? You hate school. How often did Pina spank you to get you to school? Your grades are not the best. I do not understand."

"Momma... I want to go to Horticultural College."

"Where do you want to go?"

"I want to study flowers and vegetables and trees and dirt." Francesca said, "I want to work on a farm and plant. I want to feed the world like Cenza, only in my own way. I love the outdoors and all its possibilities it has to offer me.

"Momma..." Francesca looked at her mother and said with love within her eyes, "I just love dirt!"

Anna looked at her daughter, shocked at the possibility of Francesca going to college. "Well," Anna said, "I will have to see an improvement on your grades, and then I will talk to Cenza. As far as going away this summer to work in Connecticut, that we will definitely discuss at length."

Nineteen

∽∾

Joseph said good night to Anna at the front of the bridal shop after their weekly dinner. He told Manny to head to the apartment.

"No," Joseph said, after changing his mind, "just drive through the city for a while. I want to have a brandy and look at the buildings lit up."

Manny did what he was asked but thought that was odd of a request from Joseph, but he obeyed his request.

Joseph opened the bar in his newly purchased limousine and poured himself a brandy into a snifter. He held the glass snugly tucked in the palm of his hand to warm the brandy evenly. He drank down a gulp and felt the tingling sensation of the liquid. He waited to feel the brandy hit his stomach and warm him. After he felt the warming sensation, he settled back in his seat and looked around his new vehicle. He should have been happy with it. It was large and had all the updated entities. But the plush, deep red velvet seats with their thick matching carpet meant nothing to him. He bought it because he could. He looked at his crystal brandy snifter and admired the precious bronze liquid floating in it.

He was worth millions and was liked and admired by many in the business world. His connections ranged from bankers to politicians. He was invited to all the best parties and a guest in most luxury homes in the City. When he traveled, he traveled first class. His clothes were expensive, and his watch was the best that the Swiss made. He lived on the East side, in a glorious high-rise apartment with precious antique furniture from all over the world. His apartment had enormous hanging crystal chandlers from England in every room. The view had spectacular views of the city. He was greeted by the doorman when he arrived at his residence and when he left his home. He attended the theater, the opera, and the best restaurants the city had to offer. He traveled all over the world for his business. He had some lady friends, but they meant nothing to him. His sons were doing well and were healthy. Why did he feel so empty? He knew why, because he did not have Anna.

Joseph looked out the window at all the high-rise apartments and business buildings lit up like Christmas trees. He thought of his previous night and his conversation with Anna wondering if she would ever realize how he felt about her. He had fallen in love with her the first moment that he walked into the bridal shop years ago. Joseph had never felt this way about any woman other than his wife. He thought after his wife was murdered that he could never feel passion for any other woman. But there she was, right in front of him. He longed to touch her. He wanted to touch her hair, bring it to his nose, so he could smell her scent near instead of from afar. But how could he tell her how he felt? He knew that she enjoyed spending time with him and the dinners they shared. He held on to his deep feelings for her, afraid of losing her. He enjoyed their dinner time alone without the family. They discussed so much at their dinners and became each other's support system.

"*Joseph,*" Anna's words swirled around in his brain of their dinner earlier, "*You are so pensive this evening. Is there a problem?*"

Joseph raised his wine glass. "I am worried a little, but I think all will be all right. I received a communication from my oldest son asking me to return to Switzerland and see after some business he is having trouble with. I will be leaving this coming Friday." Joseph cleared his throat, "Anna, come with me... take some time for yourself and come to Europe with me. I would love to have my sons see you again. I write to them and tell them about you and your girls in all my letters. Switzerland is beautiful. The mountain tops are magnificent. I could show you some of the most beautiful villas around. I have many friends in the country, and they are always asking me to visit. I would love to show you off." Joseph reached over and touched her hand.

Anna quickly pulled her hand away and, shaking her head, said softly. "Oh, no."

"Why not? Your daughters are old enough to take care of themselves. With Angelo and Tom, there is more supervision than they need."

"Joseph, you know I would never leave my daughters. Besides, how would it look with me traveling alone with you? What would people think? Oh, no. I could never do that."

Joseph thought of Anna's words, *what would people think*? They would have nothing to say if Anna married him. Joseph knew that Anna didn't need to re-marry. She was a survivor and did not need anyone to take care of her.

Joseph swirled his brandy in his glass. He continued to look out the window and wondered what Anna's answer would be if he proposed to her. *Could I ever ask her, or will that just jeopardize our friendship??*

Joseph remembered how Anna drew her hand away from him so quickly after touching her, and his feelings were hurt. He could not forget how handsome Franco was and how much they loved each other.

He downed the rest of the brandy. He put his hand in his pocket, pulled out a small black velvet box, opened it, and looked at four-carat square-cut center diamond with smaller diamonds set on the sides of the large stone. The settling was of yellow gold. He searched for a wedding band to set off this fantastic stone but had not found its equal yet. He knew Anna's taste and knew she would never like anything gaudy. Her taste was elegant and straightforward.

Joseph looked at the diamond and watched it sparkled as the streetlights hit it. Its glistening was magnificent. He looked at this diamond that he had purchased on one of his trips to Europe. The diamond he purchased had come from India. He bought it at a reasonable price and knew that it was worth much more. He did not purchase it because he found a bargain. He bought it because he felt that Anna was worth its intricate cut and suburb stone quality. He thought that few women were deserving of such a rare and expensive piece. Joseph closed the box and put it back into his pocket. He looked out into the night and felt very lonely.

"I've decided to get good and drunk, Manny. Just keep driving." Joseph said as he poured another brandy and proceeded to drink.

On Sunday at noon, Anna and Angie were in the kitchen preparing dinner. Joseph had arrived carrying several bottles of wine and several cartons of ice cream. The kitchen smelled better than the best restaurant in New York City. The tomato sauce was cooking, and the hot fresh bread coming out of the oven made for a perfect Sunday gathering. Only June's family was missing because one of the children had a cold.

Angelo and Tom came home to the kitchen after making a gown delivery. Tom walked over to the sink to wash his hands when Cenza entered the room. "Tom, there is a letter here for you. Sorry, it came yesterday, but I was so busy I forgot to give it to you. I put it in the desk drawer. I remembered it when I walked by the front desk just a few seconds ago. Sorry!"

Tom stopped washing his hands, reached for a towel, and asked, "What? Are you sure it's for me?"

"Yes, it is definitely for you."

Angelo walked over, "Son, are you okay? Were you expecting mail?"

"No, Angelo, I was not,"

Tom looked at Cenza and said, "Is it from my parole board?"

"No, Tom," Cenza handed the letter to Tom when Pina and Teresa came into the kitchen through the swinging door from the sewing room. The room had become hushed, and Teresa and Pina stopped at the door.

Teresa asked, "What is wrong?"

Cenza said, "Tom received a letter."

"Cenza, who is it from? Is there a return address?"

"Yes, there is a return address on it, but I think you better read it yourself," Cenza said.

Tom finally took the letter from her hand. And finally got the courage and looked inside the envelope.

He paled.

When Angie looked at her son, she went and hugged him. Angelo took the letter out of Tom's hand. "Angie, it's from the Julliard School for Performing Arts in New York City."

"Julliard? Our son got a letter from Julliard." Angie holding her heart, said, "The music school?"

Angelo said, "Yes,"

Tom said, "Angelo, will you read it for me. I need to understand what it means."

"You read it, Cenza. You are a better reader."

The family sat around the kitchen being incredibly quiet while Cenza opened the letter and read aloud:

May 1, 1958

Dear Mr. Walters,

It has come under our attention regarding your skill as a pianist. We are told that you have taught yourself many pieces of piano music. We are a school for those gifted in the arts and are always looking for new talent. Our school is designed to allow these people to join us and provide them with an education. Even though our students are of college age, we also have other programs for an older group.

We heard a tape of your playing, and it was quite impressive. Our teaching and administration staff is eager to meet you and have you audition for us. If you have the qualifications, we would like you to join our school. We would like to meet you and your family.

We will wait for your response to set a date on which we can get together.

Sincerely,

Dr. Antonio San

The room was still. Angie had her hand over her mouth, trying not to scream. Tom was standing in a daze. Finally, after a few minutes, Cenza said, "Well, we will have to work harder since Tom will be going to Julliard."

Three weeks later, Angie, Angelo, Joseph, and the Gennusa family were sitting in Julliard's auditorium. Joseph sat beside Anna. They all listen as Tom played with no jitters, no fear, and total concentration. Tom played from his expert natural ability.

Before Tom went on stage, he introduced Angie and Angelo to Dr. San and the judges' panel as his mother and father. It was the first time that Tom referred to Angie as his mother to others. Her heart burst with such pride. As always, Angelo smiled and giggled.

Anna and Joseph were introduced as his "other" mother and father. All the girls were presented to the panel as his annoying bratty sisters. Tom said this with such love as he looked at each one of his family members. Maria went to his side and held his hand tightly.

Everyone sat in the auditorium while Tom played his music. He played as if he and the piano were one. His music flowed with gentleness when needed and then with strong high emotion. He had prepared the three pieces of music which the board requested. When Tom finished his first piece, the judges and his family gave him a standing ovation. Before even starting his second number, Dr. San welcomed Tom to Julliard. He told him there was no need to continue with the audition pieces. Instead, he asked Tom to perform one of his favorites. Tom looked at his mother and smiled.

"I would like to dedicate this piece to my mother and father and my extended family." He then played *Rhapsody in Blue*.

The tour around the school was impressive. Tom kept a tight grip on Maria's hand because he felt a little unsettled, not for himself but for Maria. She seemed nervous about the chattering students passing by going to their next class

When the family returned home, the older girls served ice cream.

Cenza said, "Tom, for this occasion, I made you your favorite cookies."

"Chocolate chip?"

"Of course, but on this momentous occasion, I also made what the Americans call Brownies. Debra Simons gave me the recipe. She said you would love them. For Teresa and me, who are not chocolate lovers, she gave me a recipe for Vanilla Brownies."

Cenza pulled out a large plate of cookies from the oven and a plate of chocolate and vanilla brownies.

Tom smiled and asked, "When did you bake them?"

Cenza said, "This morning when you were asleep."

"How did you know I would get asked to attend Julliard?"

"That was easy, Tom. It is what you Americans call a 'no brainer'."

Tom and Cenza laughed while everyone else did not understand the reference.

Tom became solemn. "Cenza... how are we going to do this? How can the business afford me to go to school? How will we manage?"

Pina spoke before Cenza, "Tom, when it comes to family, we will always find a way. We will all do this together. Teresa, Cenza, and I have talked it over. We decided that Teresa will take driving lessons and work with Angelo. With Sadie working with us, we can do it. Cenza will have to spend a little longer at the factory to keep us with extra money, which we will not need too much longer. The shop is starting to do well."

Maria said. "And I will learn to make the chocolate chip cookies!"

Everyone laughed and hugged Tom.

Cenza said, "Francesca will be working with Momma and Angie in the sewing room after school and on Saturdays. She is willing as long as she promises she does not have to dress up and greet customers. It will be fine. We will manage. And yes, Tom, Francesca will have time to dig in her dirt." Cenza looked at her sister and said, "Heaven forbidden if I take you away from your dirt."

Francesca started crying, and Angelo consoled her

"What did I say, Momma? Now, why is she crying?"

"Because Francesca is so happy."

"Tom, this chance may never come again for you. Of course, you are going. Don't think you are going to get off easy. We expect you to do your share when you're not in school or practicing. Momma, what do you think if we moved the piano into the sitting room of the shop and have Tom's practice there? He can entertain our customers, and we can brag about him attending Julliard." Cenza asked.

Anna did not respond but was obviously considering Cenza's idea.

Tom looked at Angie, tears streaming. "Mom, after all the wrong things I have done in my life and ending up in prison, what did I do to deserve you and this family?"

"Tom," Angelo said, crying and giggling at the same time, "It is a good thing that you like ice cream. These women can be very unkind if you don't."

Twenty

ᕬᕫ

Her back was to her desk, and she was at her file cabinet when she heard the door squeak open. She smelled his familiar scent and started to shake. Taking a deep breath, she slowly turned around.

"Hello, Vincenza," Matt Simon said. "I came to give you my condolences to you about Mrs. Barkowitz. So sorry, she passed away. My father told me how fond of her you were."

"Thank you, Matt."

"My mother told me how you took hold and took care of the funeral arrangements," Matt said. "I was sorry that I was not able to attend."

"She was my friend, and she did so much for me when I started working here. She guided me and helped me to understand the women workers. It was the least I could do for her."

Cenza gestured to a chair near her, "Please come in and sit." Matt closed the door and joined her.

"Your mother and father were wonderful after Mrs. Barkowitz's burial. Your mother helped wash and wipe dishes," Cenza said.

"I don't think my mother ever got used to having help in our home. She always found dirt to clean that was not there and refused to have the servants clean it." Matt said, slightly raising his voice. "My father told me how well you were doing here and how much money you have saved and made for the company. He is afraid he is going to lose you."

"Your father has nothing to worry about. I will be here for some time." Cenza said. "My family and I will need the money to keep us going at the shop."

Matt's blue eyes shined as he stared at Cenza. It was difficult for her to take her eyes off his. "Are you home for long? I thought you were in Europe?"

"I am home for a while," Matt grinned.

Cenza asked, almost too casually, "I heard that you were seeing a friend and that she was very special to you?"

"Are you referring to Sherri Osborne?"

"I don't know her name. I just know you were seen in Europe with a pretty woman. I saw the picture of you and her in Paris in one of the fashion magazines in your father's office. The article said that you and she were dating."

Matt laughed and said, "Not if her brother has anything to say about it. She is my roommate's sister. I love the press. They just print to sell."

"I never saw anything written about the two of you after that."

"She is a good friend. You heard nothing after that because she got married two weeks after the article was published. Of course, you would not see anything written about it. That news wouldn't sell."

Matt rose and slowly walked over to Cenza. He leaned over her desk. Nervously Cenza took her rolled her chair away from Matt, hitting the file cabinet behind her. He smiled, "You have the most beautiful eyes. Your eyelashes are so long and thick."

Not knowing what to say, Cenza just stared at Matt. Her body was reacting to Matt's move toward her, arousing her. She felt her breasts get tender and her nipples harden as they protruded from beneath her blouse. Her face flushed.

Matt smiled at his incredible smile again, knowing he got the reaction from Cenza that he wanted. He stood up, turned, and walked out of her office. Cenza was breathless and red-faced as his scent lingered.

Embarrassed, she put her forehead to the desk and took another deep breath hating herself for not being in control. She said to herself, *"You dummy. Why do you care who Matt is seen with? What is wrong with you?"*

> *May 5, 1958*
> *Dear Momma and Papa,*
> *I told you about Tom being auditioned at the Juilliard Arts of Music School in my last letter. Tom has been attending school for some time now, and we are very proud of him. He says his playing is getting better, but I can't tell because he is so good. Angie and Angelo are bursting with pride at their son.*
> *The shop is busier than I ever expected. The money is starting to come in regularly. It is wonderful to be a part of this. Cenza has made this all possible for us. The girls are doing well. Maria has really surprised me. She is at the top of her class. She has become very quiet, but I guess her grades are her priority. She is continually studying. Enza gets taller and taller every day and more beautiful. Francesca is still the happiest when she is digging dirt. We are all well. I miss you very much. Tell Gi I think of her every day. Please write soon. Your letters are so important to me.*
> *Love Anna*

> *June 3, 1958*
> *Dear Anna and daughters,*
> *It is to Papa and my great delight to receive these beautiful letters from you and hear of the bridal shop's success. I am so*

proud of you. I just wish that your success was here in your home village with us.

It is sad to see and say, but most of our children from this island choose to move to the mainland and other parts of Europe to study. It is unfortunate, and to our regret, the children decide not to return. As the world moves further away from the war, the world is changing and becoming modern, where the island stands still. We have so little to offer our adventurous young people. The women on the island no longer want to be wives and mothers. They want to become part of the changing world and to help change it.

Thank Cenza for the money that you have sent us. Grandpapa and I are sincerely grateful for it and will accept any help you can give us. Incredibly, my daughters here in our village and their husbands do not recognize or acknowledge our needs. But you so far away have. You are a child given to us from heaven.

Please stay safe, my daughter,
Mamma

The family gathered around the kitchen table, listening to the letter.

"Cenza," Anna said, "I did not know you sent money to Sicily. How did you know they were in need? Did one of my sisters ask for help?"

"Momma," Cenza said, "No one had to tell me. It makes sense that they would need help. They are old. How can they feed themselves?"

"Where are you getting the money from?"

"It is my own money."

Teresa piped up, "I would like to help, Cenza. When you send money again, I want to give too."

Tom looked at his sisters, amazed at their collective generosity.

"Cenza, me too," he added. "They are my grandparents too. I want to help."

Angie looked at Tom with such pride.

"Tom," Cenza said, "you need to keep your money. You are a student. Besides, I have more money than I need or know what to do with."

"Enza," Cenza continued, "We need to go shopping. You need shoes.

Then she continued, "I really did not want anyone of you to know. I did not want anyone to worry about Grandma and Grandpa."

"Well... We should put a piggy-bank on the counter, and whenever one of us has extra money that we can spare, we should contribute to it. Except for you, Tom, you can contribute after you are done with school." Angie said.

Angelo said, "I think that is the right thing to do. Is that all right, Cenza? We all want to help."

"Cenza," Enza said, "I really don't need new shoes. Put the money that you would spend on me into the pig-bank."

Maria put her hand in her pocket and pulled out a one-dollar bill. "Can I put this in the piggy bank?"

Anna smiled while Tom gave Maria a big hug.

"I have another letter that came today," Anna said.

The kitchen got quiet.

"Who is it from, Momma?" Pina asked.

"It is from Lucia, Pina,"

Pina held her breath.

June 1, 1958
Anna, Daughters, Angie, Angelo, and Tom,
Congratulations, Tom, on your entering and studying in the most prestigious music school in the States! Your Palermo family

is so proud of you, but how do you practice with all the noise in that house?

We are busier than ever in the shoe store and the shoe repair shop. Vincent is now traveling to the mainland to inspect shoes at factories for our store. We have hired a person who knows the shoe repair business full-time to work with Dino. We are all working long, hard hours, but don't mind at all.

Anna, you will not believe this, but I have had to hire a housekeeper to clean my house and cook. I never thought that I could ever do that. I hope my mother is not looking down at me from heaven because she is frowning at me and objecting if she is.

I have some excellent news. I think that Dino might be interested in a girl to marry. She is nice, very pretty, and has an education. I know she is interested in Dino. I think he feels the same. Here in the city, the custom of parents finding a husband for their child is fading away. Surprisingly, her parents came to Vincent and me to tell us that she was interested in Dino.

I will let you know in my next letter if Dino is interested in her.

Please write soon.

Lucia

After reading Lucia's letter, Pina tiptoed out from the kitchen and went up the kitchen stairs to her room. She stood at her window and gazed out of it. She longed for her island, but that did not even touch on her secret sadness. Even watching the children play at the park across the street did not ease her emptiness.

Twenty-One

***

M*ay 1, 1959*

Dearest daughter,

It is to my great regret, and with a heavy heart that I must write this sad letter. Grandpa has died. He died peacefully in his sleep beside me last night. He has been feeling lethargic for the last couple of weeks, but I thought it was overworked.

Anna, you know your father always the first to be at a party and the last to leave. He still worked harder than anyone else regardless of the work that had to be done or his age. Always up early and go to bed late. Never enough hours in one day to do all he felt needed to get done.

Grandpa leaves this world with so much love behind. He was loved by everyone and did his best for the family and for me. I will miss him greatly.

Momma

June 1, 1959

Dear Anna,

It pains me to write this letter. Since the death of Papa,

I have become a source of bitter arguing in my family. My daughters' husbands are fighting among themselves over my home and my small possessions.

They feel that I owe them what little I have, for all they have done for me over the years.

Do they think of what will become of me or who will take care of me if they take away what little money I need to live on? They have all made it clear that they don't want me living with them. So, what am I to do?

Please advise me for I am frightened.

Momma

"I never hear such a thing. Just who do they think they are? The only one who helped Grandma and Grandpa was my Papa. That is the worst I have ever heard. No one will treat my Grandmother that way." Cenza was furious.

The families were all in the kitchen with June, Scooter, Joseph, and Sadie. The sadness was evident in everyone.

Anna felt empty over her father's death and sat at the kitchen table while Cenza angrily paced the floor. Francesca sobbed the hardest, for she was the one who missed her grandparents the most. Maria sat quietly beside Tom, and he felt her pain.

Teresa said, "Oh, Momma, what are we going to do for grandmother. Could we bring her here to this country?"

"That's ridiculous, Teresa. We can't do that!" Cenza said. "Grandmother is too old. The trip would kill her!"

Cenza mumbled to herself. "I won't stand for this." Cenza stopped. "Joseph. Will you help me?"

"Of course, course I will," Joseph said. "Whatever it is you need?"

August 1, 1959

Dearest daughter,

A lawyer came into my house yesterday and told me he was hired by my granddaughter Vincenza. He explained to me that she hired him to protect and take care of my financial affairs. All my income will be sent to him, and that all my expenses will be paid by him. He will be monitoring my household expenses every month. I will be given cash by him to spend when I need or want to spend it. He told me that he had access to a sum of money, which is mine, and that all I must do is ask for it, and he will arrange for me to receive it. The lawyer also told me that no one in my family has any way to get at my money.

I was so surprised to find out that Vincenza has set up a bank account for me. My wonderful and generous granddaughter has provided me with more money than I need. I am grateful to her.

When I told my sons-in-law about my new financial arrangement, they became furious. They are very bitter towards Vincenza for interfering. There are also upset about me getting more money from her to live on, and they feel that if she is giving money to anyone, it should be to them.

It upsets me to know that my daughters will not stop their husbands from being so greedy. I am sorry that I must tell you about this awful situation. I feel you need to know about the hard feelings my sons-in-law have toward my money. You might get some nasty correspondence from them.

Thank you so much for the woman who comes into my house and cleans and cooks for me. She and her husband live and stay with me and make me feel safe and less lonely for Papa.

Momma

It was a rare occasion when Anna, Angie, Sadie, and June sat around the kitchen table after a Sunday afternoon dinner without the others around. The older girls and Tom were being driven by Manny to a movie matinee. The younger girls, Angelo, Joseph, Scooter, and the boys, were playing across from the house.

The espresso served was dark, rich, and hot and laced with brandy with a twist of lemon rind floating to the top of it. The afternoon was peaceful and quiet, without the confusion with the others around.

Anna said, "June, I love watching Scooter with the boys. He is so patient with them."

"Yes! They are bundles of energy and love being with their dad. Scooter is wonderful with them. I am so fortunate to have them." Shyly she said, "Scooter and I are working on having another baby. It would be nice if I could give him a little girl.".

"That would be wonderful, June," Anna said, putting her elbow at the table and leaning her chin in her hand, dreaming. "I have not sewn little-girl dresses in such a long time. I would defiantly design her First Holy Communion dress. It would be pure white with lots of lace with little white rosettes scattered all over it."

"Scooter would love that!" Turning to Anna, June said, "Anna, would you ever get married again?"

"Me? Get married again? No... I am married. Just because Franco is not here does not mean that I am free to marry. I took my vows for my lifetime, and besides, I am too old. I wouldn't know how to go about it. How would I meet a man? Besides, I am too busy raising my daughters and working so many hours."

Angie said, "Your girls will not be around forever, Anna, and you have so much to offer someone."

"But I don't. I have nothing to offer. I have no love left in my heart. I gave it all to Franco, and he betrayed me. I have nothing left. All my strength and trust are gone."

"Well," Sadie said after drinking her third cup of laced espresso dreamily, "I would love to have sex." The women got quiet. "What? What did I say? Sure, I am old, but I am not dead?"

"I think we need more brandy without the coffee," June said, laughing.

"Yes, I agree!" Angie said, rising to reach in the cabinet behind her to get the brandy glasses.

At the same time, Sadie blushed, and June started laughing harder.

Twenty-Two

❧

Cenza minded the shop's front for Pina as she was modeling a gown for her mother and Angie. They needed to see their finished work that Angelo had to deliver that day. They promised it would only take a few minutes since Cenza hated being late for work.

"Miss Gennusa?"

Cenza looked up from the desk and smiled at the stranger, "Yes, may I help you?"

He was a tall, dark-haired man in an expensive suit holding a large leather briefcase. "I am Arthur Greensborough, and I'd like to discuss something with you..."

Later that day, "We are not going to do that, Cenza. What do we know of such things? We sew gowns. That is all we do."

The families were seated at the kitchen table since Cenza had called a family meeting. Joseph was beside Anna, with Sadie on her other side. June and Scooter were at the table while their boys watched television and ate cookies in the family room.

"Momma, it is a chance of a lifetime. Think of the exposure we will get. Think of the people we will cater to. Think, Momma, think! Think of the money we will make." Cenza said.

"Money...! Since when did money mean anything to you?"

233

"Since I can remember, money brought food for us and anything we need to survive. Money is what I have worked for every day. I have not used it to spend myself except on books and art. But, yes, I like what I can do with money for others. Yes, money gives me pleasure. I am no different from anyone else. I love money, and this will lead us to make the kind of money we've never dreamed of."

Anna looked and at Joseph. "Joseph, please reason with her."

"Cenza, you know how hard it is to change your mother's mind. But I think if you explain the ramifications of this kind of exposure where it will lead too, she will not be able to refuse you."

"Momma," Cenza looking at her mother, "Think of what will happen to us. With this exposure, we will need to expand. We will need to hire more people. Think... Momma... think of providing jobs for women who are in need. Think... Momma... think, instead of using your emotions. Think about the money we will be making. We can send the younger ones to college and send more money to Sicily to our family there."

Angelo added. "Anna, your daughter, has never steered us wrong. Let us all listen to her again, but this time to her whole idea."

The room was quiet when Cenza waited for her mother's permission to repeat herself.

Anna nodded.

"Like I said, we have a chance to put one of our designs on the runway for the Govina Couture House. This runway is the most prestigious show in New York. Its attendees are the wealthy and famous movie stars who can't take the time to go to Europe for the yearly fashion shows. It is our opportunity to place our work and name out to these people. The show will be televised, and the exposure is enormous. Momma, you are so talented. You belong up with today's great designers, not just here in America but also in Europe. Eventually, you will be known in Europe. Don't count yourself short. You have a gift, and that gift should be shared, and hopefully, you can encourage young new talent."

Cenza paused. "I hope you are not mad at me, Momma, but I have accepted Mr. Greensborough's offer to be in the show. I could not turn it down. I have it all planned. The first thing is for Momma to design a new look, and it must be ready for the fall show, which is in August."

"Where do we get a model for the runway fashion show?" Teresa asked.

"That was easy to decide. Pina will be our model,"

Pina's eyes widened, and her face went pale at Cenza words. Everyone looked at Pina.

June said, "You could not have picked a better person for the job. Pina, you are so beautiful!"

Teresa, beside Pina, put her arm around her and hugged her. Pina jumped from the table, her chair falling backward, hitting the floor, making a big thumping noise.

"No, I will not. I refuse."

Cenza – and everyone else - looked surprised. "Why would you refuse? You're tall, beautiful, and elegant. You are perfect, and you would represent the family. It will open doors to you and maybe a career in modeling. This is about family. Pina, what is your problem?"

"Cenza, you always think that whatever you think can be done is easy. Well, it is not easy for me. All you see is what you want to see. I am not a model."

Pina looked at her mother. "Please, Momma, don't make me do this. I can't do this. I already take care of our customers out at the shop, which I hate. Don't put me on display. It's not me. Please, Momma, do not make me do this."

Pina lifted her head, tears running down her cheeks, ran to the kitchen stairs, and ran up them.

The room became hushed. In the near distance, noises came from the family room's television.

"Is Pina all right?" Joseph asked later that night, sitting beside Anna on the park bench facing the house.

"Yes, she is, and she agreed to model. Cenza told her that she would get lessons to feel more confident about her being on display. Pina is perfect for the job. It is hard for Pina to think of herself as anything other than a farmer. Her beauty means nothing to her. When she investigates a mirror, all she sees is a person, not an incredibly beautiful tall, elegant creature." Anna said. "She has no clue about her soft demeanor or that she walks like an angel. People stare at her because of her beauty, but she never notices. Men fall all over themselves over her, which worries me because she never sees what they see. I keep an extra eye on her."

Anna hesitated, "During the War, Franco was always by her side, afraid of what the Germans would do if they took her. She was his biggest concern. He made me cut her hair and putting her in loose male clothing, so she looked like a boy. I did this with all the older girls. I even had to bind Cenza's breasts because she was well endowed."

"Maybe that is why people react to Pina the way they do because she doesn't set herself above them."

"There so many times I wish she was vain. Then she would be more aware of her surroundings, and I wouldn't have to watch her so closely. Even Tom watches over her when they go to the movies, aware of the men looking at her."

"Anna, your reaction to Cenza today when Cenza asked you to put one of your designs in the fashion show was a bit strong. I know you well enough to know when you are scared, which is not often. You become testy. Today I saw you afraid. Am I right?

"Was it noticeable to my family?"

"Anna, it was noticeable just to me. What is it that you are afraid of?

"Afraid...yes... I am afraid. I am afraid to change my life again. I am a farmer's wife, not some high profiled person Cenza wants me to be. I have had so many changes in my life how can I handle any more? Joseph, what is my daughter asking of me?"

"Your extremely ambitious daughter is asking for a chance to grow and to expand her abilities. She is asking you with your talent to help her advance. Be proud of her because she is asking you. She could go elsewhere." Joseph said. "Cenza has the need to feed her family, feed her co-workers, and now has a great need to feed the world. She can't do it without money, and at this stage of her life, she needs to make a lot of money because the world she is finding is bigger than she thought.

"Cenza wants you to help her make money, so she can save the world. With all that she has done and her motives to do more, first for her family and then for the world, how can you say no? I wish my youngest son would want to feed the world instead of being a ski-bum. Soon your younger daughters will want to go to college. Look at Maria's grades. Look at how hard she works. Think about what you can give her. I don't see how you can say no to Cenza. Don't be afraid, my friend. I will help you make those changes. You know those simple restaurants we go out to once a week?"

"Yes," Anna said.

"Well... starting next week, we'll go to the best restaurants in the City. I have been to all of them and will enjoy sharing them with you. You'll find them enjoyable and learn a bit about other cuisines and cultures. Don't let fear hold you back." Joseph said as he and Anna got up from their park bench and walked toward the house.

Anna put her hand into her pocket and held on to her spool of thread for comfort. "Anna, it's about time you taste Asian food," Joseph said. Anna scrunched her face with distaste. Joseph said, laughing at Anna's reaction. "You will be surprised how good Asian food is, especially their fish dinners."

They walked across the street towards the house. "I will educate you on wine, fine dining, jewelry. It's about time you started wearing more fashionable clothes, especially shoes." He thought of the diamond ring he bought for her.

Anna sighed. She knew he had a point about promoting herself. She was just fearful of change, as always.

"Have you ever noticed how beautiful Enza is?"

Anna looked at Joseph, took a deep breath, and sighed. "Yes, Joseph... how could I not? With her creamy olive skin, dark hair, and those incredible hazel eyes with those thick eyelashes. I can never describe those eyes of hers."

"Exotic," Joseph said.

"Yes, that describes them... Beautiful daughters can be a curse to a mother. But I don't worry so much about Enza because she knows that she is pretty and rare. She knows about the attention she gets. Angelo spoils her so and tells her every day how beautiful she is. He also warns her of the dangers around her because she is so lovely. She keeps a sharp eye out, and she has good senses."

Joseph turned toward the stairs, and Anna followed him together, climbing the stair to the bridal shop. More lightly, Joseph said. "And I will give you a good deal on a few pieces of jewelry that I think you should start wearing."

Anna just shook her head, laughing. "This is where friendship ends. You will give me a good price, right?"

As Joseph opened the door, "For you because you are a good friend, I will give you my pieces at cost!"

"You are going to enjoy making an American out of me, aren't you?" Anna said.

"Yes," Joseph said, smiling. "I am."

The door shut behind them as they laughed, going inside.

And Joseph did just that. He took Anna out to the best restaurants, parties, and to the theater. Anna enjoyed her adventures if Joseph was at her side. Anna met many men interested in her, but she did not encourage them. She had Joseph's friendship, which was safe, and she didn't need more.

When Anna returned from her new adventures, she took off her fashionable clothes, expensive jewelry, and wore her simple house dress. Anna was most comfortable in her own home, cooking or at her table in the sewing room, designing her first runway gowns. Once she was over the shock and fear of Cenza's request, she put all her effort and energy into her work.

The whole family gave their opinion on all of Anna's new designs. When she finished a drawing the family did not love, she put the sketch in the hall closet for later review. She started over again, taking in each family member's suggestions.

Anna found her new challenge invigorated her. She had so many ideas. She sketched, cut patterns, and stitched until her fingers hurt. Neither tired nor discouraged, she kept at it. Finally, everyone agreed on the gown. Anna had more work ahead of her. She needed the right fabric and design a headpiece. Again, the whole family got involved.

Anna's first runway designed gown was beautiful. Pina's beauty elevated the design, making it more exquisite. The combination of both Anna's design and Pina's beauty brought the fashion show to a stop.

Even though uncomfortable and unhappy about modeling, Pina practiced her walk and in her mother's creation. Her lessons took up countless amounts of hours because Pina was so awkward about displaying herself.

Twenty-Three

After all these years in New York City, Anna was still amazed when she went to the corner market stand, one block from the bridal shop. She shopped for her daily produce at the open-air market. It was her favorite time of day, looking at all the food varieties available. She enjoyed the walk and saying hello to all her neighbors. She was away from her daily concerns and appreciated her surroundings. She gave herself time to clear her mind of designs. After getting fresh air, she returned to her work, feeling refreshed with more creative thoughts. This morning she really needed a reprieve because she was putting extra time into the fashion show's gown.

Anna liked it when the owner of the local market greeted her by her name. She never noticed the extra smile that the grocer had for her or the time he spent chatting and bagging her groceries. He was intrigued by Anna and knew she was a widow. He watched her closely as she passed by him. Anna just noticed the pleasant atmosphere of the small market and its fresh smell. She strolled through the small market isles marveled at all the choices of products at hand. She felt so rich to have all these choices. She was always in awe that even in cold weather, she still had a selection of fresh fruit and vegetables.

Even bitter icy winter days, when the sidewalks were covered in snow, and the streets were ice, Anna's daily shopping spree never stopped.

After leaving the produce market, she would go to either the fish-monger for fresh fish or the butchers for meat. Her last stop was always the bakery when she did not have time to bake. On occasion, she would buy a fresh-baked pastry for dessert.

Anna felt that her daily marketing and picking out the best products was her way despite her busy day to care for her family. She never cared for the price of the food. She budgeted her money in other ways since getting the best food for her family resulted in her – and their - hard work and was her priority.

On an already warm morning in the middle of summer, Anna was on her daily markets run. On this day, she enjoyed inspecting each fruit and vegetable piece by touching, smelling, and examining it thoroughly before she purchased it.

While there, a person stood behind her and spoke to her in Sicilian, "Please do not turn around. I am here to ask for your help. I will not harm you. I will stand beside you and start looking at the fruit and tell you who I am. Please do not look and me until I am done telling you my identity."

Anna did not move. She could tell that the voice was noticeably young and male.

He stood beside her, picked up an orange, and examined it. Anna realized he needed to bathe. She felt no fear, just curiosity.

"My name is Daniel Stevens. My father is Joseph Stevens." Anna began turning, "No, don't look at me."

Anna looked at the bin of fruit and raised another piece. Daniel went to the next bin, looked at the vegetables for a few minutes, and then returned to Anna's side.

"Go to the bread section and wait for me. I will take my time before approaching you again. I need to make sure I am not being watched. I need your help. Please help me."

Anna strolled over to the bread aisle, where she examined all the different loaves of bread, squeezing, and smelling them.

Daniel found her. "I need a place to stay and hide for a few days. May I stay with you? I know you have a big cellar. I am doing vital work, and it is perilous. I have no one else here in the city to ask for help."

"Your father thinks you are in Europe. You must go to him. He must know that you are in danger."

"No... I don't want any connection to my father or my brother. They must not know. I need a place temporarily. May I stay in your cellar?"

"My cellar? What about my daughters?"

"They will be safe. No one knows that I am connected to you, and if they did, they would not think I would be foolish enough to go to you because of the enormous activity in your home."

"How can I get you into my house without anyone knowing?"

"There is a window attached at the back of your house that leads to the cellar. If you can manage to open it for me, I will crawl into the cellar from there. I also need food and water, for I have not had any in several days." Daniel pleaded.

"Come after 2:00 A.M. I will be waiting for you in the cellar. If you need my help, you need to tell me what is going on."

Anna moved to the register to pay for her purchases without buying the one thing she came into the store to buy, and those were fresh tomatoes.

Anxiously, Anna awaited Daniel in the cellar of her house. It was 2:30, and he had not come. Waiting in the dark, Anna paced the floor, getting more worried. What had the young man done? Wondering about the boy, she remembered a sweet, cute little fellow with dark curly hair and big bright eyes. How had his life come to this?

Anna thought of the time Joseph and his family lived with them during the war and how hard it was to keep the small children calm during that stressful time.

Anna heard a scraping sound and looked toward the window. She saw Daniel came through the window and looked at the stairs to make sure that no one was coming into the cellar. She looked at this young man and hugged him tightly, remembering the boy. She quietly instructed him to follow her. They walked through a couple of sizeable rooms to the back to the cellar; Anna pushed a huge old dresser away from the wall and crawled behind it, beckoning Daniel to enter.

Earlier that evening, Anna went to the cellar to find a hiding place for the boy. She searched every inch of the basement closely when, by accident, she discovered this room. She tripped on a large old piece of furniture and skinned her knee. She held on to this piece of furniture, rubbing her knee. After she rubbed her knee out of desperation, she put her hand in her pocket and around her spool of white thread. She worried that she would not find Daniel a safe hidden place to hide without being caught. She pulled the spool from her pocket and dropped it. It rolled under the furniture. She knelt on the floor, reaching beneath the chest, but could not find her spool. She moved this massive piece of furniture to recover her prized possession when she noticed a small door against the wall. She opened the door and, to her amazement, discovered a little room.

Anna loaded warm blankets, soap, towels, and a disposable bucket for a urinal.

Daniel stood in the room felt safe for the first time in days. It was just large enough for him to lie down. He stammered out his thanks.

"I don't think my daughters know about this room. It has a light over in that corner, but you must not use it unless you have to. After I close the door, I will put a piece of old furniture against it. There will be no way for you to leave this room without assistance, which is a concern. I am amazed that my younger daughters have not found this room. There are some newspapers and books for you to read. Here are warm blankets and a pillow. I also put a can for you to urinate in. Here is food and enough water until tomorrow night, and I will bring you more."

Daniel was relieved to see all the comforts of home. He had been on the run for some time and was exhausted and in need of sleep.

Daniel sat down on the floor and drank the water.

Anna sat down with him. "Daniel, what is this all about?"

"What I about to tell you is in strict confidence. You must promise not to say a word, especially if I am caught by my enemies, no matter the circumstance. In that case, you must never reveal to anyone, not even my father, that you knew me. Do you understand? It is vital not only for your safety and for your family but also for mine."

Anna looked at Daniel, no longer containing her anger. "You are still a child. What have you gotten yourself into?"

"I hoped that someday I would see you again. I wanted to thank you and your family for taking care of my family and me during the war. It is disheartening to meet you this way, but now I will have the opportunity to thank you myself. We never forgot your family and for your bravery, kindness, and your generosity.

"Daniel, you were just a child. How could you remember?"

"I might have been a child, but I remember the bombing in Palermo and watching my house being destroyed. I remember the cold nights in the mountains frightened. I remember the warmth of your kitchen and all your children who became my friends."

Daniel started crying. "I still remember a tall light-haired man with beautiful blue eyes who ruffled my hair with such love and strength. I remember everything, even hearing about the German soldiers who killed the young boy and his father in the village center during the olive season when getting their oil harvested. Yes," Daniel said, "I remember it all, including the Nazi who shot my mother. She died for no other reason but because she was trying to survive the war and because she was a Jew." That day that my mother was shot, I promised myself that I would get revenge on those people, and now I am getting my revenge."

"So, this is all about revenge? But how?"

"After my father, my brother, and I left Sicily, we got to Switzerland. My father put us boys in a Catholic school because he felt my brother and I would be protected. Well, the nuns took good care of us. They did not care that we were Jews and not Catholic. The nuns fed us, prayed for us, educated us, and kept us safe. During those years in the school, many Jewish boys were hidden by their parents to protect them. They were several boys who experienced similar tragedies as mine. We became good friends. We promised each other when we were old enough, we would track down the Nazis and any communist party member that escaped the war and bring them to justice.

"Yes, we may be young, but we know how we feel. All of us come from wealthy families. We had money available to us without our parents asking where we spent it. We pool our money, and we travel to find leftover war enemies. Being young, we're never asked about our traveling because no one thinks a young person wants responsibly. For the past several years, we have moved freely. At times like now, when there is a possibility of being exposed, we find a safe-haven. I feel that I am being followed. I apologize to you for being here, but I had nowhere else to go.

"With all the funds we share, all of us boys, we have captured some German officers who drove the Jews to the death camps. We sponsor and deliver their surviving victims and send them to the trials they hold of Nazi officers who killed Jews. These victims tell their stories and aid in imprisoning many of those who tortured them. These are the men that sent millions of Jews to their deaths. Many of these Germans were in high-level jobs and are still in hiding. We will find them and bring them to justice. I will get revenge for my mother's murder.

"Daniel, you are so young to hold on to such hate. You should forget it. Get on with your life like the rest of us. We have all been

246 - *Mary B. Patterson*

touched and left with scars from the war. It is not good to carry so much of this burden on yourself. You are but a child."

"It is not hatred you hear from me, but strength and commitment to do what is needed. We owe it to ourselves never to let one man submit to such atrocities and never do this again in the history of this world. I am not talking about the Jewish people. I am talking about all people. Yes, you are right. I still need to grow to manhood, but I am filled with purpose inside this young man's body. I will fulfill this purpose so that when I am old, I will be able to live with myself with pride." Daniel said. "To me, it is why my mother gave birth to me and why she had to die the way she did. In my heart, I know my mother has directed me into doing what I am doing."

"How did you get started to find these people that should be brought to justice?"

"One night, several of my friends and I were in our bedroom at school. They usually gathered with my brother and me because we were all lonely and missed our parents. One night a boy we did not like joined us. His family was much richer than any of ours. He was loud and a braggart, even bragging how he stole whiskey from his father's car. He was already drunk when he staggered into our room, holding several packs of American cigarettes. We were surprised when we saw the cigarettes and wondered how his father obtained them. We grabbed them and lit up. I started to choke, but I continued inhaling, trying to act all grown-up. He watched us laughing and, as usual, pretended he was superior to us. We all knew his father gave the school a great deal of money just to keep him there. We assumed his father was keeping safe from the Nazis, just like our parents were doing.

"We passed the whiskey around, hoping it would ease our loneliness for our parents. I was only ten, and my brother was twelve, and here we were puffing on cigarettes and getting drunk. The older boys giggled and talked about the girls they would someday fuck. I did not know what that meant, but my brother did. I listened to boys describing their breasts and how they would feel. They all longed for girls, wondering how they would have sex. I knew my brother understood, but all the talk confused me. But I started feeling things in my groin, and it worried me.

"I longed for my mother more that evening than I had for a long time. I knew that she would have explained all these feelings I was having."

Daniel took a deep breath, "My brother handed the whiskey to me. I coughed and choked a bit at it burned, sliding down into my stomach. I handed the bottle to my friend beside me, and the bottle was passed around several times. The kid we hated drank a lot and said things to us that we were shocked and horrified to hear. As he kept drinking, he bragged how his father had connections with Hitler and his high-ranking officers."

"When we heard of the extermination of Jews and the mention of death camps from this person, we were shocked, sick to our stomachs. To this day, it is hard for me to describe what I felt finding out this kid's father was connected to such horrors. He talked about how his father had dealings with banks all over Europe and how he helped the Germans make money for war."

Daniel stopped. Anna watched him, horrified at what he was telling her.

"We listened as he bragged on... and on... and on. He was so pleased with his story. He never noticed our reactions to what he was saying. My brother asked him, 'How does your father justify his action?" Arnold Mann - that was his name - said it was easy. Power and money and ever more power and money! Besides, the Nazis promised his father some famous art they would retrieve in Europe, any chalet his father wanted. Then there were the connections to all the high officials running Europe after the war was over. Mann's father was already part of the upper echelon of Hitler's regime. He was involved financially in the invasion of France and the alliance of Italy. *"My fa-*

ther's," Arnold said, "*proudest moment came when he was the guest of Mussolini, along with the heads of state from Austria and Poland. He has acquired some of the most beautiful and exquisite stones from the Africa Continent.*"

"He just continued bragging. '*No doubt that the Germans will win this war, and when it is over, my father will hand all that money and power to me...*He almost laughed and instead responded said, "I will take it willing." My brother controlled his emotions and asked, "Even at the expense of all the death that comes with it? The deaths of Jews mean nothing to you?"

Arnold answered, "*They are worthless. They can't even be called human.*"

"I had never seen my friends so lost and longing for their families like they did that evening. Later that night, I heard my brother crying, and I knew my other friends were in the same state. Our youth was gone, and even going to mass the next day did not return our childhood

"We realized, though, that Arnold was filled with information. I can't tell you what it felt like to hear him talk. We exploited him for everything he knew and kept notes.

After that night, a friend and I decided on our future. We needed to rid the world of these monsters. After that, it became a natural progression. I must admit that we were happy when Arnold and his father had a fatal car accident several years later. I am immensely proud that we were able to transmit information to the 'right' people and are indirectly responsible for their deaths."

Anna was shocked to hear what Daniel told her so coldly. "Is your brother a part of this group?"

"No," Daniel replied, "He knows nothing, and neither does my father. Knowing about me will bring great danger to them, and I am sorry, to your family, too."

Anna kissed Daniel's tear-stained cheek. She encouraged him to lie on the blanket tucking the pillow under his head and kissed his cheek again. "Sleep well, my son. I will be back late tomorrow night to bring you fresh food. Do you need anything?"

Daniel did not answer. Anna looked at the young man, barely seeing him in the dark, and knew he was sound asleep.

Anna tossed and turned all night, thinking about Daniel. She felt guilty for promising him not to tell his father of his whereabouts and Nazi-hunting involvement.

Anna rose early, desperately needing coffee. As she drank her cup of coffee alone in the early morning, she grateful for the solicitude.

As the day lingered, Anna felt as if it would never end. She continually looked toward the basement, watching everyone who went down there. She even insisted on doing the days' laundry and refused any help.

In the afternoon, she was hand sewing the gown to be worn by Pina in the fashion show and pricked her finger. Angrily, she grabbed some scrap fabric and brought it to her finger before blood got on the garment.

Teresa seeing her mother's reaction took the dress. "I will finish it. You have not been yourself today. You seem to be out of sorts."

"I am only tired. This whole fashion show has put such stress on me, with Cenza's constant demands."

"Cenza has put us under so much pressure, especially Pina. I will talk to her and make sure she lets up on all of us. I noticed that our even-tempered Angelo is showing stress."

"I need a break... I am going into the kitchen for coffee. Maybe that will wake me up."

Teresa watched her mother walk out of the sewing room when Tom entered. "Why aren't you in school?"

"I don't have to go in until late this afternoon. My instructor had an emergency, so I will see him later for my lesson."

Teresa smiled. "You look so happy, Tom."

"How could I not be? When I was in prison, I never thought that I would be attending the best music school in the country. Your families made this all happen for me, and I can never repay them."

"Tom, you have repaid us in more ways than you know," Teresa said.

"Can you get away for lunch and go to the deli with me. We could get a sandwich and sit in the park. I promise it wouldn't take too long."

Teresa put the dress down on a clean surface, stood up, and stretched. "Yes, I am so hungry, and the park sounds wonderful. I could do with a break and some fresh air."

Anna watched them leave. Two fewer people to worry about going into the basement

The evening finally arrived. Anna waited for the family to be asleep when she approached Daniel's room. She entered the room with a plate of food. She also carried a bag with breakfast and lunch for the next day.

Daniel greeted her with a big smile and a big hug. "I know this must be difficult for you to understand what I am doing. Even though the war is over, it is still dangerous for any Jew in Europe. There are Hitler sympathizers still killing anyone Jewish. My brother and father are protected by their business and their new identity. My enemies will kill anyone who knows me right now and what I am doing. They don't care if they are Jewish or not."

"You are very brave. Your father would be so proud of you. Is there any way I can stop you from continuing what you are doing?"

"No... I have another dangerous request from you. Tomorrow I am supposed to meet my contact at Grand Central Train Station at one p.m. He is supposed to give me a passport and money to get back to Europe. I am not comfortable leaving here in the daylight. Will you go for me? I know I am asking a lot, but you are the only one I can trust."

Anna rubbed her forehead, agonizing over Daniel's request. She looked at him and sighed. "Yes. I'll make sure you get this package."

A tall, middle-aged man got off the 1:00 train, carrying a brown leather briefcase with the day's newspaper under his arm. He had just lit an English tobacco pipe when he heard a young man yell his name, "Rory!"

A young man waved briskly, smiling, and came towards him. "Rory Redman."

The two men embraced and began strolling away from the train. They behaved as if they were having an animated conversation between the two people, happy to see each other. Grand Central Station was crowded and very noisy with mobs of commuters, station personnel, and tourists walking through. The noise level was so high it almost hurt their ears.

The pair walked outside, still chatting as the middle-aged man hailed a cab. A taxi stopped in front of them, and they got in. The younger man leaned over to the cab driver and told him where to go.

Once settled, the middle-aged man asked softly, so the cab driver would not hear him, "Who are you? Is Daniel safe?"

The young man whispered, "Daniel did not feel it was safe for him to come. I took his place. He has been residing at my house, hidden in a very secret location, for the last few days. I'm Tom Pertucci. I go to Julliard, so it was less conspicuous for me to meet you since I travel out of the neighborhood every day to go to school."

"Do you know what you are into?" Rory Redman handed Tom a small package.

"No," Tom put the package into his school bag. "It doesn't matter. I'd do anything for the person who asked me to do this. No questions

252 - *Mary B. Patterson*

asked. I do know it's vital this the package gets to my home without anyone seeing it."

Rory nodded. The cab stopped in front of Julliard. Both men got out of the cab and hugged each other. Rory said softly, "Thank you, son. We are indebted to you."

"It has been my pleasure, Sir."

Rory Redman returned to the cab. Tom went into the school, neither one to ever to see the other again.

After school, Tom entered the kitchen, looked at Anna, and gave her a small nod to let her know that all went well. Anna sighed, relieved he was safe.

Anna handed Daniel the package that night. He quickly inspected its contents: his passport, plane ticket, money, and a note.

"Oh, no!"

"What is it?" Anna asked, "What is wrong?"

"I need to stay one more night. My plane ticket is not until late tomorrow night."

"I have a dinner engagement with your father tomorrow night. What shall I do?"

"You must keep it!"

"I can't do that. I would not be able to think straight around your father. I will be lying to him, even if he doesn't know that you are here. There is no way I can do that."

"You must not break your dinner plans with my father. Everything should look as normal here as possible." Daniel said. "How will I get out of here without being detected tomorrow night? This is the only time I can leave this country. The date on my passport says tomorrow evening at 8:00 PM."

As Anna left Daniel that night, she asked herself, "*Will I be able to get through the night with Joseph? How can I handle so much stress? The fashion shows? Daniel?*"

The next night as Anna was out with Joseph having their weekly dinner, Tom moved the furniture that Anna told him hid their 'visitor.'"

Tom crawled into the tiny space, sure that no one was watching him. "I have some clean clothes for you, and I think my jacket will fit you. It was more fashionable than what you are wearing and less conspicuous. Anna said to make sure you ate this plate of food before you leave."

"You must be Tom," Daniel said. "Anna has told me that you went to the train station for her."

"Yes. I love Anna and would do anything for her. I would never question her motives for what she asked me to do for you."

"She loves you like a son."

Tom reached out his hand, and the young men shook hands

"You are truly fortunate to have her. She is so generous and kind and gave us so much during the war. I am Daniel Stevens, Joseph Stevens' youngest son. My father doesn't know what I am into, but I can promise you he would be proud of me.

Tom was shocked to find out that the young man hidden in the basement was Joseph's son.

"My father must not know that I was here or that you helped me. It is too dangerous for you and your family."

Tom didn't question their visitor. He handed Daniel the plate of food and was quiet while Daniel ate. After Daniel was done eating, he started to straighten up his temporary home when Tom said, "Don't worry about the room. I will clean it."

Daniel looked at the urinal in the corner across the room. "But?"

"Don't worry, my friend, I have cleaned worse. It's time for you to leave. I was told not to drive you to the airport, so you're on your own when you leave this house. I'll close the window when you are gone."

Tom handed Daniel a piece of paper, "Our phone number. Put it in your pocket. If you need help, I will come and help you. I know ways to be hidden within the city if you need to. I will stay close to the phone until your flight leaves. If I don't hear from you, I will know that you are safe and traveling to your destination. After you are on the plane, throw the phone number away. Maybe someday, under different circumstances, we can become friends."

The two young men stood by the window. Daniel changed clothes and was ready to leave when he turned to Tom, "Thank you. Maybe we can share a bottle of wine sometime soon."

Tom smiled, "That would be nice. Have a safe trip."

> *August 30, 1959*
> *Dear Anna and families,*
> *I was so pleased to hear about the fashion show you will be in and its exposure to the shop. It looks like a big success is on its way. Pina will be fantastic, representing the family. With her absolute beauty and your creativeness, Anna, great success will come with it. Vincent is sending you a pair of shoes that would go with the gown you will show. When you explained the creation for the showing, Vincent knew what shoes would go with it.*
> *By the time you receive this letter, Vincent will be in Rome buying shoes for our store. It amazes me how Vincent's shoes bought from the mainland sell so fast and are the first to be sold in our store. Women asked when the shoe shipments will come so they can have the first choice. Vincent is taking a few matching handbags to see if his customers like them on this trip that he is taking. If they do, he is going to stock more bags for our customers. Vincent is delighted with his traveling and our store doing so well.*
> *As I told you that in my last letter, Dino was almost engaged. To my regret, Dino has backed away from this girl whom I was telling you about. I am not sure why, because I know he liked her.*

*Write soon and let me know if Vincent and I can help with
your show.*
> *My Love always,*
> *Lucia*

"That is good, Pina. You got it. Remember, don't look at the audience. Focus over their heads against the wall. Spot something and keep looking at it. You are doing great." Cenza said.

Pina shook her shoulders. She was stiff from practicing her walk on the runway. "Cenza, I think I've got it. How do I look?"

Cenza sighed, "Oh, Pina, you are so beautiful! You will be the hit of the show. I have seen some models rehearsing, and none of them have your stature and your natural grace and beauty." Cenza sighed again. "I know how hard this is for you, and I feel bad that I have pushed you into this." She hugged her sister. "I am so proud of you. Thank you, Pina. This is so important to the business and the whole family."

Anna and Teresa watched, not saying a word. Pina lifted her shoulders, straightened up her back, and started practicing again.

Cenza was not nervous. She was confident that Pina was ready, the gown was ready, Anna was ready, and all that was left was to wait for the two weeks to go by. Cenza paced to stay calm, no matter where she was, and it drove them nuts. They were all nervous enough waiting until the time to pass.

On Saturday morning, Anna was making coffee in the kitchen and enjoying a quiet moment before the house bustled with noise from her family and the customers from the bridal shop.

After the coffee finished brewing, Anna poured herself a cup, went to the table, sat down, poured heavy cream into the coffee, and stirred it. She sipped it, "*MMMMM the cream is almost as good as the cream we got at the farm in Sicily.*"

She opened the early edition of the morning newspaper, scamming the fashion section for words about the fashion show. She turned the page, and an extensive article sprang out at her. She smiled with pleasure at the illustration of the show. She read every word, absorbing its contents. Happily, she saw Anna's Bridal Shop on the bottom of the page, and her name was listed as the designer.

Contented but nervous at the same time, she lifted her head from the newspaper as she heard the commotion start making her home come alive. As she listened to an unusual heaviness of footsteps coming from the kitchen stairs, she saw Teresa.

Teresa was standing on the bottom step. Anna became concerned when she saw Teresa's face. Teresa started sobbing. "Momma, I am so sorry."

Teresa walked to her and handed her a folded paper.

Anna opened it up with fear and read the letter. Her hand fell to her side, and the note fell out of her hand. She rose and unsteadily walked to the sink, staring out the window.

Cenza walked into the kitchen, still in her robe and slippers. Her hair was a mess, but her face was pink as she rubbed the sleep out of her eyes. "The coffee smells good!"

Cenza poured herself some coffee, went to the table, sat down, and reached for the cream. She noticed that Teresa had not moved from where she was standing, and her mother stood motionless, gazing out of the window.

"What is it? What is wrong?"

Teresa went to the note on the floor, picked it up, and handed it to her. Cenza knew it was not good. She unfolded it slowly.

The other girls came downstairs still in their nightclothes. They immediately knew something was seriously wrong. They quietly approached a chair to the table and sat down quietly.

Cenza read it aloud:

September 1, 1959

Dear Momma,

Please forgive me for what I have done. I know it is wrong and very selfish of me to think only of myself. It is to my regret that I had to take such measures.

I have tried to accustom myself to our new ways here in this country, but it did not work in my heart. I have tried in every way to do what was best for our family. While we all work hard here, you and my sisters adjusted well, but I did not. I die slowly every day.

My heart is in Sicily. It has always been in Sicily. Please forgive me. I left on a ship early this morning to go back to my homeland, where I belong. Not only have I gone back to my home, but to the man I love and could only love. Since the first day when his family came to help at the farm, I have loved Dino. Dino has felt the same since that time. When we arrived in this country, I thought it was just for a few years. As the years slowly passed by, it was evident that we would never return. Between Dino and me, we saved enough money for my trip back home.

Don't be disappointed or blame Lucia, for she had no idea the love I have for her son and the love we have for each other.

When we received Lucia's letter about Dino almost getting married, I felt my life was over. The days were long and dark for me, and I shed many tears. When Lucia sent the second letter telling us that Dino would not marry that girl, I searched my heart and prayed to God to give me the strength to do what I had to do.

Dino and I have corresponded privately several times during the past years. Dino asked me to marry him, and I have said yes. We will be married as soon as I arrive in Palermo.

Please forgive me and try to understand. I want to live and live in happiness, which can only happen if I am with Dino.

Do not worry about my voyage on the ship. I have prepared well. I brought plenty of clothes and some medication, and I'm carrying a large bag of fruit and cheese. I will drink the water, whatever it tastes like, and any liquids that I will be served. As far as my safety goes, I will watch and stay in large crowds.

As I sit and write this letter, I write with a heavy heart. Not to just you, Momma, but to my sisters who I dearly love. I love you, Momma. Please understand. Tell Cenza I am sorry. I need to breathe and start to live again. I can only be fulfilled and whole as a person in Sicily in Dino's arms. I will send a telegram when I reach Sicily.

Your loving daughter,
Pina

Anna did not move after absorbing what Cenza had read in a deep and sad voice. "Teresa, did you know that Pina was going back to Sicily?"

"No, Momma, I did not."

There was dead silence in the kitchen.

Tom entered from the kitchen stairs and noticed that the room was eerily silent. It frightened him to be in such quiet, and it brought him back to his nights at the prison where he was vulnerable and alone.

Instead of remembering the cries of cellmates when he closed his eyes, he only heard Francesca weeping. He slumped his shoulders from heaviness, and his body felt iced. It had been a long time that he felt these feelings, and it scared him.

"Good morning, everyone," Angelo cheerfully, as he did every morning when he entered the kitchen, "It is going to be another beaut..."

Angelo stopped and looked around the room. As Angie reached the kitchen, she walked to Angelo and felt the uneasiness in the room.

"Son, what is wrong?"

Angie saw Anna looking out the window and knew she needed her. She went to her side. She stood still beside her, and they both looked out the window together. Angie slowly put her arm around Anna's shoulder.

Angelo put his arm around Tom and felt him shaking. "What is wrong?"

Cenza kept staring at the letter. Enza sat quietly, as always.

Finally, Teresa turned to Angelo. "It's Pina... she has left for Sicily on a ship this morning."

Angie put her head on Anna's shoulder to console her. The rest, lost in their own thoughts, needing to resolve their feelings, stayed quiet.

Cenza walked to the door and stared out of it. "What have I done? What did I do to Pina? I kept forcing her to work and work hard for the good of the family, never thinking of her and what it would do to her." Cenza started crying. "I have made her life so unbearable."

Teresa asked, "What do we do about the fashion show? I guess we will have to cancel our showing."

Cenza turned from the door. She took deep breaths while she took long strides to calm herself. Tom and Angelo walked to the table and sat down to give Cenza room. She stopped after a few minutes, wiped her tears from her red face. "We will not cancel the show. We will do the show."

Teresa said, "How can we do the show? We have no model. Hiring a model is out of the question. We don't have the money."

Tom said, "I have money. I have the house that I inherited. I could borrow against it."

"No, Tom, you cannot. You may need to borrow against it some-day for your music career."

Angie turned from the window, looked towards Tom with pride. "Teresa, you are right. We don't have the money. We do have a large problem, but" she continued with conviction, "We do have Enza."

"What!" Anna exclaimed, turning from the window.

Enza was shocked.

Cenza looked at Enza. "She will do the show."

Anna pushed Angie's arm from her shoulder and snarled. "No, she will not, Cenza."

Cenza looked sharply at her mother. "She is perfect. She is almost as tall as Pina. She certainly is as beautiful. I have seen her practice with Pina, and she walks more naturally than Pina ever did. We have no choice, Momma. What is the problem?"

"The problem is that she is just a child. She is only eighteen years old. I will not have one of my daughters exposed to that kind of noto-riety at such a young age."

"Momma," Teresa said, gently trying not to get her mother mad-der, "Cenza is right... Enza is perfect."

"No," Anna said.

The bickering went on for several minutes. Cenza and Anna's voices got louder.

Angelo got angry, raised his voice over the shouting, which he barely ever did, and said, "Stop both of you... Stop immediately!"

As Angelo was yelling, Maria walked to Tom. She sat frozen beside him. Tom felt that she needed him and slid closer to put his warm arm around to let her know that she was safe. She raised the back of her hand to her lips and started to rub them hard. Tom reached up and took her hand away from her mouth with care. As always, he won-dered why she kept doing that.

Anna and Cenza stopped, surprised at Angelo's sharp voice, and turned away from each other.

Enza said quietly, "Cenza, I will do the show."

"No, you will not," Anna said harshly.

Angelo walked to Enza. "Your mother is right, my beautiful angel. You are so young."

Angelo reached her, and Enza went to his arms. She turned to Anna. "Cenza is right. I am perfect for the show, even better than Pina. Pina is pretty, but so am I. I can give the show the one thing that Pina could not, and that is my wanting to be there and to be noticed."

"Momma. We have made a commitment. We cannot back out. We back out, the name we have worked so hard to build will be destroyed, and opportunity will never come to us again." Cenza said.

Teresa added. "Momma, Cenza is right. We may never have the opportunity again. We have to use Enza."

Cenza turning Teresa, said, "Enza is so flat-chested, we will have to fill out the bust line in the gown."

Enza said. "That won't be necessary."

"What do you mean it would be necessary?"

"If I am to do the show, I will not wear that dress designed for Pina," Enza said.

Cenza looked at Enza, surprised. "What?"

"You heard me, Cenza, I will not wear that gown."

"Well, Enza, what do you plan on wearing? May I ask?"

"I will wear, and only wear, a duplicate of Momma's wedding gown when she and Papa got married. I also want a duplicate of your veil and flowers, except the dress will be off-white, not pure white or maybe ivory."

Enza continued, mesmerizing the family, "Yes, ivory would look better on me. The soft pearl look of the gown would look better on me. In fact, I think if satin material is used under the lace, it will make my skin creamier looking. Yes," Enza said as she looked at a Cenza. "I know that ivory satin would look better against my skin. The lace has to be the best we can find," Enza added stubbornly, looking at her mother.

Enza's demands caused the entire room to pause. Then she saw at Maria, still rubbing her lips. "Maria!"

Maria jumped at Enza's harsh tone. "Stop rubbing your lips. Why do you do that?"

Tom raised his hands to Maria's lips and took her hand away from her again.

"Also, I have to be last on the runway. My performance must be the showstopper."

Cenza angrily asked. "How do you expect us to get that gown done in time for the show, my little whinny bratty sister?"

"That's your problem."

"We could do it, Cenza," Teresa said, looking at Angie.

"Yes," Angie said in an excited voice. "We can do it. I know the lace that we could purchase is perfect. Enza is right. Pure white would not look as good against her skin.

Cenza asked in a low deep angry voice. "Well, how do I get you to be the last on the runway... Enza?"

"As I said, that is your problem. You find a way, or I will not model!"

"Why are you acting this way, Enza?"

"Because I can!" Enza said, "It is my way, or I don't model. Also, I want to update Momma's dress. Instead of a high neck, it should be a boat neck with sleeves a little lower from the elbow. The bottom of the dress should be full, with a long train. The veil should be the same with the same fabric flowers as before. I want the same lace bottom from the top of the dress to its waist in the back."

Cenza shook her head, wondering how this situation got so out of control.

Enza moved out of Angelo's arms and stood straight. She was acting beyond her young years. "Also, I need to change my name. I can't be called Innocenza Gennusa - it is too long and ethnic while Enza is too common. I want to shorten it to Innu, which is more intriguing. I will be called Innu. No last name. And Momma, there is something I need to know."

Anna looked at her daughter, shocked by her cold attitude, and said nothing as Innu continued, "I need to know who my father is?"

Anna stopped breathing, a sharp pain cutting through her body. Everyone looked at Innu, horrified.

She lifted her hands to the ceiling and appealed to God, "Do I deserve this. What have I done?"

Anna closed her eyes with a flashback of the night in Sicily, where Franco asked her the same question after striking her. Anna put her hand to her face and rubbed that spot. There was no evidence of the hit from Franco's hand, but the tenderness on her face and the hurt in her heart was still there. How could he think that she was unfaithful to him after all the years and loved they share together? How could this daughter believe that she was anyone else's child but hers and Franco's?

"You heard me, Momma. Who is my father?" Innu looked straight into her mother's eyes with iciness and bitterness in her voice.

Anna slapped her face hard.

Cenza screamed. "Momma, her face... Not her face!"

Everyone in the room watched, paralyzed.

In Tom's arms, Maria brought the back of her hand to her mouth and started to rub her lips hard. Tom reached up and took Maria's hand away from her lips and held her hand firmly. She felt a sharp pain in her groin area. Her body went limp, and she folded over on to Tom's shoulder.

Francesca ran to Angelo and buried her tearful face against his shoulder, trying to shut out the surrounding horror and crying harder

Anna grabbed Innu's hair, pulled her toward a mirror against the wall by the stairs, and pushed Innu's face close to it. Look!" Anna pulled and squeezed Innu hair harder and said again, "Look at your grandfather's face in you. You are an image of your grandfather, your father, and the Gennusa family. I don't know where you get your dark skin from."

With more hate in her voice, Anna said, "Maybe you should study Sicilian history. I am sure you will find Arab blood there and in you."

Innu looking into the mirror as Anna squeezed her hair tightly for the first time in her life; she looked at every part of her face and saw her grandfather and her father. She now knew her identity. All her father's rejection throughout her life now meant nothing to her. For the first time in her life, she felt that she finally belonged, and she belonged to her extraordinary family.

Anna let go of Innu hair.

Cenza screamed, "Teresa get ice for Innu's face." Cenza ran to Innu. The rest of the family stayed frozen.

"You are the daughter of the only man I ever loved." Then with hate, she added, "But today, I despise him and you."

Anna walked out of the room.

"Momma, how blind were you and Papa? Did you ever see how Pina and Dino looked at each other? How they worked together every chance they could get to be close? Their love was so evident to me. How could you not see?"

Anna and Teresa were in the park sitting at a bench together, facing the house. Anna did not look at her daughter but sat quietly listening to her. She tried to remember the farm but could not remember Dino and Pina spending time together.

"How could Lucia not see what was happening to her son? Pina and Dino both were so happy being with each other. I saw them and knew. Pina knew what she felt at a young age, but she never talked to me about her feelings. She never had to tell me of her feeling for Dino. She kept that secret to herself. But I knew."

"She was just a child," Anna said remorsefully.

"You think of all of us as children, but we are not. Even back then and even when Pina was younger, did you not notice the attention she received because she was so beautiful?"

"Yes... I did, but the war. Your father and I had so much to worry about. We never took our eyes off you girls. It was a constant worry that the Germans would have their way with you, especially Pina. Her skin so creamy, so soft and those big hazel eyes of hers," Anna said to herself, "How could I be so blind?"

Teresa cuddled her mother and put her arm around her. "I am sorry about Innu and how she treated you. Can you ever forgive her?"

Anna said nothing.

Later that evening, Innu went looking for Angelo and found him alone in his sitting room. She went to him, and he held her close. "You know, my little one, you can be extremely tough on your mother. She loves you so. You should take care of her. She is the only Momma you will ever have, although it is debatable who loves you more, her or me."

He hugged her tight, giggling.

"I will be good to her... I promise because I love her so much. She does so much for this family and me. She brought me here to you, and she placed me into your arms lovely, knowing that you were always around me to protect me."

"Yes, your Momma gives so much of herself. She brought you and your sisters to Angie and me. We found Tom because of her. I can't tell you how grateful and how blessed we are." Angelo said. "Now go find your mother and spend time with her telling her how much you love her."

Innu walked out of Angie and Angelo's master suite and found her mother in her bedroom. Before entering, she knocked softly on

266 - Mary B. Patterson

the door, peeked in, and saw her mother sitting at her makeup dresser brushing her hair.

Anna did not respond. Innu entered her mother's bedroom, kissed her cheek. Then she took the hairbrush and continued to brush Anna's hair.

"Momma, I love you so much. I am sorry I hurt you. My life would be so empty if it was not for your love and my sisters' love..."

Innu continued brushing Anna's hair. "When we were in Sicily, I always felt that the village people would look at me strangely like Papa used to. Like I did not belong in my family and to the village...Here in this country, people look at me for all my attributes and not my skin, hair, and eyes. Here I am accepted for my beauty, which makes me proud of who I am and where I came from. I come from you and Papa. I knew he doubted whether I was his, but I always knew. You and Papa both made me into this beautiful creature that I am. I am so proud of my looks, but mostly I am proud to be your daughter. If I am cruel, sometimes it because I am trying to protect myself from people that have hurt me in the past. From this point on, I promise to be more aware of my cruelty and become a better person, not just for myself but for you. I know you are worried about me and what will happen to me after the fashion show. Please... do not be concerned. I am ready. I am ready to be noticed, and I have wanted and waited and was born for this. Give me the chance to be noticed. I promise I will not change, and I will always be true to myself."

Innu stopped for a second, smiling, "Besides, I don't think my Angelo will let me forget who I am." Hesitating again for a second, "Thank you... Momma...for making me! For bringing me into this country where I can be noticed and mostly for giving me Angelo. Can you forgive me?"

Anna still said nothing when Innu added, "Momma, I am so sorry about Pina."

Anna turned to her magnificent olive-skinned daughter and

smiled, "There is nothing to forgive. But could you be less spoiled around Angelo?"

Innu smiled while Anna turned to her mirror, and Innu continued to brush her Momma's hair.

Anna said proudly and motherly, "I like your new name."

New York City's high society was ready for the new fall collections, even during the heat of summer. Each was being shown by all the prominent dress designers of New York and Europe. As the women sat in their chairs in their cool crisp clothes, the models modeled their fashion-forward wears.

Cenza was behind the curtain, waiting for Innu to show her gown. She cringed when she remembered how earlier that day, Innu declared, "*Know I will not go on unless you get what I want!*"

Anna was heading towards the backstage door, "I will go to the store and buy it. Please stop your ranting."

The other models looked toward the commotion as they were getting ready. A hairdresser stepped toward Innu to do her hair. Innu sat down on a stool for the hairdresser and told this man how to do her hair.

The hairdresser looked at Innu, ready to walk away when Cenza intervened. She persuaded the hairdresser to do Innu hair the way she wanted.

Innu watched as the hairstylist started to work on her when she erupted, pushing him away and said, "Take your hands off me. I will do this myself. You have no idea how to do my hair like I can."

The hairdresser became so irate that he threw the comb he had in his hand on the table in front of Innu and huffed away. "Bitch!"

As the announcer was ready to announce the second last model on the runway, Innu, Cenza went boldly to the announcer on stage and gave him a paper slip. Then quickly, with a pit in her stomach, she went back behind the curtain, praying as the announcer read the note.

The announcer smiled at the audience, "My apologies, but we have a change to the program." He then announced the next model's name and her designer. The model who was to go last was confused by the announcement. However, she walked the runway with her head held high and smiled.

Innu was in place, ready when the announcer called her. "Our final model is Innu. She represents Anna's Bridal Shop, wearing a gown designed by Anna Gennusa."

Innu walked the runway slowly with confidence and maturity. Her olive skin glowed with the olive oil she had made Anna buy and had rubbed into her skin. The stage lights on made her skin look soft and creamy.

Innu's instructions were to stop at her end of the runway, turn around and walk back slowly.

The audience was awed by the beautiful gown, satin roses and lace from the dress repeated on the long veil and headpiece, tucked into Innu's head. She carried a bouquet of pink and ivory white lace roses. The room was silent as Innu stopped at the end of the runway. She grabbed her veil, held it, turned in a full circle slowly so that the audience could look at every inch of the ensemble. She displayed the beautiful diamond bracelet that Joseph had insisted she wear and the matching diamond earrings. She raised her dress to reveal her matching lace-satin shoes. As she did this, the audience clapped boldly.

She stopped at each side of the stage, repeating her actions. Everyone received a closer look at the gown, the shoes - and her. She turned and returned upstage. She turned, looked at the audience, and walked down the runway again with only a brief hesitation. At the end of the stage, she swirled again, detached the veil, and showed the handmade lace flowers tucked into her long dark curls. She dropped the veil on the runway and walked back. The audience exploded in applause, giving her a standing ovation as Innu showed her mother's creation to its fullest. She turned to the audience, and the women went wild.

Cenza was blinking back a stream of tears as Anna and Angie hugged her. "When we get home, Innu is going to get an ear full about the end of her walk. She will never do anything like that again without me knowing."

The three stood beside the stage as Innu was not allowed to leave because of the ovation. Innu smiled and stopped to talk to potential customers. In a surprise move, she brought her mother onto the stage to share the accolades for the magnificent gown she designed.

Women flooded the stage, and the security guards swarmed to protect them. They escorted Innu and Anna backstage. On the main floor, the room was in chaos. The announcer proclaimed the end of the show and said catalogs were available in the corridor.

Angelo escorted Innu from the building, where the press was waiting for her. She was ready to greet them. Her newly applied mascara showed off her exotic thick eyelashes, and she wanted everyone to notice her eyes.

She wore one of Anna's casual pantsuit designs, with cropped legs and a short, colorful jacket. The outfit was in silk. Her purse and red shoes had arrived from Vincent that morning from Palermo. Her dark curly hair flowed softly on her shoulders. She selected this outfit because she wanted to press her mother's creativity in all fashion areas. She knew she looked good in bold colors. The cameras flashed as Innu stood sure of herself and allowed the press to take pictures.

Innu stood tall and confident while the cameras flashed, and the reporters asked their many questions. "My name is Innu. It's short for Innocenza, which means innocence. My mother is the designer and owner of Anna's Bridal Shop..."

As Innu chatted with the press, Cenza, Anna, Teresa, and Angie listened. They were thrilled that she discussed the fashion show and how even her after-show outfit was designed by her mother

Cenza was shocked at her little sister having so much natural flair and the ability to keep the press interested in her as she spoke to them.

One reporter asked, "Where did your beautiful hair and your olive skin come from?"

"I come from an island in the Mediterranean. I was born in a small village south of Palermo on the island of Sicily. I am a mixture of ancient history that consists of the many nationalities..."

As she was explaining her heritage, the other models hurried by her. They were furious and hated her for the stunt she pulled on the stage. Several other models tried to get the press's attention, but they were not interested in them. The night belonged to this new and upcoming young star, who stood in front of them, answering all their questions with style and grace.

By the backstage door, Anna, Angie, Teresa, and Cenza hugged each other.

"I can see now that my Angelo is going to not only Innu's father but her bodyguard."

Cenza added, "She has such stage presence!" Shaking her head, "She is so demanding to the point of being obnoxious... How am I going to be able to handle her now?"

Anna and Angie both looked at each other, and Teresa laughed, "Like you are not?"

Cenza looked at them in confusion and said, "What?"

Anna put her arm around Angie, "Let go home. I am tired, and I need a glass of brandy."

Angie whispered, "I thought the brandy was just for us women when we're alone talking about sex."

Anna blushed, "Tonight, we will make an exception."

Cenza and Teresa caught up with Anna and Angie.

Cenza asked, "What did you say about brandy?"

Anna and Angie looked at each other and laughed. Anna said, "Let pack up and go home."

Cenza said, "I want ice cream."

Teresa said, "I want my bed."

All the prominent New York City newspapers had an extensive article in the fashion section about the fashion show and the showstopper. Anna's gown was described flawlessly, and Joseph's diamonds were described as extravagant, elegant, and magnificent. The whole extended family, including June, Scooter (and their boys), Sadie, Mrs. Green, and Joseph, sat around the table reading each newspaper and passing them around. Everyone praised the show and especially Innu.

The sun was shining through the windows that warmed the room as Tom reached for his second donut. The room smelled of rich coffee and bakery goods. The oldest of June and Scooter's sons came to the kitchen table and tried to put his hand in the plate of donuts, looking at his mom, hoping she would not see him try to sneak a couple for him and his brother. He knew that he had his limit, but today was exceptional, and he thought he could get away with eating a few more.

Tom stopped Patrick's hand from getting the donuts. He looked at Tom, and Tom smiled. Tom reached for the last two chocolate donuts, handed them to him, and then put his finger to his lips, indicating not telling his mom on him. After Patrick took the donuts, he ran into the family room, watched by Tom and Angelo as Angelo giggled.

Mrs. Green sat beside Francesca while they read the garden section. Mrs. Green said to Francesca, "The showroom would have looked better if there were fall flowers around the room."

Francesca said, "I tried, but Cenza would not listen to me."

Innu read the article about her incredible performance and her presence on stage. The night belonged to this new young model that dominated the scene with her flair, grace, and exceptional beauty.

She muttered to herself, but everyone still heard, "I knew Momma's wedding gown would get the highest praise. I knew I could model it and bring the crowd down to their knees. I knew...

"Innu," Angelo said, "Come sit by me. I need you to sit by me, so

I can tell you how beautiful you are but also to remind you where you come from and where you belong."

Innu went to Angelo and sat beside him. "I know Angelo beauty comes from the heart, not the face." She kissed his forehead.

"Yes," Angelo looking at his beautiful Innu, "From the heart."

Innu planted another kiss on Angelo's forehead. She turned and looked at her mother with pride and smiled.

Anna placed her newspaper on the table and got up. She poured a cup of coffee. Joining her, Tom asked quietly, "Have you seen anything in the papers about Daniel and his group?"

Anna shook her head. They both turned to Joseph reading one of the newspapers, each feeling intensely heavyhearted.

Maybe no news was good news.

Epilogue-Anna Across From the Brownstone

"The children go to the movies all the time. They've seen "Some Like it Hot" and "Ben-Hur." They even dragged Tom to "Gigi," which won the Oscar.

Cenza has Boris Pasternak's "Doctor Zhivago" by her bed, ready when she has the time to read it. Tom is reading James A. Michener's "Hawaii."

It's been twelve years since we landed in New York. Sometimes it feels as if it were yesterday, and other times so much longer. I am still caught up in the events of the Fashion Show and our success. I can't believe we triumphed at the show!

I like sitting here, looking at this house. It feels good to rest. We've had long days and nights working to survive in this land. I try not to remember Sicily too often or my family left behind.

Although I am usually lonely, I don't have the luxury to think about the past.

Or about you.

I feel your warm, callused hand on mine when I touch my shoulder. I keep asking, "Could this really be? Is this you? I thought you had...? And then I breathe in your warm smoky wintry scent. Now your hand on my thigh, and I know you're here with me. I need you. Enter me. Feel me. Your breath is so warm, so moist. I can't stop shaking. I need you so. Don't stop...

Franco, where have you been? I needed you to help me raise our children; I needed you to protect them from this hostile country.

Why did you leave me? I was so angry when you made us come here, but I never thought I'd be here alone, without you.

Raising our daughters in Sicily during World War II was not easy. But because we were in our homeland, we were somewhat protected by our people. The danger was less of a burden. It has been a struggle for me and still is after all these years. I am naïve about this country and how to survive in it. I have done wrong.

Franco, I committed murder. I submitted myself to a monster. I am not ashamed, nor do I have any regrets. I would do it again. Our daughters were being stalked by a sexual predator. I did it to protect them from losing their innocence. I had to protect them from the evil that lurked around them. I watch them every day and try to protect them the best that I can. But it is so hard. Please don't leave again. I need you desperately. I love you. Stay with me.

Do you remember our wedding day? I was so afraid of you, and I wanted you to touch me so badly. I was young. I was inexperienced. I want you to stay here with us forever. I want to feel my head on your shoulder as you caress my breasts. I want you to be here to support and care for me as you did in those early days. Please don't stop. Keep touching me. What happened to you? Why did you turn away from me? I try not to dream about those passionate years that we spent together, but those dreams are still with me. Your touch, your breath, and your strength carried me through so many hard times, and they felt natural to go through because I had you.

What was that burden that you carried that took you away from me? You should have talked to me. You should have trusted me. Nothing could have kept me away from you, and I would have understood. Together we could have conquered those demons that tortured you.

Look, Franco, look at our home. Our daughters are waiting for you there. Wait until you see how beautiful our daughters are. Teresa, after all the years she rebelled against us now, is my best friend.

Pina is more beautiful than she was when she was a child and walks like a swan. She was so unhappy in this country, and the polluted air always made her feel sick. Pina ran back to Sicily, and you will be happy to know that Pina married Dino. She has loved him since the first day that his parents and his brother come to our farmhouse.

Your most prized daughter Vincenza is beautiful, brilliant, and has a keen business sense. She found a way for us to buy that massive house and start our own business. She has grown more in the business world than you could have ever imagined. She is so unselfish and gives to everyone. She never spends on herself. Even sends money back to Sicily and helps to support our family.

Francesca, on the other hand, has not changed much. She still loves dirt, and she still hates to wear a dress. She still cries her big tears with her deep dimples that get deeper with every tear.

Innocenza, your daughter, yes Franco, your daughter, will be the biggest surprise of all. When she was a small child, she was so quiet. Do you remember? When we came to this country, she was no longer placid. She grows more beautiful than all the others. She looks more like you and your family as she gets older. She has talent agents screaming to represent her. She has a considerable career in modeling ahead of her if she chooses.

Your Maria, our youngest and most active, has changed the most. She is not like the child we knew in Sicily. I don't know what changed her, but I worry about her the most."

No, I won't let go of your hand. You are my love, the only man I've ever loved, and I want you to come and meet your beautiful daughters."

Let's go home."

Mary B. Patterson was born in Bisacquino, Sicily, and was brought to America when she was three years old in 1947. She spent her childhood in Enfield, Connecticut, during the 1950s. It was difficult for a young woman raised in an ethnic Sicilian family and fitting into American's young society. Mary found creative ways to fit into her small-town life. She was never inspired to study or be educated in writing. Her love of reading fiction brought her to a point in her life when she decided to write her own novel. From art to writing, she discovered her creativity and voice. Mary combines her two distinct cultural life experiences into her work. She lives in Maryland and is the mother of three grown sons.

Acknowledgments

I want to thank Paula M. Kalamaras and Paul T. Kraly, my editors and publishers, for all their help in making "After Love – The Life of Anna Gennusa – A novel" possible. Many thanks to both of you. I am looking forward to many more writing adventures together.

Lightning Source UK Ltd.
Milton Keynes UK
UKHW020932270221
379459UK00009B/2203